Books by David Griffith

The Border Series

Blackwater Crossing
The Death Dealers
Without Redemption
Brothers of the Blood

The Freedom Series

Free to Run
Vengeance is Mine

VENGEANCE IS MINE

BOOK 2 IN THE FREEDOM SERIES

David Griffith

© Copyright 2019 David Griffith
Published in Canada by Bar 7 Publishing

www.davidgriffith.ca

All rights reserved

No part of this publication may be reproduced in any form, or by any means, electronic or mechanical except by written permission of the publisher, except for reviewers who may quote brief passages.

ISBN 978-1-9994873-2-4

VENGEANCE IS MINE

Prologue

MAYBE IT WAS THE excitement of grad night combined with the euphoria she'd felt after Greg had convinced her to smoke the crack cocaine. After that first toke, there were no limits. They'd piled into his dad's Mercedes. She tipped her head back against the seat, her teeth bared as the drug exploded into her brain. The speed hadn't mattered – until Greg missed the sharp corner at the county line. The expensive car careened end over end. Glass shards exploded over the dashboard, puncturing airbags and flailing limbs. Eventually, the twisted, metal hulk settled on the rocky floor of the gorge and – for a long time there was only silence until the distant wail of sirens broke the quiet, rural calm. The ambulance attendants rappelled to the bottom as quickly as they could, but there was no need. Both the once supple bodies lay silent, mangled beyond recognition. The brilliant, full moon stared uncomprehending and uncaring as the teen lifeblood spilled onto the plush gray upholstery.

Fifteen hundred miles to the south, in that spiny ridge of mountains they call the Sierra Madre, the same moon threw an equal amount of light on a villa barricaded by assault rifles and razor wire. Two men counted hundred-dollar bills, pile after pile. Both smiled. Another immensely profitable week in the cocaine trade. The Lord of the Skies would be pleased.

Chapter 1
DINA

DINA TUGGED GENTLY at the rangy bay gelding as he charged wildly into the first barrel. His approach was still too wide, but she smiled and kept him collected as he drove into the turn. Before they were even around the barrel, she was looking ahead toward the second, planning her approach, firmly positioning the gelding to power into the sweet spot. He needed to learn to control that wild, crazy momentum. In this game, speed was of no value if it couldn't be managed. At the third barrel, he cut too tight, and she winced as her shin thudded against the padded rim of the barrel. Not that it hurt. She always wore lots of protection when training young horses. They often knocked barrels over, but this time had been her fault. She'd cued him a split-second too early because he was usually slow to respond. Not today. His response had been instant. So even though he'd knocked the barrel over, he was learning, and that's what counted. Benito was a horse with great talent, the first and only colt out of her old Piñata mare. Tomorrow, they would do better.

For twenty minutes, Dina walked the colt around the arena, then eyed him critically as she unsaddled and scraped the sweat off his bright bay coat. Benito was bred to run, and with young, hot-blooded horses like this one, ramping down was part of the process. It was crucial that before they quit for the day, he was calm and relaxed, inside and out. She blanketed him, then led him into the barn and down the long row of stalls.

Dina's father had planned well. Ricardo Rodríguez had built this spacious facility with a firm grip on the future. And since Dina had returned to the ranch, the barn had been more than full. Always there were new colts from the broodmare band. Most were trained as roping and ranch horses. A select few were slated to run like the wind around three forty-five gallon drums in the sport they call barrel racing. These talented athletes were the mainstay of the Rodríguez horse program. Early in their career they were shipped to the Arizona satellite ranch. From there, they were marketed to the human stars who competed in a mad dash where a hundredth of a second might decide a world championship.

Dina walked Benito into his stall, slipped off the halter, and trudged toward the barn office. She'd be so glad when Raul returned. He'd been their *Segundo* for as long as Dina could remember. Nobody understood more about horses and training than Raul Altamirez. What was even more valuable was his ability to communicate those skills to the other trainers.

At the office Dina slumped into the dust-covered chair at Raul's desk. Nothing had changed since Monday morning when he'd been called to Juárez on business. Raul had been vague as to the exact nature of his mission, but he had promised to be back by Wednesday night. She glanced at the calendar. Today was Thursday, and there had been no word from their *Segundo*. What had held him? It wasn't like him not to call if something had happened to keep him away. In fact, Raul often called every evening when he was away on business, just to make sure everything was running smoothly. Not for the first time, a small knot of worry formed in the pit of her stomach.

One last time, Dina's gaze swept the office before settling on the phone. Should she check with Raul's wife Juana to see if she'd heard anything from Raul? She hesitated. No, Juana would have called. She knew they were all worried. Dina flicked the light switch and shuffled wearily toward the house. As she reached the long circular driveway, she saw Juana's Jeep Renegade barreling down the road, though that meant nothing. Juana always drove like the Russian Red Army was about to close her account. Dina grinned, momentarily forgetting her worries about Raul as Juana braked in a cloud of red dust.

"Hi Dina." Juana's thousand-watt smile sparkled with life, her flashing brown eyes filled with laughter. "I had to run into town. There's a quinceañera celebration for Camilla Portillo next week. Raul is her godfather, and I haven't a thing to wear, and of course I looked all over Agua Prieta and found nothing suitable. Now I will have to go to Douglas, and if there's nothing there ... I'll probably end up shopping in Hermosillo or Tucson." Juana threw up her hands in frustration, then stepped out of the vehicle and crossed her arms in disgust. "I just wanted something nice to surprise my husband. He already rented a tuxedo, so it's clearly a big deal to him."

"Did you try Top Fashion Boutique?"

"Yes. They do have a blue gown to die for, but it makes

me look fat."

Dina chuckled, wondering how any gown could make the willowy Juana look overweight. "I think you should go back tomorrow and buy it."

"Well, it was a good price, and I'm already tired of looking. I certainly don't want to have to drive to Tucson, just for a dress."

"How about we both go into town tomorrow? We'll look at the blue gown again, and if it isn't right, we'll slip across to Douglas and find a dress at Victoria Prom. I've shopped there before, and they have a good selection."

"Oh Dina, I can't imagine what I'd do without you. After an afternoon of trying on dresses, I'm frazzled. If you come with me tomorrow I would be forever grateful."

Dina reached over and squeezed Juana's arm. "Consider it done."

"Thanks." Juana patted the hand Dina had laid on her arm. "Oh, and I picked up the mail. After I unload the groceries, I'll bring it over."

"No, I'll come over later and get it. We can have a cup of tea. Any word from Raul?"

"No." Juana's brow instantly furrowed. "Dina, I'm starting to worry. He always calls, and if he has cell coverage, we text back and forth several times a day — always have."

Dina grinned. Raul and Juana had a rare love affair, one of those increasingly uncommon ones that had "lifetime" written all over it. "Okay, I'll come over right after supper."

They parted, and Dina followed the walkway around to the back of the house. She glanced back as Juana parked and stepped out in front of the rust-colored adobe rancher a hundred yards to the east. Dina smiled and walked inside. Her father had built the house for his oldest friend, the man he had trusted to be his second in command. Why hadn't Raul called? Even if he had gone out into the mountains to look at horses, or possibly followed up a good deal on a herd of cattle, he should have at least texted Juana. He always had before. However, some of those places had limited cell service. His truck might have broken down, or perhaps he'd been caught on the wrong side of a river in a flash flood or ...? Well, those things happened. That's probably all it was, but he might need assistance. Later, she and Juana would sit down and figure out where he'd gone. Then she could send one of the men to look for him. That seemed reasonable, but it did nothing for the growing knot of worry over his absence.

After a light supper with her mother and Frederick, Dina helped mama up to her room, while her husband retreated to the ranch office. She could faintly hear his voice as he barked orders to one of his agents. She trudged back down the stairs, the worry grinding deeper into her soul. Mama wasn't doing better. Every day she seemed more tired. Too often, she didn't even have the energy to come down to dinner. Dina slipped by the office and stepped outside. Instantly, a frown creased her face. Even from this distance, she could see Juana's screen door tilted open at a crazy angle. It looked as if someone had used it for a trampoline. Dina shrugged. No worries. Fixing it would be a good job for the new man.

Raul did all the hiring of new men, but Mama had hired this one. Oscar was apparently a handyman and gardener. Her mother seemed to get along with him alright which was great, but Dina had disliked him from the first moment.

Anyhow, she would have him fix the damaged screen door in the morning. She sauntered down the gravel driveway, savoring the cooler evening air and the last cooing dove song of the day. Her knock sounded loud on the wooden door, but it engendered no response. She studied the broken screen door while she waited. Fresh scars marred the wood where the screws had ripped out. She chuckled. What had Juana done to cause this? Undoubtedly, it would be an entertaining story.

Finally, Dina opened the door and hollered. Still no answer. Had Juana stepped out – gone somewhere? She wouldn't likely be down at the barns. Juana loved the ranch, and would often spend hours at the barn with Raul, but that was because she loved being with her husband. She had little interest or affinity for his equine charges.

Dina stepped inside and let the screen door bang behind her. Again she called Juana's name. No answer. She kicked off her manure-stained boots, and padded down the hallway that led to the open dining and living room area. The ornate wood and leather furniture stood solid and familiar, the wedding picture of Raul and Juana in its usual place on the fireplace mantel. Dina stopped in front of it, unaware of the small frown lines creasing her smooth, olive face. Her full lips tipped upward in a familiar smile as she stared at Raul's picture. He looked so happy, and Juana was certainly beautiful.

Raul's whole life had revolved around horses. He'd always said he didn't have time for a wife – until Juana. Six weeks of courtship had culminated in a wedding. And Juana? With her bubbly, warm personality she'd quickly fit in at the ranch, and she and Dina had become instant friends. Though

Juana spoke little of her past life, Dina had gathered enough to know that somewhere in her distant past Juana had been married for a short time and lived in Juárez. Snippets of conversation indicated her family was reasonably wealthy, and that she'd traveled extensively. As time passed, they'd become close enough that Juana had one day volunteered the details of her abusive first marriage. Occasionally, she'd visited her family. Twice, Raul had accompanied her. Both times when they'd arrived back at the ranch he'd been subdued, and though Dina threw out oblique opportunities to talk, her oldest friend and mentor refused to divulge any information. Whatever occurred during his visits to Juana's family stayed private.

Dina turned away from the wedding picture. Dusk had silently enshrouded the room, turning it sinister and gloomy. Suddenly, she felt as if she'd invaded Raul and Juana's privacy. She shouldn't have walked into the house. No, that was silly. She'd never knocked before, other than to announce her presence, and Juana's Jeep was still outside. She must be out back in her little flower garden. Dina called again, her voice hollow in the cavernous silence. She tiptoed through the kitchen, then down the hall. The master bedroom door stood partially open. Perhaps Juana had opted for an early bedtime. Yes, that was it. She'd just peek into the room, then slip quietly out. With Raul gone, she should at least check and make sure Juana was alright. Quietly, she placed her fingers against the heavy wood bedroom door. The hinges creaked as she pushed it back. The floor came into view. Dresser drawers hung open at crazy angles. Clothes littered nearly every inch of the beige tile floor. Dina choked off a scream of horror before it ever reached the surface. The sheets lay wrinkled and torn, spattered with drops of what could only be blood. She peered into the bathroom and closets, then steeled herself for the shock of what would surely lay on the floor on the far side of the bed. But there was no sign of Juana Altamirez.

Chapter 2
DINA

TERROR THREATENED TO freeze every nerve in her body, but Dina forced herself to back out of the room. How had this happened? There were always people around. No vehicle could have driven into the yard without several of the ranch employees noticing. And why Juana? What had she done to draw this kind of treatment? Silently, Dina tiptoed through the still open front door in her sock feet, grabbed her boots and fled. When she reached the driveway, she ran toward the main house. Fear lent wings to her sock feet, and she barely noticed the coarse gravel that cut into her soles. Frantically, she pushed open the side entry door and rushed through the kitchen, screaming her husband's name.

Before she'd reached the end of the room, Frederick's massive frame skidded around the corner of the study.

"What's wrong?" His worried voice caught as she buried her head momentarily in his chest. Just as quickly, she pushed away.

"Juana's gone!" she gasped.

Frederick's jaw dropped. "Where? What happened?"

Dina backed away, until her breathing slowed enough

to answer. "In their house. There's blood everywhere – they must have killed her."

Frederick stared at her. "Juana? Who? How could anyone ... we've been here all evening. That's not possible." He stepped forward and grabbed her shoulders as she slumped against the wall. "Sweetheart, we're going to find out what happened. Did Raul get home?"

Dina took a deep breath before answering. "No, I went over to talk to her and to pick up the mail. Frederick, I'm worried. Raul hasn't called since he left Monday morning, and he should have been home last night. Juana hadn't heard from him either. I talked to her in the driveway when I came in from the barn, just before dark, and now this has happened."

Frederick strode to the massive front entry. "I'll call Luis, and go over there. You stay here."

Dina scurried through before he could close the door. "Not a chance. I'm not staying alone."

Frederick grabbed her hand. "I understand. Is anybody still at the barn?"

"I don't think so."

"Then call the bunkhouse, and have Luis meet us at Raul's."

Dina pulled out her cell. She punched at the dial pad, then gave rapid instructions in Spanish as they walked the short distance to Raul's house.

At the bottom of the step, Frederick unholstered the ever-present nine millimeter Glock under his left arm. He hated carrying it, but he'd long ago become a marked man by the drug cartels. To go without protection was to invite death.

When Luis met them in front of Raul and Juana's house, Frederick broke the news of Juana's disappearance. His instructions to Luis were explicit. "Just follow me inside, and stay with Dina while I have a look in the bedroom and through the rest of the house."

Luis nodded soberly. Dina followed him up the steps, glad for his presence. Their trusted *Segundo* had come to the ranch as a child. Always he'd been treated like every other Rodríguez Ranch employee, as family, but of late, Luis had seemed unhappy, as if ... Dina wished she could put her finger on why. Luis never let on why, and she was afraid to ask.

Luis and Dina paused while Frederick stepped inside. In the entry, he studied the hallway, paying careful attention to every inch of the tile floor. Halfway through the living room he pointed to a couple fresh scuff marks. "Try not to step on those."

Dina and Luis carefully skirted the nearly obscure marks Frederick had indicated, signs few others would have noticed. They might be nothing, but to Frederick, every little item was important. Dina slid into a chair, her fingers nervously rubbing at the varnish on the table while she waited with Luis in the dining room. He paced through the room, his head down, brow furrowed with worry.

"Luis, did Raul talk about where he was going?"

Luis's clenched jaw muscles flickered with tension before he answered. "He said he was going to Juárez. He didn't say why, but he has not been himself lately. Often he has been sharp with the men, and that is unusual. I think that wherever he went, it had much to do with what we are facing here today."

Lines of worry crinkled Dina's smooth features. "Have we had trouble with one of the cartels?"

Luis shrugged and continued his pacing. "They are always a problem, but there is nothing new that I'm aware of."

Dina studied Luis's face, but he quickly turned away. Was he hiding something to protect Raul?

"Luis, this is not about betraying a trust. Juana may be dead, and Raul could be in trouble. Please tell me whatever you can."

Luis walked over to the east-facing window. He stared through the now dark pane as if he could see beyond the sandy flat that dropped off to the dry creek bed and the Big Coulee.

"I don't think Raul and his wife were getting along. One night last week, I rode in late from the south range. It was nearly midnight, and when I passed by this house, the lights were still on. Though I tried not to eavesdrop or intrude in any way, I couldn't help hearing their conversation. Both were visible from the window, their voices angry and loud."

Dina tried to digest what Luis had told her. What did *that* mean? Surely, it could only be a domestic spat. And what did that have to do with Juana's disappearance? She eyed Luis, again wondering whether he was holding back information. Was it because of loyalty to Raul, or something more sinister? She sighed as memories of the father she'd learned to love too late washed over her. It had been Papa who built that fervent loyalty. Was that what she was seeing in the man in front of her? He wasn't just an employee. He was family, but for reasons nearly as old as he was, his first loyalty would be to Raul.

"Luis, I know the regard you held for my father, and I understand the tremendous respect you have for Raul. Frederick and I are absent a good part of the time, and it's not likely that will change, at least not for a while. I wish it was different, but for now, it is only Mama, Raul, and you to keep the ranch running as it should."

Luis raised his hands and turned from the window. "Dina, that is no longer acceptable. We need you. Your mother no longer has a strong enough hand to run this ranch." His voice cracked with a pent-up frustration he'd never before verbalized. His next words were dropped like shotgun shells. "You. Need. To. Come. Home."

Dina recoiled at Luis's unaccustomed anger, avoiding his accusing eyes. "Luis, I can't, at least not now. You and Raul have to keep going, make the day-to-day decisions and do whatever is necessary to meet the needs of those who depend on us."

Luis took a deep breath and exhaled slowly. He stepped forward, as if to place a hand on her shoulder. At the last second, his fist clenched, and his hand fell. Anger flickered across his face, but as quickly as it had appeared, it vanished. When he spoke, his words were measured, the tone indifferent. "You are right, of course. All of us understand the importance of Frederick's job, but it is difficult here without your father. He had a great work as well, but the ranch never suffered because of it. I wish you could do the same."

A forced smile played across Dina's face, disguising the frustration she felt. "Luis, my heart is always here."

For a long and confusing moment, Luis held her eyes. Then he glanced down the hallway toward the master bedroom. "I understand." Instantly, he turned away and resumed his pacing.

Dina stood awkwardly, her hands braced on the table in front of her, wondering if Luis understood anything. Several times she glanced at the dark lines that marred his expressive face. Had he misunderstood her words? Surely he couldn't think ... no, his long ago declaration of youthful love was when they were scarcely more than children. She had made her choice. Never could it have been him.

Dina marched to the far side of the table and slid into a chair where she could face Luis's pacing figure. It was time to return to the reason they were here. "Did you hear what Raul and Juana were arguing about?"

Luis shrugged. "Only a small part. I rode by as quickly as I could." He shrugged. "Their voices were very loud – or at least Juana's was. She kept shouting, 'Why? Why did you not tell me you were related to ...?' And then he answered. He said he didn't think it mattered."

"You didn't hear the name?"

"I thought I heard it, but I couldn't be sure."

Dina folded her hands on the table and leaned forward. "And?"

"Amado."

"No last name?"

"It did sound like Carrillo, but I must have been mistaken. Amado Carrillo is the leader of the Juárez cartel."

Dina raised an eyebrow and shook her head in disgust. "As if I or anyone else in Mexico didn't know *that*. Who else ferries jet-sized loads of cocaine from Columbia to America?" Dina tapped her index finger on the top of the table until she realized that's what her husband did when his mind engaged in overdrive. She instantly folded her hands in her lap.

Luis must be wrong. Raul could never be involved with the Carrillo crime family, but what about Juana? Was there a dark secret buried in her past?

Frederick suddenly appeared in the doorway leading into the kitchen, his face haggard. Dina searched his face, dreading the answers she hoped not to hear.

Frederick slipped a hand over her shoulder. "What time did you see her last?"

"Just before supper. We talked in the yard for a few minutes. Juana had been in town most of the day shopping for dresses for Camilla's quinceañera party."

"I didn't do a thorough check of the room, but she evidently fought like a tiger. The police may have further to add. The good news is she's probably not dead, or they wouldn't have taken her." He wiped one of his big hands across his brow. "Do you have your phone?"

"Yes." She dug in her pocket for her cell.

"Call the police. My deficient Spanish won't cut it."

Dina's finger shook as she punched in zero six six, the emergency number, then reported the details of Juana's disappearance.

As they walked toward the door, Frederick reached over and hugged her as she wiped at a tear. "One way or the other, we are going to find who took her."

At the top of the driveway, Luis spoke. "I will be at home if you need me for anything else."

Dina thanked him, her earlier suspicions forgotten. Luis disappeared into the darkness. Frederick slipped his arm around her shoulder, and they trudged wearily toward the ranch house veranda to wait for the police.

"Raul disappears, and now Juana is kidnapped," Dina

said. "I can't believe this. Luis said they were having trouble, but they were so much in love. Neither of them deserved this."

Frederick's brow furrowed. "You mean they were having marriage problems?"

"It was probably only a squabble. Luis said he heard them arguing – something about Amado Carrillo. He indicated they'd had other quarrels, but I'm not so sure."

Frederick rubbed the back of his neck, then ran his fingers through his hair. "So you're saying one of them may have ties to the Juárez cartel?"

Dina glared at her husband. "Anything this well-planned and brutal has to be a drug cartel hit. I can't imagine Juana having any blood connection to that crime family? Even, if she did, she would never be involved with any of their business."

Frederick thought for a minute. "Then it's likely she was kidnapped to send a message to somebody else, possibly Raul."

"Why would he be targeted?" Dina's voice rose. "He could no more be involved in drug cartel business than you or I."

Approaching car lights interrupted Frederick's reply. They walked to the bottom of the steps and greeted the four Federal police officers who stepped warily forward. All were heavily armed. After a summary of what they'd found, Dina and Frederick led them into Raul's house. Frederick informed the ranking officer they'd be available at the main ranch house if they had further questions. Then he and Dina left the officers to do their investigation.

Frederick sighed as they walked through the arched

kitchen entry. "They may find something I missed."

Dina arched an eyebrow. "Hmm, not likely." She filled the brass kettle with water and slid it onto the stove.

"I did spend enough time in there to know that Juana is in deep trouble. If we just knew why they targeted her? Anyhow, it's important that we not tread on the toes of those who should have jurisdiction."

Dina folded her arms and walked to the window. "What I can't understand is that if Juana's disappearance has something to do with Raul's activities, why haven't we received a ransom note? The cartels always leave a message. It's part of their fear tactics. Why didn't they leave demands or conditions? Wouldn't they want money?"

"Yes, and that may still come."

Dina shrugged, walked over to the table and sat next to her husband. "Are we presuming too much? This may not have anything to do with Raul. Possibly he just got held up – "

Frederick raised an eyebrow. "And if pigs could fly?"

The kettle whistled its shrill warning. Frederick turned off the hot burner before pouring the boiling water into two cups. He dumped a teabag in one and handed it to Dina.

Her eyes flickered upward from the cup. "Thanks. I know Raul would have called if he could, but can't we still hope?"

Frederick stirred the tea bag into the hot water and laid it carefully beside the cup. "We can always hope, but right now his disappearance and Juana's kidnapping make no sense. How well do you know Raul's past?"

Dina bristled. "Meaning … ?"

Frederick pointed a finger at her and scowled. "Meaning

whoever did this didn't just pick Juana out of the phone book. Either Raul or Juana has something they need, or one of them has a past that can be exploited."

"Raul wouldn't do anything wrong," Dina snapped, "and I resent your insinuation that he might have a connection to the drug trade." She slammed her cup onto the counter and stomped out of the kitchen. Leave it to Frederick to come up with a ten cent theory that would utterly destroy a reputation. Raul had been at the Rodriguez Ranch before she'd been born. His whole life had been dedicated to training horses. He would never have anything to do with a drug cartel, even if he *had* the time – which he didn't. She paced around the spacious living room, her arms folded, while her mind flitted from Raul to Juana's blood-stained bedroom scarcely a hundred yards away. She stared out the window and across the yard toward Raul's house. Light streamed from every window which meant the police must still be doing their investigation. Even if they'd found anything, it wasn't likely they'd share the information. She turned away from the window as random childhood memories battered at the foundation of her carefully laid defense against Frederick's allegations. Papa had been a CIA agent. Part of his cover was smuggling contraband, occasionally even small quantities of marijuana. Raul had been his trusted Lieutenant. He would have been part of every operation. Could Raul still be smuggling illegals across the border – or even drugs? Had some event from the past now come back to slash and kill those whom her father had loved?

Chapter 3
DINA

FREDERICK WALKED INTO the living room and stood just inside the arched doorway. "I'm sorry. I didn't mean to insinuate that Raul had done anything wrong. He's a valued employee *and* a friend. I just think there's something going on here we don't understand, but the federal police will get to the bottom of it – at least I hope they will." He sighed. "We need to be back to Albuquerque in the morning, but we'll come back as soon as we can get away."

Dina's shoulders stiffened. She turned from the window, her arms crossed as if she were holding off an invading army. "I can't go anywhere as long as Raul and Juana are missing."

Frustration flashed across Frederick's face, instantly replaced with the professional demeanor he reserved for colleagues who crossed his path. He stepped forward, as if that would drive his point home.

Dina recognized *the look*, and it infuriated her. He never seemed to realize – she was not one of his precious agents. The animosity built into a seething cauldron of anger as they stared at each other.

Frederick turned back to the window, as if it suddenly

didn't matter. He spoke, his voice icy. "Of course. I understand. Nevertheless, I have to be in the office tomorrow." He deliberately turned and walked out of the room.

Dina bit her bottom lip as Frederick disappeared. This felt like another milestone in their relationship, and not a good one. Slowly, she trudged up the wide staircase to the second story bedrooms. Even though she tiptoed by her mother's room, the door opened and Mariela peered out into the hallway. "I heard cars pull up, and voices downstairs. Is anything wrong?"

The last thing her mother needed was more stress. Nevertheless, Mama was still her backstop. As much as Dina wanted to shield her mother from the stressful events, she needed her calm, measured counsel. Dina even considered a small lie before she answered. "No – well yes, I guess everything isn't okay, Mama. Raul is still gone, and now Juana has disappeared."

Mariela's face fell. "Oh-h no! What happened?"

"Mama, we don't really know, but I don't want you to worry about it. The police are there now, and Frederick will be talking to them. I'm sure everything will be fine." That was really a lie. The blood stains in Juana's bedroom said everything wasn't fine, but there was no way she was going to tell Mama that.

Dina avoided Mariela's eyes. There was no way she could look her mother in the eye and make that story pass for the truth.

Mariela studied her for a few moments, then stepped forward and hugged her. "This is very distressing, but I will pray that our Lord will provide an answer." She slipped her hand under Dina's chin and tipped it up so that their eyes met. They held a glint of mischievousness. "Praying is probably the best thing for a sick old woman to do – yes?"

Dina colored. Her mother suspected she was holding something back. "Oh Mama, thank you. Your prayers are treasured. We all appreciate them immensely. How was your day?"

Mariela smiled. "It was not one of my better ones, but the doctor says we must do this chemotherapy, and so I suppose I will. I refuse to just lie down and die."

Dina put her arms around her mother's thin shoulders and bit back the tears. "Mama, you are such an inspiration. Why don't you come downstairs? I can warm up a bowl of that good tortilla soup that Lupita fixed for lunch."

"No honey, I'm not hungry. I think I'll just go to bed. I'll see you in the morning."

Dina kissed her mother goodnight and stepped back into the hallway. Frederick's voice floated up to the landing as he talked to the police officers. She padded down the stairs, arriving in time to catch the officer's last few questions about Raul's whereabouts.

Frederick and Dina exchanged glances, the recent icy exchange between them carefully concealed while the officer jotted notes onto a palm-sized pad. After a few more perfunctory questions, he thanked them, indicated he would be in touch, and left.

Dina avoided Frederick's eyes and in the awkward silence escaped into the office to catch up on the ranch bills. Frederick plodded upstairs, presumably to pack for the trip home. After all was quiet, she tiptoed to the side door, closed it quietly behind her, and walked to the barn. Heated anger erupted through her chest. Why couldn't her husband understand her need to stay until Raul and Juana were found? And then there was the worry about Mama. The cancer had weakened her enough she could no longer manage any day-to-day activities, and without Raul's firm hand on the reins, ranch function deteriorated rapidly. Whatever else Luis didn't understand, he was right about her being needed with Raul gone. Frederick would just have to understand that.

Clouds scudded overhead, obscuring the half-moon just rising over the eastern horizon as she followed the worn and familiar trail to the barn. She scanned the sky. Would they finally get rain? If it didn't arrive in the next couple of weeks, they would have to start selling cattle. The ranch couldn't survive more drought, which meant that whatever grass was left would have to be saved for the broodmare band. She sighed. Somebody had to be here to make those decisions.

At the barn, she fumbled for the latch, pushed the door open, and flicked the light switch. She hated to do that because Frederick would be able to see the barn lights from their upstairs window. For a perverse reason Dina couldn't even identify, she didn't want him to know she was here.

Slowly, she walked down the line of stalls, stopping to inspect each occupant. Most of the stalls were filled with young horses, three and four-year-olds that Raul and his apprentices were training. Benito, the colt out of Piñata stuck his head over his stall door and watched her approach. She spent a few minutes stroking his bright bay coat. Further along, Pico, a bright sorrel gelding whickered at her. He was a horse with huge speed and talent, undoubtedly destined to be a barrel racer. Both were colts that Raul had trained from their first day under saddle. Dina choked back panicky tears that threatened to overflow. What if he didn't come back? How would they ever go on without him?

Frederick had never understood that Raul was part of a tight-knit family. He'd been at the ranch before her father had married her mother. Luis had arrived before she was born. She had a duty to every employee. This ranch, and the people who worked on it were as much a part of her life as intelligence work was Frederick's. She couldn't walk away and expect everything to run smoothly, and he shouldn't expect that.

Dina reached up and flicked the light switch, instantly plunging the barn into inky darkness. She slumped onto a bale of hay and leaned back against the rough-sawn wall while she idly catalogued each sound. Pico had gone back to eating, the muffled grinding of his teeth against the stalks of sweet-scented grass hay. The palomino filly in the corner with the crib-collar around her neck still attempted to bite at the creosote varnished boards in her stall. Nervously, the mare pawed at the rubber matting on the floor of her spacious quarters. Who could she contact about Raul? She had no acquaintances in Juárez – for good reason. Who *wanted* to know anyone in that city of death? This year, it was again the murder capitol of Mexico. Everyone at the ranch avoided the place, so why would Raul have gone there? It wasn't likely cattle or ranch business. All the ranch accounting and legal work was either done in Agua Prieta or across the border at Douglas. Supplies were readily available in either place so whatever had drawn Raul to Juárez had to be outside his ranch duties. Dina flicked off the lights and slipped outside. Juana's disappearance almost certainly pointed to either the Sinaloa or Juárez cartels. Did that have anything to do with Raul's continued absence? As she felt her way up the trail to the house, she clenched her fists. All she had were more questions – and no answers.

The trail to the house didn't seem long enough. She strolled along, gazing at the sporadic stars on the northern horizon. Hopefully, Frederick was asleep. The last thing she wanted was a late-night argument. They'd had too many of those. However, the more likely scenario was he'd give her the silent treatment. She hated that. Besides, there were enough issues here without him putting a guilt trip on her. Halfway to the house, she stopped and stared down the lane toward Raul's house. Though the police had long departed, the lights were still blazing inside. Hardly thinking, her feet moved toward the sparkling windows. They should have at least turned the lights out. Oh well, she could do that. Probably it was only the living room light, and she wouldn't even have to go inside. There was a switch in the hallway just inside the door. She would quickly flip it off and leave. Still, her eyes flickered nervously to each side of the path as she padded along the dark drive. A hoot owl in the dry creek bed to the south announced the start of the evening hunt. Up on the south ridge a big dog coyote yapped his evening territorial announcement to all who cared. In their stygian hiding places a chorus of crickets chirped, because that's what crickets do when they're content.

Dina stopped at the bottom of the walk and stared at the front door. Momentarily, she shivered. She should have gone to the house and asked Frederick to turn out the lights. No, that was ridiculous. This she could manage. Besides, Frederick would already be in bed. He was never one to stay up late. She walked softly up the sidewalk, opened the front door, and peered inside. Everything was as it had been before. Nothing seemed out of place. Everything inside her shouted a warning not to step over the threshold. She did it anyway. Turning the lights out would only take a second. Despite her resolve to avoid the bedroom, one step followed another down the tiled hallway. Her fingers gripped the door jamb, every muscle tense, ready to run – to escape. Carefully, she peered around the corner. The blood-stained sheets had not been disturbed. Suddenly, she was glad she'd thought to come. This mayhem was not a scene Raul should have to face. Quickly, she swallowed back the fear and loathing and ripped back the sheets. A mattress pad had been an ineffective barrier at stopping any blood from staining the mattress. She stripped off the pad and walked to the other side of the bed to tip the mattress up against the wall. Tomorrow morning she would have a couple of the ranch hands take it to the dump. She checked the tag for the brand name. She would go to town and get another one before Raul returned. He might not want to sleep in here again, but if he did, the mattress should be sterile, and new. His wrenching sorrow would be difficult enough without having to face the physical evidence of his wife's kidnapping. She heaved the mattress off the bed and up against the far wall. It was then she spotted the cell phone that had been tucked between the bedspring and the mattress. Stunned that the police had missed it, she picked it up. It had to be Juana's. She took it into the kitchen, sat at the counter and opened Juana's email account. Within minutes, she understood where Raul had gone, and why he hadn't returned.

Chapter 4
RAUL

I'VE TRAINED HORSES at the Rodríguez Ranch for more years than I care to remember. Honestly, I can't imagine working anywhere else, and I've always been thankful for that night Ricardo, Dina's father, stopped at a small cantina in Nogales. It was a rowdy, wild place, inhabited by pimps, prostitutes, smugglers, and those wishing to be smuggled. At the time, I was barely out of my teens, trying to make a few extra dollars as a *coyote*, spiriting my countrymen and others across the border and through the Arizona desert.

That night, I sat at the bar sipping a Coke while I waited for my contact, a man who apparently had a small group of Hondurans who wanted to cross. A slight, well-dressed *ranchero* walked in, sat on the stool beside me, and ordered a drink. Without looking directly at him, I tried to figure out whether this was the man I was supposed to meet. Somehow, he didn't look right, but several times his eyes met mine. Finally, I spoke to him. He returned my greeting and introduced himself. When he said his name, I nearly fell off my stool. Ricardo Rodríguez was a legend. Though he rarely took people across the border, he'd built a reputation as one of the very best smugglers of contraband. His price and record attracted only high dollar goods, and of course the very wealthy who could afford to pay. Even his family didn't know of Ricardo's connection to the CIA, though later Mariela his wife became a part of the charade. After we'd talked, Ricardo turned on his bar stool and offered me a job on his ranch at Agua Prieta. I will never forget his words. He said, "Raul, I am looking for a few very good men." His eyes bored into mine, like he could see deep inside me. That's the way he made you feel, and that night, I accepted his offer. It was the best decision of my life. Ricardo became my boss and best friend for thirty-one years. Though I seldom left the ranch during the many years we were together, Ricardo kept me well-informed of the problems along the border. Often I was privy to the dangerous assignments he took for his country, but because of my background with my father, my real job was to train the horses, stay at the ranch, and give it the necessary façade of legitimacy. Don't get me wrong. It was a real ranch, and my life revolved around the horses. I loved every minute of it, and I humbly submit that I became quite good over the years at understanding how horses think, and why they react the way they do. As time went on, I was asked to do clinics in faraway places so that other people could learn what had taken me so long to understand. But through all those dangerous years, the real reason for my job was to provide cover for Ricardo, for everything he did to keep America safe from terrorists. I like to think we were successful, though today it seems things are worse in both America and Mexico than ever before.

When Ricardo, my friend and boss was killed, all our lives changed. The children, Alejandro and Dina, had already spread their wings and left the family home. Mariela, Ricardo's wife, is a wonderful woman who supported him unconditionally. She took the reins, and carried on with the ranch as best she could, but it was never the same. Then Dina started coming back, and for a while, it was almost like old times. She loved the horses the way her father had, and when she was at the ranch, there was hope. But Dina had married, which meant she had other responsibilities. Her husband, Frederick, was a good man, but he had his own work and she wasn't able to come to the ranch as often as I would have liked. Nevertheless, we carried on.

None of the ranch people left after Ricardo died. Most had been there many years, and like me, they were desperate to re-create what we'd had when Ricardo was alive. The only time that seemed possible was when Dina was at the ranch. More and more, Mariela either refused or was incapable of making the necessary decisions to move the business forward.

I'd never taken the time or had any interest in searching for a wife. But a few years after Ricardo died, I found, and fell in love with a woman in Juárez. What was I doing in that God-forsaken den of drug dealers? Good question, one I hesitate to answer. After all, Ciudad Juárez is over four hours from Agua Prieta, and it certainly isn't a necessary supply depot for the ranch. We dealt in nearby towns, or even across the border at Douglas, but never in Juárez. My only reason for being there is because of my family. You see, my cousin is Amado Carrillo Fuentes. That probably means nothing to you, but in Mexico, it is the same as if I said I were a cousin to Al Capone, or maybe one of the other Cosa Nostra dons like Joe Bonanno or Carlo Gambino. In those days, most of the cartel bosses used Cessna Citation size jets to fly cocaine from Colombia for transshipment to the United States, but my cousin Amado, the Lord of the Skies, had a whole fleet of Boeing 727's. He ran the Juárez Cartel like a Fortune 500 company, and nobody in the country could come close to his power and wealth.

In Mexico, family is everything. Nevertheless, when my cousin Amado's number showed on my call display, I ignored him. The problem was that he knew I'd smuggled contraband and illegals with Ricardo, so in his mind a refusal to help him in *his* illegal activities was a slap in the face. Cousin or not, one did not do that to Amado Carrillo and enjoy a long life. He did not understand my refusal to help with the family business. Nor could he comprehend my loyalty to the Rodríguez family who were much dearer to me than he could ever be.

When Amado sent me the first email, I ignored it. The second came shortly after. What could I do? In our country, those who think they can escape the clutches of the cartels are naïve. The cartels know all, and they can reach you – anytime, anywhere. That was something I'd known all my life, but one tends to forget those disturbing details when training horses. My life continued to revolve around dusty arenas, clients, and employees.

A week after the email, on a late Thursday afternoon, I received a phone call. My new wife, the love of my life had left a sticky note by the phone before she went into Agua Prieta to buy groceries. The message was simple, innocuous to anyone who wouldn't have known what it meant. "Your cousin Amado called. He wanted you to call back as soon as possible. I love you." And underneath she signed it with her flowery and familiar signature.

This time, I couldn't ignore him. With dread in my heart, I picked up the phone and dialed the number Juana had left. He answered on the first ring. Obviously, he wanted to talk to me. That feeling was in no way mutual. Though I'd not seen him since we were young men, I recognized his voice immediately.

"Raul, this is such a pleasure. It has been too many years since we have connected."

To say what was on the tip of my tongue would not have been polite, and possibly not smart. I tempered my reply, and answered as best I could.

"That it has, Amado. We travel in different circles."

"Of course." His friendly ebullience never wavered. "We can never see what life will bring. Though we are family, our paths have diverged. We don't even get together. That is not as it should be. Tell me, how are you? Often, I hear of your successes in your chosen profession. You have become very famous in your field of training horses."

Somewhat taken aback at Amado's praise, I thanked him, but remained wary. I couldn't bring myself to return the tribute to his own notoriety. Though we'd worked together as teenagers, harvesting marijuana for our Uncle Ernesto Fonseca, I wanted nothing to do with the son of my mother's brother. Nevertheless, I listened to his continued compliments, then politely inquired about his family.

Amado had four children, all apparently doing well. Somewhere in the conversation he volunteered that the oldest was involved in the family business, which meant he was in the drug trade, and not yet in prison. He then gave me a short history of his two daughters, but curiously left out the second son. Amado was a cousin I neither needed nor wanted, but it seemed only polite to inquire about his unmentioned son. That was a mistake because his next words meant I had to make a choice.

"Yes – about Rodrigo. I'm glad you asked because it is why I called. He has no interest in the business. He wants only to be a *ranchero* and train horses. He was so excited when I told him that our cousin is one of the best trainers in the world. Ah, Raul, we have not done our duty as family, but I am to blame. He should know his family, and be able to visit. Would it be possible for him to come to your ranch? Would you spend some time with my son, work with him, perhaps teach him a little of your skills?"

Inside, I breathed a sigh of relief. Why had I been afraid to talk to Amado? After all, what could it hurt to take this kid and try to teach him the basics of training horses? As much as I might wish differently, he *was* family. I'd often done as much for others. Why wouldn't I do it for my own flesh and blood? Though I had an uneasy feeling in the pit of my stomach, I told Amado his boy would be welcome. We ended the conversation on amiable terms.

Three days later, Amado's son arrived. The uneasy feeling I'd had quickly turned into a lead sinker. Rodrigo Carrillo Leyva was trouble. The boy did have a bit of talent with the horses. He also had unbridled ambition – and a cocaine habit. We clashed the first day, but it was too late. I understood now why his father had sent him. Rodrigo was as dangerous as a coiled rattlesnake, but for the foreseeable future, I was stuck with him.

Chapter 5
DINA

DINA SCROLLED THROUGH the recent messages from Raul on Juana's phone.

His first text read: "Hey love, thanks for the note on the fridge. I have to make a quick trip to Juárez. Explain all when I get back. My bad news family!" A scowly face emoticon followed the text.

Dina peered nervously around the kitchen, ears attuned to the faintest sound of danger. Her fingers gripped Juana's phone as her eyes darted toward each dark corner. Should she just turn out the lights and go back to the main ranch house? At least Frederick was there, which would be more comforting than the eerie feeling here. Her eyes darted to the bedroom door. Was Juana really dead, or did one of the cartels just brutally rough her up to send a message? Either option was bad, but any hope that Juana might be alive was comforting. She scrolled down to Juana's return message.

"Hmm, must be important. When are you going to be back?"

Dina thumbed through the rest of the text messages. Pangs of guilt sent warm crimson to her face. A portion of this correspondence between a man and his wife was none of her business — and yet it was. Both of her friends were missing, and unless she found out what happened, neither might return.

Raul had sent his last message at 2:30, Monday afternoon: "Be home Wednesday night for sure. Probably sooner. Issue concerns our new HT — and your brother."

HT? What did that mean? And who was the brother? She read on to Juana's reply.

"My bro can be bigger trouble than HT. You should have X'd both of them! Whatever Marcos wanted, say no!!!"

Right, HT was the new guy, Rodrigo, the 'wannabe' *Horse Trainer*. That was easy enough. Juana had wanted to send him home, but Raul had refused, which was so typical. Trouble or not, Raul gave every employee the benefit of the doubt. In this case it made perfect sense. Raul had introduced the young man as his nephew, so it was natural that he'd stick by his own kin, even though it rapidly became apparent that the man was a liability to the ranch, to himself, and to everybody around him because of his cocaine habit. She turned to the next message and stared at the screen. Raul would have still been on the road. He couldn't have reached Juárez when he'd sent this text.

"You know I can't. He's the C of P. Big trouble, but I *will* be careful."

She stared at the message. Marcos? C of P? None of it made sense. Suddenly, she wished Frederick was beside her. He'd figure it out. His analytical problem-solving skills were light-years ahead of his husband abilities. For a moment, Raul and Juana's problems faded into the background, eclipsed by her rapidly deteriorating relationship with her husband. Their unsolved issues continued to fester, and it seemed Frederick had less and less desire for anything to change. Dina wrapped her arms around her shoulders and bit back the tears. How had this happened? Their marriage wasn't at all what she'd imagined. She took a couple of deep breaths, trying to focus on the real issues. This wasn't about her, or Frederick. Dwelling on their escalating marriage troubles would not help Juana or Raul. She scrolled to the next message on Juana's phone. Her reply to Raul's last text was caustic.

"What did Marcos want?"

Raul: "Don't know. Not there yet. He called as I was reading your last post ... been listening to him for twenty minutes."

Juana: "So ...?"

Raul: "Long and complicated. Call you tonite from the hotel."

Juana: "Ok. Talk to you then. Luv yu."

Raul: "Love you too. Later."

Seconds later, the screen in Dina's hand went blank. She tried to imagine what had happened. Had Raul called Juana that evening with an explanation of his mission in Juárez? Obviously, he was there to see Juana's brother. Raul had referred to him as the C of P. She turned the cell phone back on. If she was going to snoop, then she might as well be really guilty. Would Juana have emailed or texted this brother? Probably not. They didn't seem to be on the best of terms. Rapidly, she flicked through the old mail messages on Juana's phone. As she'd suspected, nothing had been sent or received from anyone named Marcos. After she'd checked the inbox, sent, and trash files, she returned to the main menu. Even if Juana and her brother were not on speaking terms, he'd probably be in her contacts list. She scrolled through the alphabetical list until she found a Marcos Ortero, and suddenly Dina understood. C of P meant Chief of Police. Marcos Ortero, the most feared law enforcement officer in northern Mexico was Juana's brother? Dina slid the phone into her vest pocket and paced the room while she sorted through the mixed messages and crazy rumors that floated like a river of human misery out of the murder capitol of Mexico.

After reeling through three thousand murders in one year, Juárez had hired a former army colonel to clean up their city. The controversial Marcos wasted no time – and few bullets. Within months he'd garnered a long list of human rights abuse charges. But Juárez had the beginnings of a new and honest police force, and if not on the run, the two dominant cartels who had paved the city with blood were at least wary. Dina stared out the window toward the bunkhouse and cabins that housed each valued employee. Why had Raul gone all the way to Juárez to meet with Marcos Ortero? Sure he was his brother-on-law, but that didn't mean they had anything in common. What could a horse trainer and ranch manager have that the iron-fisted police chief could want? From the sound of Juana's texts, there was little contact or love between them, so a social visit would have been out of the question. Juana had warned Raul to stay away from her brother? That sounded like more than a garden variety family feud? Wearily, Dina stood, flicked the lights off and carefully closed the front door to Raul's house. Nothing in this puzzle fit, and no answers were forthcoming.

Several times Dina glanced over her shoulder as she

trudged back to the house. Whoever had kidnapped Juana was long gone. Nevertheless, she was glad to reach the three steps that led to the veranda. Frederick's presence would be comforting, and he would be able to access every bit of intelligence there was on Marcos Ortero and everybody around him. Whatever marital problems loomed between them could wait. She needed his quick mind and intelligence network, now more than ever before. Quietly, she slipped through the double door front entry and into the expansive hallway. The stairs to the upstairs bedroom were to her left, and she took them two at a time. Quietly, she slipped through the door, then closed it softly behind her while her eyes became accustomed to the darkness. Every item in the room was immaculate, like a high-end hotel. The bed was exactly as Paulina the housemaid had left it. The two bath towels remained folded in the exact center of the bedspread like ivory swans. Obviously, Frederick had not been here. Or had he? Her eyes moved to the unsealed envelope leaning against the vase of fresh flowers on her end table. She pulled out the single sheet of paper and started to read.

"As you are not able to come with me, I see no sense waiting until morning. I have returned to Albuquerque ..." She looked up from the page. Frederick stood in the doorway. For the longest time, neither of them spoke.

Eventually, Frederick's eyes flickered toward the sheet of paper in her hand. "I see you read my note."

She nodded. "Why can't you understand? Is it too much to ask you to stay one more day? I need your help. You could delegate whatever you have at the office, and – "

"Dina, I understand your need to remain here during this difficult time, but I haven't a choice. I *have* to return to

Albuquerque." He picked up his suitcase and walked out the door.

Dina stared daggers at the back of Frederick's bomber jacket before he disappeared on the stairs. Angrily, she turned away. Let him go. She would not beg. But when she heard the downstairs door close softly behind him, she had to fight back tears. Their marriage was disintegrating, and now, when she needed him more than she'd ever needed him in her life – her husband was gone.

Chapter 6
DINA

EVENTUALLY DINA'S TEARS dried, leaving behind a simmering cauldron of anger and regret. What had gone wrong? It used to be different. A night together was precious. Never before would Frederick have just walked away. She'd tried to understand his work. He had a dozen agents in the field, often in tense situations. But did he really have to be at headquarters tomorrow? Up until now, they'd dealt with the stress. It was part of their life, and often Frederick was unapproachable during those times. Yet they'd survived – until now.

Dina walked over to the spacious walk-in closet, slipped out of her clothes and slipped her nightgown over her head. A shower could wait until morning. She was too tired, and after all, what was the use. It wasn't like anyone would care.

Angrily, she grabbed the two white-towel swans, flung them into a corner and crawled between the sheets. Why couldn't Frederick understand she needed him? Her body ached with exhaustion, but she knew from experience that the anger and hurt would hold sleep at bay until the wee hours of the morning. Eventually, her hand fumbled for the switch on the lamp beside her bed. Perhaps if she read for a while, she would be able to put aside her anger with Frederick, and her worry about Raul and Juana. Certainly she had no energy to think about the ranch, or the cattle and horses. The ranch would always survive. It was solid; an ingrained, immovable part of her life that would never change.

Several books littered her bedside table, none appealing. She turned off the lamp, slipped out of bed and padded over to the open window on the east side of the room. The window looked out over the dry wash they'd always called the Big Coulee. It snaked southwest for miles, clear to the foothills of the Sierra Madre. In the bottom left-hand corner of the window, she could just glimpse a part of the front of Raul's house, now dark and silent, lonely in the light of the three-quarter moon. A rustling breeze carried the last of the day's warmth and stirred the long drapes on either side of the window. She reached for the braided cords to fasten them. Perhaps it was that movement that caused her to see the figure in the moonlight. The silhouette of a man hugged the wall of the now burnt-out structure. The man's movement had caught her attention. As she peered into the darkness, she could now see him clearly in the light of the rising moon. Was it one of the ranch hands, or Luis? Suddenly afraid at being so exposed, she stepped to the side, so she was partially hidden by the drapes. The man scurried out of sight along the east wall. Who had it been? Tomorrow, she would check with Luis. He would laugh and tell her ... well, what *would* he say? That it had been one of the men? Or that, unable to sleep, he'd been out for a late-night stroll? Of course, that had been it. Luis was just as worried as she was, and like her, he'd be scrambling to find answers.

Dina closed the drapes and trudged back to bed. Exhaustion now trumped the stress and horror of the day. Shortly after midnight, sleep overtook her.

When the cell phone on her dresser played its raucous "jump to my command" tune, Dina stumbled out of bed. In normal times, she might have ignored it. Well, probably not. With a mother battling cancer and ranch problems that ran from calving or foaling difficulties to employee dilemmas, ignoring a call, no matter the hour, would never be an option.

"Hello?" Her voice was dogged with sleep.

"Dina." It was Luis, his next words rapid and abrupt.

"Yes."

"Raul's house is on fire."

Dina's pulse raced. Raul's house on fire? What had happened? Had she ... what had she done? She had been the last person in it. "I'll be right there." Her feet hit the floor. She flung the nightgown onto the bed and scrambled into shirt and jeans. Socks and bra she could do without. She rushed down the stairs and across the gravel path, but there was little anyone could do to stop the spreading flames. Dina stood in a semicircle with the men. Nobody spoke. When the roof caved in, she shuddered and reached for Luis's hand. He slipped an arm around her shoulder, but it was little comfort.

How had the fire happened? As much as she wanted to avoid that answer, she knew the man she'd seen last night had been responsible. She should have investigated, then alerted the men. Instead – what had she done? Gone to sleep. What a wonderful manager she had proven to be. Under her breath, she swore at Frederick. If he had been here, this might not have happened. As soon as she uttered the words, she was sorry. This wasn't his fault. His responsibilities were back in Albuquerque. Still, Frederick *would* have investigated, and that's what she should have done. Dina's face warmed, and her jaw set against the sudden chill of the night. She had failed. Wearily, she turned away, but before she left she glanced over her shoulder and scanned the faces of the men who stood in a huddle, staring at the flames. Every one of the ranch hands had turned out to do what they could. She studied the group. They were all there – except for Oscar – and Rodrigo. The gardener and the budding horse trainer were conspicuously absent.

Chapter 7
FREDERICK

FREDERICK'S HAND GRIPPED the wheel as he slowed for the harsh lights of the border crossing. No matter how many times he went through successfully, he always tensed up, just like everybody in this lineup, he thought. There was good reason for it. American border security had changed. It wasn't like the old days where you pulled up, flashed a driver's license, made a quick declaration of American citizenship, and went on your way. He rummaged in the console. Now an American passport and a good story were mandatory. Armed agents with underbody mirrors and drug sniffing dogs scoured the bottom of each vehicle. Cameras snapped pictures from multiple angles, not that it did much good. Even with all the added safeguards, contraband drugs and illegal immigrants still poured through every crossing.

Frederick handed his passport to the agent in the glassed-in booth as he met her eyes. She was young, Hispanic, probably had less than five years with the agency. Her questions were correct, the same probing inquiries every agent made as her eyes roved over the vehicle. "How long have you been out of the country? Where do you live?" Inane, irrelevant questions that seldom trapped any who were a threat to the country's security. The questions were only asked to give the agent time to assess the truthfulness of the declaration. The next questions were the real kickers; whether he had tobacco, alcohol, or firearms. A negative response was always the easiest. The agent handed his passport back. He stuffed it in the console and drove away. The system didn't work, but this was not the place to argue the point, or attempt a fix.

By morning, he'd be in Albuquerque. He'd not told Dina the real reason he had to be back, nor could he – ever. As he accelerated away from the border, he sighed. What would it be like to have a job where you came home from work, sat in the cool of the evening and discussed the day's events with your wife? He'd never been able to do that. For Dina to know anything of what he did was too dangerous, not only for her, but also for the agents he handled. And if it was an infiltration operation like this one, the danger increased astronomically. Her unreasonable anger at his leaving had built the wall between them even higher. It wasn't like this was the first time, but he didn't have a choice. Maybe after they solved the Juana and Raul issue, they could plan a few days in Hawaii or the Caribbean and try to solve their own marriage problems.

His fingers idly flicked the dimmer switch in response to the passing cars as he wound through the small Arizona towns north of the border. Once he hit the interstate, he'd make better time. He glanced at the digital clock on the Sierra's dash. Just after midnight. He should be in the office long before anyone else.

Several agent handlers would be on the duty roster, but

other than them, the building would be deserted. Agents in the field didn't take the weekend off, which meant their handlers couldn't either. They were expected to be on call, ready to offer whatever assistance an agent needed at a moment's notice. But he did hope he could wind things up at the office by three. He really wanted to watch the Saturday night performance at Roswell. There would be a handful of big names there, and the bucking horses and bulls would be the best that Butler Brothers Stock Contractors had. It promised to be an excellent performance.

Frederick clocked through the security gates at Stirling Associates at 7:17 Saturday morning, locked the pickup and walked to the three story, gray brick building. He stood in front of the scanner until it cleared him. Why couldn't Dina understand? His need to get back to headquarters was every bit as pressing as the issues she faced at the ranch. His shoulders slumped. There were so many problems they needed to sort through, but he refused to listen to another harangue about his spending too much time at the office, and how work was more important to him than their marriage and her family's ranch and ... on and on. It was just easier to leave. Let her vent without him having to listen. It would be less stressful for both of them.

Other than the security gate, no sign or identifying marks ever graced any Stirling Associates properties. The Albuquerque headquarters building was no exception. Frederick opened the front door and walked into a central vestibule area. The slightly-worn green carpet and beige walls would have fit in any small company's building. Nothing in the appearance or care of the building shouted successful – or secure. The three desks in the room were without inhabitants, as they were on most weekends. Frederick walked quickly to the elevator. At the third floor, he stood for a moment in front of a scanner, then opened a heavy steel door. Here, the security started, and though the biometric recognition system was never visible, it was the best and most up-to-date anywhere in the world. This floor was never still. No matter what time of day or night, operators and agent handlers were on duty, actively making decisions that could and did affect their people on the front line. Frederick's jaw muscles tightened. He wished his wife could see this. Though it would change her perception, he knew that she could never be allowed to walk through the doors of this facility.

Frederick slid into his worn leather office chair as he continued to agonize over his failing marriage. He'd tried to take the time at home that Dina needed. But when there were an average of a dozen agents deployed, it was not possible to walk away and leave them in compromising situations.

This morning, he had two situations that were critical, one in Venezuela, the other just across the border. Venezuela was deteriorating even further – if that were possible. The security downgrade was becoming a regular weekly occurrence, which precipitated almost daily calls from the state department with requests for updates. Frederick grimaced as he glanced at the line of clocks set into the north wall of his expansive office. Washington time was 9:30. Mentally, he rehearsed his briefing if the phone rang. As usual, they'd want up-to-the-minute knowledge on Venezuela's tortured status, as well as any new updates on the Russian and Chinese operatives inside the country. His instructions were to have agents close to the action, which was always problematic. If one of Stirling's agents was caught in the country, the State Department would claim no knowledge or responsibility, which meant no one in Washington had to fall on their sword. Stirling Associates would take the rap. They would be chastised and criticized for overstepping their boundaries, publicly fired – and privately rehired. And because adequate intelligence was paramount, nothing would change.

Frederick checked the last situation reports. The Venezuela operative was assigned a typical agent routine. Watch key people, quietly develop intelligence assets inside the country, and be prepared to instantly evacuate if the situation deteriorated. Frederick's teeth clenched as he scanned the encrypted digital message. The agent's report detailed a growing unrest in the country, and he wanted directions from headquarters. Frederick spent several minutes making notes, then flipped to the next report, this one much closer to home.

The current Mexico operation should have been simple. Pablo Martinez was a veteran agent. He'd infiltrated the Juárez cartel, accomplishing what they'd all thought was the impossible. Like most operations, what he'd done was the end result of a long-term play, one that had already gone on for the better part of a year. But last night the agent had called, which meant an immediate emergency. He punched in the handler's office number.

"Good morning, Ricky."

"Mornin' boss."

"Come to my office. We need to talk." Frederick slipped the intercom phone back onto its cradle and waited for Ricky to appear. Within five minutes, Ricky Stanwick strode through the door and slumped onto the faux-leather sofa.

Frederick stepped from behind his desk and pulled a chair closer as the man in front of him slid several sheets of papers onto the coffee table between them.

"What's happening? This doesn't sound good."

Ricky raised a hand. "I know. I've never been more afraid for the safety of an agent, but Pablo is confident he can pull it off." He leaned forward, his sport-jacketed elbows resting on the knees of his fortrel pants as his weary voice sketched in the details of last night's message. Frederick tried not to focus on Ricky's attire. In an office with no dress code, where everybody mostly wore short-sleeved shirts and jeans, Ricky was an anomaly. Casual for him was a sport jacket with a pair of five-year-old dress-pants. Frederick doubted he even owned a pair of jeans. It didn't matter. Ricky Stanwick was first-class. He shepherded agents with the tenacity of a Border Collie sheep dog. The man missed no detail, and no agent ever wanted for direction or support on his watch.

Frederick glanced at the log-in details. The call had come in at four minutes after midnight. Amado Carrillo, the undisputed leader of the Juárez Cartel was apparently in trouble. The *Federales*, with considerable help from the U.S. Drug Enforcement Administration, were closing in. For the next twenty minutes, Ricky's monotone voice described each minute detail. Frederick tapped the end of his pen on the blotter in front of him while his mind wandered to tonight's rodeo performance at Roswell. Would he still be able to slip out of the office early enough to make it to the performance? Suddenly, the agent's words smashed through his reverie. He scooted his chair forward.

"Go over that again. I need to – "

Ricky chuckled. "Gotcha, Frederick. Let me guess? Your wife wanted you to buy eggs and milk at the store on your way home, and you couldn't remember that third item. Trust me, it's always bread."

Frederick growled. "Never mind. I'm listening now. This is bigger than I thought. Carry on."

Ricky grinned. "Amado is going in for plastic surgery. Both hands and a complete face job, which means no more fingerprints, and no recognition. He instantly becomes a new man. No law enforcement agency can touch him."

"You gotta' be kidding, Frederick scoffed. "Nobody can touch him now. He just bought another Boeing 727. That gives him at least twenty of them, so he's now flying even more cocaine out of Colombia, and the Mexican authorities have done nothing. Anyhow, where's he going to have this surgery done?"

"Pablo says it's all going to happen in Juárez. Amado's personal physician will be one of the attending surgeons. He didn't know who would do the actual surgery, and he wasn't sure he'd be privy to that information. Our man Pablo is still pretty low in the ranks, but here's the trump card. Amado trusts him. Because of Pablo's extensive experience as a paramedic, Amado wants Pablo in the operating room to make sure everything is done as it should be."

"But Pablo's not a doctor. I don't see – "

"True, but Amado is betting that Pablo has enough medical knowledge to stop the procedure if there is anything out-of-line."

"But I thought you said his personal physician would be in the room."

Ricky shrugged. "Amado may be afraid. He wants

double insurance he'll survive. And I doubt any of the goons who surround him can match Pablo's three years of med school, plus paramedical certification."

Frederick stood and paced through the room, his eyes searching the beige carpet for answers that weren't there. His hands remained firmly jammed in the bottom of his pants pockets. "Alright. Let's meet again in the morning. This whole situation with Pablo worries me. He's so vulnerable if things don't turn out well." He turned to Ricky. "Keep Carlos and Fernando in the loop. I'll want them here in the morning as well. This is the biggest play we've had in the last year. We need everybody's input.

After Ricky left, Frederick returned to his desk and made notes of the conversation, not that he needed that. He would remember every detail of Ricky's report, but putting details on paper often helped him categorize and identify solutions. After he'd finished, he stared at the checked items on his list. Pablo's situation worried him, but no answers jumped off the page. He glanced at his watch, stuffed Ricky's papers in the safe, then hurriedly, made his exit. Twenty minutes later, he hit the highway to Roswell.

******

The bareback riding had barely started when Frederick found a seat in the outdoor arena. The evening was gorgeous, the temperature a mild seventy-five degrees. The horses and bulls always bucked better if it wasn't scorching hot. He scanned the program, immediately recognizing some of the better matchups in the rough-stock events. This could be an exceptional performance.

Three of the bareback riders were in the top fifteen. His eyes moved across to what they'd drawn. Two were matched with mediocre horses, but the third one, Luke Perry had Tommy Gun. If he rode him well, he'd win it all, but it was by no means a done deal. Luke had the skill, but he'd been plagued by injuries for most of the year.

Frederick hunched forward as the announcer's voice rose an octave. The second bareback rider was out, spurring well, a no-name kid who clearly had enough talent to make the big-time. He made a solid ride, and Frederick mentally calculated what his score should be. When the points from the judges were tallied, Frederick figured the kid had come up short. The crowd clapped enthusiastically. Under his breath, Frederick muttered his disgust at the judge's decision. "That's okay kid. They can't hammer you forever. Your turn will come." He sighed. It wasn't that the judges were consciously biased. It was human nature. If one of the big names had made the same ride, the judges would have awarded at least another five points. Probably the same happened in any sport or contest that relied on the subjective judgment of other humans. Frederick muttered under his breath. "Just go on kid, and give it your best shot at the next one."

The other rides were from forgettable to good, but nothing fantastic. The last, was Luke Perry. Even from across the arena, Frederick could see Luke's heavily taped riding arm as he wedged his hand into his bareback riggin.' Luke was still winning, but he was getting close to the end of his career. He scooted into position, tucked his chin and nodded. The gate swung back, and Tommy Gun bailed into the arena. Luke's spurs were over the points of the horse's shoulder, right where they should be. He had too much experience to make a careless disqualification mistake. After that, things got bad. The man was obviously hurting, and

Tommy Gun did everything but turn him upside down. Every third jump, the horse dropped a shoulder and swooped off in a new direction. Though Luke was still there at the eight second horn, he did not do well. The pickup men boxed in Tommy between them. One of them tripped the flank strap. The other rode alongside until Luke got his hand loose. He bailed across, grabbed the pickup man's cantle, and slid to the ground. Frederick suspected that Luke had wasted a spectacular opportunity to win. The judges had a different opinion. He went to the lead, well in front of the no-name kid. Frederick chuckled. Today hadn't been completely fair, but they couldn't ignore the kid's talent forever.

The tie-down roping was mostly forgettable, with no accidents or injuries. Whether at the ranch or in a rodeo arena, when a horse and a calf are running at thirty miles an hour, the result is not always predictable or controllable. Tonight, there was nothing unexpected; just good solid roping by some of the best in the business.

The saddle bronc riding was the event Frederick had come to watch more than any other. The quintessential ranch event, it has always played out wherever there are horses and cowboys. He scanned the program for the names of the seven who would ride tonight. As with every Saturday night performance, Bobby Butler had lined up the cream of his bronc string. Frederick's knowledgeable eye picked out the three who had the best chance of winning. There was Clint Harmon. Though he'd never been a world champion, for years he'd consistently been in the top fifteen. He'd drawn Feather Foot, a big Clyde-cross gelding. If Clint rode him he would place high, or win this rodeo. Feather Foot bucked hard, but at least at the professional level, was easy to ride. Then there was Jack Jacobson. He'd drawn the chunky bay mare they called Viceroy. She was trouble from the first jump, and could jerk the swells away from an unwary rider. If Jack didn't do everything just right, she might buck him off. But if he put in a solid performance, she would definitely take him to the pay window. Then there was the wild card. It was that new Indian kid from Canada. Frederick checked his name again on the program. Lonnie Bowers. The dusky-haired young man with the lean, tough jaw. He'd always seemed moody and sullen, but he could ride like nobody Frederick had seen in a long time. If he had a fault, it was that he made a rank horse look too easy.

Idly, Frederick watched the first four bronc riders. None of them were memorable, though still fun to watch. Two of them were rookies, and way overmatched. One barely made it past the chute gate, and the other valiantly tried to spur his way to a decent finish, but the good Butler Brothers' horse tossed him into the stands. The other two cowboys were good enough, but the horses they had were less than stellar. They were filler material, horses that on a good day and with a bit of a gift from the judges might garner some gas money for a cowboy that rode them well.

Whether it was the cool evening, or she was just feeling extra frisky, Viceroy had an excellent day, and Jack Jacobson made a good solid ride on her for seventy-nine points. He'd be hard to beat, but Clint Harmon was more than capable of doing it. Feather Foot bucked hard and spectacular, right from the first jump, and Clint showed the crowd why he was in the top fifteen in the world. It was a faultless ride, and the judges thought so as well. They gave Clint eighty-three points. The Indian kid would have to make an exceptional ride to beat either Clint or Jack. In fact, it was hardly possible on the horse he'd drawn.

Lonnie Bowers had drawn a black stud horse with an unremarkable name. Frederick had seen the horse a number of times. First, it was hard to get out of the chute on Midnight without getting hurt. The stock contractor had a special muzzle they put on him because he would try his best to bite any part of the cowboy's anatomy he could reach. Overall, he was a bad actor, and cowboys had a healthy respect for him. But even though Midnight was trouble in the chutes, sometimes he would buck as good as any horse in the business. He would duck one way, then dive the other, and every jump he would kick straight over his head. But it was nearly impossible to make a good spur ride, so even if you did manage to stay in the saddle, you didn't win anything. More times than not, he would slam his unlucky rider into the ground.

Frederick leaned forward in his seat, watching intently as the Indian kid gingerly lowered himself into the saddle, all while staying well away from Midnight's dangerous teeth. Quickly he nodded for the gate. When that horse hit the arena dirt, it was like everything went into overdrive. Never had Frederick seen a horse buck like Midnight did that day. He rolled and dived. He made every bad move a bronc could do, and that Canadian kid sat up there and spurred him as if he were a rocking horse. Nobody could believe it, including the judges. They gave him eighty-eight points – which wasn't enough. Nevertheless, Lonnie Bowers won the bronc riding by a wide margin.

Frederick eyed the young man as he vaulted over the pickup horse and strolled back to the chutes. If he kept riding like he had tonight, his name was going to be around for a while. Frederick watched his easy, athletic walk, the cool, dark eyes and slow grin, as those around him slapped him on the back and offered their congratulations. He studied the kid's face. It could kindly be described as rugged. Few women would call him handsome. In fact, unlike his riding, his features were completely forgettable.

Chapter 8
RAUL

THOUGH I WAS MARRIED to Marcos's sister, I had little doubt the outcome of my coming meeting would not be in my best interest.

At a small plaza I stopped and ordered some greasy, tasteless tamales, made worse by the thought of having to deal with my arrogant brother-in-law. My family status had never carried any weight with the current police chief of Juárez. I suppose I should have been more sympathetic. He had a tough job. His fight with the cartels was a fight to the death. Some days he lost, and the Sinaloa Cartel or one of their proxies carried the big stick, but as time passed, Marcos had consolidated his hard-fought gains. He was winning in a city the whole world had given up as lost to crime. Two assassination attempts had only made him more determined. In the last year, he'd cut the murder rate in half. Businesses could actually operate without fear – or at least less of it. His street-beat cops were, if not incorruptible, at least less corrupt than the citizenry had come to expect. Overall, Marcos had been as good for Juárez as he'd been for Tijuana. Though the disagreements we had were many, I had to admit, he was one tough *hombre*.

After I'd left the plaza café, I strolled the half-dozen blocks to the police station. For the last year, Marcos had lived there, simply because to live anywhere less secure would have been suicide. As a former lieutenant colonel in the army, he'd studied war tactics, and for him this was war. He stayed with, and was available to his troops, no matter the time of day or night.

Like everyone who found it necessary to access police headquarters in Juárez, I wound my way through a maze of concrete barriers. Two guards on duty in front of the building eyed my approach, their assault rifles cocked and ready. Near the door, I stood in line with the rest of the citizenry.

An hour later, I made it to the front desk. The officer asked the nature of my complaint. I said I had none, gave him my name, and told him my brother-in-law, Marcos had requested an appointment. He eyed me, then picked up one of the phones. Somebody, gave the okay, because another officer appeared and led me upstairs. Halfway to the end of the hallway, he slipped a pass card into a slot next to a steel door, then pushed it open. Inside, a bevy of officers worked at different desks. A two-striper waved me over to his desk where I grudgingly sat through a whole multitude of questions. Unfortunately, I passed, because he stood and motioned me to follow him. We walked down a hallway to an open door. He waved me inside. A large, cherry-wood desk took up the majority of space. It held a laptop and a cut-glass bowl of peppermints. No papers, files, or family pictures. Marcos's unsmiling eyes watched my approach, an AR-15 propped against the wall behind him. At the last moment, he rose and held out a hand.

"Raul, welcome to Juárez."

I nodded, tight-lipped and wary. "I have no wish to be in Juárez, or this office."

Marcos thanked the young officer who had escorted me, then politely dismissed him.

"Please, sit." He indicated one of the two chairs as the door closed behind the retreating sergeant.

I'd spent a good part of the day driving two hundred miles. I had no intention of staying here or letting Juana's brother waste more of my time. "What do you want?" I glanced at my watch.

Marcos folded his arms. "How is my sister?"

"I didn't have time to ask before I left, but I'm sure she sends her best," I lied.

One side of Marcos's mouth twitched upward, but he made no comment.

We eyed each other like two circling mongrel dogs in one of his Juárez barrios. Though I wanted no more acrimony, the past separated us. Marcos hadn't even come to our wedding, and Juana had neither forgotten nor forgiven. It was just one of a long list of snubs by her bombastic brother.

Marcos closed the laptop in front of him, then leaned back in his chair. "I hear you have a new horse trainer."

My face stilled. "Perhaps. What is that to you?" Where was he going with this? If he knew about Rodrigo, did that mean he knew I was related to Amado? If he did, so what? He could rule Juárez however he wanted. That had nothing to do with his sister, me, or the ranch.

"Is that why you wanted to see me, to talk about some ranch hand? If so, we've both wasted our time." I stood and walked toward the door.

"Raul, I have no wish to waste your time or mine. But when you attempt to hide a *Sicario* who has now killed two of my policemen, I'm coming to get him." He pointed his finger at me. "And whoever is hiding him."

Momentarily, my jaw dropped. Quickly, I clamped it shut. Anger exploded through my chest. Two steps brought me back, and I placed both hands on his desk and leaned toward his insolent face. "You know better – or you should. I am not, nor have I or the people I work for ever harbored criminals at the ranch. You know what we do, and who we are, and this is inexcusable." I spat out the words, but a budding caution and the door opening behind me stopped any further words I might have spoken. I glanced over my shoulder. Two tough looking troopers blocked the doorway. I swiveled back at Marcos. "What's this?"

Marcos grimaced.

"I'm under arrest?" I laughed in his face. "I had no idea your family feud was this acrimonious."

"This isn't about family, and no, you're not under arrest. Until a few hours ago, I had no intention of holding you – but your *Sicario* relative killed another of my men."

I stared at him. Marcos did know I was related to Amado. I backed away, trying not to betray the sudden weight of worry. "Rodrigo was at the ranch last night."

Marcos reached into the top left drawer of his desk, pulled out a file, and slid it across the desk. "I don't think so." He flipped open the cover. A half-dozen pictures chronicled the shattered body of a uniformed policeman on a narrow street. His life spilled into the gutter to join the blood of thousands more who had died in this violent city. The last photo was the typical perp mug shot. Rodrigo's cocaine-deadened, angry eyes stared back at me. There wasn't any doubt. It was him, and for a moment, I was happy. No more would I have to pretend to teach him about the subject that was dear to me, and he would no longer juggle his divided interests. The boy had talent, but in the end, the cocaine and his cartel connections had won.

The brief thrill of having Rodrigo gone faded quickly. He was family, and as much as I disliked him and his father, I still grieved for what might have been. What if drugs were not a part of my family's destiny? What if we were involved in manufacturing, or real estate, or ... God, why this?

Marcos gathered up the photos and nodded to the two burly cops behind me. "You will stay, Raul. You aren't under arrest – at least not now. But you will remain here at the station. You are to contact nobody during the investigation – not even Juana."

Slowly, I nodded. It wasn't like I had any other choice. In this town, Marcos made the rules. "And how long will this investigation take?"

He shrugged, avoiding my eyes. "We are working as quickly as possible."

******

My third floor room with the barred windows was comfortable. It wasn't a jail cell, but neither was it freedom. My brother-in-law had made sure to supply everything I needed, and I had to admit that as much as I disliked him, my incarceration quarters could have been worse.

My mind led me back to the police photo of my nephew Rodrigo, and the lifeless body of the Juárez policeman who had died at his hand. I slumped onto the edge of the bed and rubbed my face in my hands. If Rodrigo had done it, he should pay. But then what about his violent family upbringing as the son of Amado Carrillo, charged with the murder of hundreds of his countrymen? Did the boy have a chance to be anything different than what he was? I reckoned that was beyond me. His guilt or innocence had to be left to a judge bigger than me. God created every man with a free will. Regardless of circumstances, we are responsible for our own choices, or at least that's what Dina would say, and I'm inclined to think she's right.

Marcos pounded on the door at ten o'clock that night to see if I needed anything, I found it in my heart to be grateful. As an old adversary of my friend and employer, Ricardo Rodríguez, he could have treated me much worse. His perception of Ricardo was that he was a criminal, one of the many prolific smugglers on the border. What he could never know was that ninety-eight percent of the drugs and illegal aliens that went through Ricardo's hands were funneled right into the arms of U.S. Customs and the Border Patrol. Ricardo's CIA mission had always been to cultivate deep enough contacts in the Mexican underworld so that he would be the first to know when foreign operatives who were dangerous to America reached the southern border. Often, that meant he had to smuggle a few bales of marijuana, or a group of illegals. It was a trade-off, and nobody had done it better or longer than Ricardo.

After Marcos left, I showered, then lay on the bed wishing I could call Juana to say goodnight. Even if I'd have risked that, it wasn't an option. Not only had Marcos discovered my family ties with Amado Carrillo, he'd taken my phone. I understood his need for security, but not being able to call Juana made me angry all over again.

It was a long night. I turned back and forth on the hard bed, trying to find a comfortable spot while I wondered how Marcos had found out about the family I'd walked away from so many years ago. Who had told him? Juana? Never. Dina, or any of the others at the Rodríguez Ranch? Not a chance. Everyone at the ranch was intensely loyal ... or were they? Mentally, I ticked off each man in my head. Ramon? Not a chance. Sandy? Absolutely trustworthy. Luis? How could it be him? Luis would die before betraying anyone at the ranch. What about the new man, Oscar? He'd been with us the least amount of time. He always made me uncomfortable, though I could never pinpoint why. Certainly there was nothing in his work that gave me reason to dislike him. But something in his eyes didn't ring true. And that face – somewhere in the past I'd seen him before, though I couldn't remember where. Possibly in some cantina in Agua Prieta, or even here in Juárez? I tried to elucidate why I distrusted him. The man did his job. He was properly respectful to the *Señora*, so really, what else mattered? And if he'd heard somewhere I was Amado's cousin, so what? Why would he inform Marcos?

Sleep wasn't coming, so I catalogued everything I knew, along with every bit of gossip about each of the men in my care. All were good men, honest and trustworthy. Luis did have a distant blood connection to one of Amado's former wives, but he was as much a part of the Rodríguez Ranch as me. Besides, our relationship had always been like a father and son – for good reason. Luis doing anything behind my back was unthinkable.

My mind wandered to that long ago night in the Sonora desert, south of the Papago Indian Reservation. Often,

Ricardo used that desolate stretch of border country to accomplish the task given us. When we moved people, and sometimes contraband across the border, our real job was to monitor those who presented the most danger to Ricardo's country. Operating in that sun-scorched hell of lizards and rattlesnakes made it easier for the U.S. Border Patrol to quietly confiscate our night's work. Occasionally, they let a few of my countrymen slip through their fingers to give us a cloak of legitimacy. A few illegal aliens were a small price to pay to maintain Ricardo's cover. Besides, Mexican illegals were not why we were there. The people we targeted spoke no Spanish. Their mother tongue was more likely to be Farsi or another of the Arabic languages.

After one of our more intricate smuggling operations, we rode hard to be back across the border by daylight. We were no more than a couple miles south of the rickety barbed-wire fence which is all that separates Mexico from the United States in that uninhabited wasteland when we heard the shooting. We rode forward cautiously, not knowing whether we'd run into Mexican Border Patrol agents in a firefight with drug smugglers, or something worse. After topping a long rise, the brilliant moonlight illuminated the scene below. In the bottom of a steep-walled canyon, two young *Sicarios* with automatic rifles backed away from the bodies they'd so recently created. We took cover before they saw us. The damage had been done, and there was little we could do. No matter how much we despised the two men below us, we had to pick our battles wisely with the cartels. I dearly wanted to obliterate these killers from the face of the earth, but between the three of us, all we had were a couple of Browning nine millimeters, and an old Colt forty-five. The distinctive curved magazines on their two AK-47's meant we were badly outgunned. As hard as it was, the best thing for us to do was to slip quietly away. Justice for those below would have to wait for another day.

I watched as the two swaggered back to the truck they'd apparently used to transport the two unfortunate souls they'd left for dead. They were nearly there when one of the bodies moved. Both stopped, and sauntered back. One of them rammed a fresh clip into his rifle. Now things had changed. Never could I sit up here and watch as they coldly murdered another one of my countrymen. I glanced at Ricardo. He nodded, and I clicked the safety off the nine millimeter in my hand and nodded to the others with me. We gave them everything we had, which wasn't much. I doubt if any of our bullets came close, but we made lots of noise, enough that they changed their minds. They bailed into their pickup and headed south toward El Patricio.

Single file, we rode into the bottom. The two bodies lay where they'd fallen, shot to doll rags, and quite dead – or so we thought, until the little guy moved. He appeared to be about twelve years old. I leaned over and looked into his pain-filled eyes while I swallowed back the rising anger and tears. How could anyone do this to a kid? He had a big hole in his chest, and should have been dead. When he looked up at me with those big brown eyes, I decided I was going to do everything in my power to keep this kid alive. The site was on the Mexican side so we called in the *Federales*. They dealt with the dead man, and Ricardo, bless his sainted soul, pulled enough strings to get that kid medevacked into the trauma center in Tucson. That was how our Luis came to the ranch.

Luis had grown up to be a quiet man, with big hands and a bigger heart. Sometimes he could be moody, and for days he'd go about his work with hardly a word to anyone, but I'd never had any reason to question his loyalty. So why did I now have doubts? Was it his poorly kept secret attraction to Dina, despite the fact she was married? I didn't think so. Though he idolized her, his loyalty had never given me any cause for concern. Though I lay awake trying to find an answer, I had none. However, my last thought was not Luis. Whatever, or whoever was at fault, my current problem was my brother-in-law Marcos. To leave here, I had to convince him neither I nor any of my men had anything to do with the cartels. Could I do that? The odds were not good.

Chapter 9
DINA

AFTER A RESTLESS FEW hours of sleep, Dina crawled out of bed. The first thing she noticed was Frederick's hastily scrawled note on her dresser. She wadded the paper into a ball. Why was it such a big deal to ask his precious agents to be on their own for a day or two? Once more, they carried priority over her needs, or the ranch. Well, so be it. She'd return to their home in Albuquerque when she was good and ready, and that wouldn't be for a while.

Weary from the night's stress, she gazed out the window at the smoldering ruins of Raul's house before sponging the sleep from her eyes. This morning, she would check to see if Oscar had made an appearance. The man left her feeling uncomfortable every time she was around him, but surely he had nothing to do with the fire.

Normally, Raul hired any new employees. However, he hadn't objected when her mother had hired Oscar to look after the yard and garden. He had more than enough responsibility looking after the horses, cattle, and thousands of parched acres that made up the Rodriguez Ranch without worrying about the yard flowers.

Dina smoothed cream into her face, a first line of defense against the merciless Sonoran sun. Oscar Ortega had been an enigma from the first day. A shifty-eyed loner, he was older than most of the other men, but he'd been respectful toward her mother, and saw things that needed doing long before she thought to give him orders. To this point, he'd been a reasonable addition, even if he didn't mix with the close-knit ranch crew. So why didn't she trust him? And where had he been last night? Why hadn't he turned out with the rest of the crew at the fire?

Dina slipped into jeans and a worn, red blouse, then trudged downstairs. Mama wasn't awake yet, but Lupita was in the kitchen. She glanced at Dina's haggard appearance.

"You don't look like you should be out of bed yet. Why don't you eat breakfast and then go sleep some more? You will feel much better."

Dina patted Lupita's back as she walked past her to the coffeemaker. "If I could, I might. But this morning, that isn't an option. Has anyone heard from Raul?"

"How should I know? Talk to Luis."

"How about Oscar? Has anyone seen him?"

Lupita raised an eyebrow. "No. Why?"

"I just wondered where he went. He wasn't at the fire last night."

"Probably he slept through it." The big stove griddle sizzled with several patties of chorizo. "You think he had something to do with Raul's house burning down?"

"Maybe. Everybody else was at the fire – except you and Mama of course."

Lupita carried plates and silverware into the dining room without comment. Dina stared after her, suddenly realizing how her distrust of Oscar sounded, and yet she couldn't let go of her growing doubt. She buttered toast and poured a glass of juice. Jousting with Lupita wasn't going to get her anywhere. It would be more productive to ask the other men in the crew where Oscar had been. Besides, she needed to speak to Luis. Something had to be done today to find Raul.

Dina smeared marmalade on a piece of toast and ate it standing over the sink, then gulped down the juice. After rinsing her hands under the tap, she stomped into her boots and hurried toward the training arenas and barn. Purposely, she swung by her mother's big garden that Oscar tended at the back of the house. He wasn't there, though admittedly it was early. She pulled the door open to the small shed where they kept the hand tools and other yard necessities.

"Good morning."

Startled at the voice, she stepped back and bumped her head on the low door sill.

Oscar chuckled at her discomfort. "Is there something the Señora needs me to do?" His voice carried the usual carefully measured, flattering contempt.

Dina rubbed the top of her head and backed outside. "No ... well, yes. Perhaps ... you went to town last night – late. I thought you'd stayed there."

His lips flattened, the obsidian eyes suddenly hooded and cold. "No. Actually, I was back at the ranch before midnight. You wanted to know – "

"No, Oscar. It's just that I didn't see you at the fire, and all the other men were there."

"I'm sorry. I slept right through it. Such a tragedy."

Dina gritted her teeth at the phony concern in Oscar's voice. "Yes, you have no idea how much." She turned, and left. Deep in her soul, she doubted everything the man had said.

Silence greeted her when she arrived at the barn. The deserted alley, devoid of any activity stretched in front of her. She strolled across the hoof-worn planks, taking time to glance into each stall. Angrily, she kicked a piece of manure out of her path. Had Oscar been the man she'd seen skulking around Raul and Juana's house last night? Had he searched for the same item that now lay on her upstairs dresser, or was it something else? Juana's cell phone contained no incriminating text messages other than she had disliked her brother. So – big deal. Marcos Ortero wasn't exactly Mister Personality.

At the end of the alley, Dina opened the massive grain bin, scooped out several five gallon buckets of feed, then carried them down the line of stalls. The men would be here shortly, but she'd get a head start on the feeding. Besides, she liked doing it. It gave her a chance to watch each horse to make sure they were eating well. Raul always stressed to everyone who handled the horses. "Watch them eat. If a horse has a health problem, that's where you will discover it first." When she'd poured the high-protein grain ration into the last rubber trough, she went to the door and stared out into the rising sun. Luis appeared around the corner of the tack shed.

"Good morning." Dina smiled wearily at him. "Are you as tired as I am?"

"Probably."

Both of them turned and stared at the wisps of smoke that still rose from the burned house. Dina slipped her hands into the pockets of her windbreaker. "I've decided to go to

Juárez this morning to look for Raul. Wherever he is, he needs to know about Juana."

Luis nodded. "Yes, but be careful. Something is wrong. He should have called by now. And Oscar? Perhaps you were right to be concerned. He just loaded up his pickup and left the ranch."

"What about the new horse trainer?" Dina made little effort to keep the scorn from her voice for Raul's recent charge.

Luis's eyes shifted away. "I don't know. He's been gone since Sunday." He brushed past her and into the barn, his eyes flickering down the long line of stalls.

Dina eyed his retreating figure. Did Luis have more information about Rodrigo's whereabouts than he was telling? If he did, she needed to find out.

"So he didn't work any colts at all this week?"

Luis whirled, and his expressive face darkened. "I don't know – nor do I care. He is Raul's charge – not mine. I want nothing to do with him."

Dina set the feed buckets at the end of the alley. "Hey, I get it. I was just asking. So do you know anything about the new man, Oscar?"

"No, I don't." His voice was almost belligerent.

"I think he's trouble."

"Really?" Luis threw two bales into the stall cart and wheeled them down the alley as Dina followed. At the last stall, he stopped and dug for his knife to cut the strings on the top bale.

"You may be right," he said. The other men disliked Rodrigo, but he and Oscar were instant *amigos*. I think they knew each other before they arrived here." Luis measured off flakes of hay and passed them to Dina to place in the feed bunks.

"I suspect you're right, but even if they didn't have any prior acquaintance, it didn't take them long to become friends."

"So what was the connection?" Luis fidgeted, his hands twisting several pieces of sisal twine into a knot.

Dina shrugged. "Drugs?"

Luis angrily threw the twine into the wheelbarrow. "Where Rodrigo bought it is anybody's guess, but he was doing coke even while he was here."

"How did you know that?"

"It wasn't hard. He was trouble on several fronts. I've stayed as far away from him as I could."

Dina stuck her hand in one of the water bowls to clean out some residue hay. When she'd finished, she looked up. Luis now stood quietly, all anger gone, his dark, Latin eyes glued to her face. She instantly averted her eyes.

Dina felt, rather than saw Luis finally turn his intense gaze away. She was certain he was holding something back. But what bothered her most was the sudden smoldering intensity she'd first seen when they were barely into their teens. She'd made her choice, married Frederick, and had long ago forgotten their teenage romance. Luis apparently hadn't.

Chapter 10
DINA

When Dina pulled out of the yard, the heat of the day had already pushed the thermometer close to a hundred degrees. Not that the outside temperature mattered in the air conditioned King Ranch Ford. She hadn't wanted to take *that* truck to Juárez. She only used it for heavy hauling over long road trips across the border. In Sinaloa country it was wiser to drive older vehicles. Unfortunately, today the other ranch pickups were all needed. Though everyone lived under the threat of the cartels taking whatever they wanted, it was often the small "wannabes," angry, grasping young hoodlums who were the most dangerous.

Dina shook her head. So many things had changed since she had grown up here in Agua Prieta. The morality and discipline she'd known a few short years ago seemed a thing of the past. What had happened to make faith and the moral teaching of the church so irrelevant? And it wasn't just the young men. The aftermath of many cartel fights now left the bullet-riddled bodies of barely pubescent girls right alongside the men, painted fingernails clutching at the assault rifles in their slim and lifeless hands.

She punched the cruise control and adjusted the seat to a more comfortable angle. Though weary, she wasn't sleepy. Too many questions ricocheted around inside her brain. Where had Rodrigo gone? Actually, who cared? She was just glad he was off the ranch. Several times she'd been on the verge of confronting Raul about this new and scary addition to the crew. Why had he hired someone with an obvious cocaine addiction? Raul hated drugs. And then there was Oscar. What was his connection to Rodrigo, and why had Raul let her mother hire *him*? Were these two newest employees just another dreadful result of the unraveling ranch administration? Maybe Luis was right, and it was time she came home to oversee the day-to-day operations.

Dina gripped the wheel tighter. More time at the ranch had already birthed a cool reserve in her relationship with Frederick. She felt like giants she couldn't control were pulling at her limbs, intent on tearing her to pieces, but Mama couldn't do it all, not when she was so sick. Dina shook her head. Enough! She made a conscious effort to drive away thoughts of spending more time at the ranch, and what that might do to her marriage. Better to concentrate on issues she could actually solve. There were plenty of those to ponder, like additional pasture during the current drought, and how they would market this year's crop of young horses in a crumbling economy.

Three hours later, Dina pulled into the outskirts of Juárez. After crunching through a couple of quick *gorditas* at a market stall in the central Mercado, she drove the five blocks to the downtown police headquarters and parked as close to the station as she could manage. She stepped out and locked the doors, then made her way through the police barriers on Calle Juan Carranza. She clenched her fists and gripped her purse closer to her body, fighting the urge to run back to her pickup and drive as fast as she could out of this dangerous city.

The central reception area, crowded with every conceivable description of humanity looked and sounded more like a street market than a police station. A uniformed guard searched her purse while two other eagle-eyed policemen with assault rifles watched her every move as they motioned her through the obligatory metal detector. She passed through without incident, then joined a long lineup that inched toward a long, scuffed counter manned by three duty officers. Benches lined the perimeter of the room, filled with those waiting for the next step in their pursuit of justice, or at least a listening ear. In front of her, a steel barrier topped by bulletproof glass separated the unwashed from the three uniforms.

Dina looped the strap of her purse over her neck before joining the line shuffling toward the glass barrier. This could take forever. Perhaps she could find out about Raul if she just placed a call on her cell. Surely if she informed Marcos about Juana's disappearance, she would get a quicker audience.

The call produced nothing but a recording, and an invitation to press one, two, or three for further assistance. That was a scam, because she punched every number twice with no result. Resigned to her fate, she stuffed the phone back in her purse. An hour later, she faced the officer behind the desk.

"What is your complaint, Señora? His monotone delivery did nothing to mask his disinterest in whatever answer she might give.

Dina put her hands on the counter and leaned toward the metal-covered hole in the bulletproof glass barrier. "I would like to speak to Marcos Ortero."

There was no hesitation from the officer. "That is not possible. What is your name?" His pen poised over the duty form in front of him.

"Dina Rodríguez-Roseman."

"Address?"

Dina rolled her eyes. It did no good. The probing queries that every duty officer in the world is trained to ask, continued.

"And your complaint, Señora Rodríguez?"

"I already told you. I want to see Marcos Ortero."

The duty officer smirked. "Señora, whatever issues you have can be dealt with here. I will decide where it goes in the chain of command, but it will not be possible for you to see the police commander."

Anger blew caution to the four winds. "Well, sir." Dina's voice rose. "You may tell your police commander that his sister Juana has been tortured and kidnapped. And while you're at it, you might ask him whether he knows the whereabouts of her husband Raul, his brother-in-law." With that, Dina turned and stomped toward the door. She never made it. The two officers with assault rifles she'd passed when she entered the building closed the gap between them. The one on the right pointed toward the duty sergeant behind the desk. She glanced back at the glass window. He had one ear to the phone. With the other hand, he waved her to come back. Still angry at the man's arrogance, she considered trying to push her way through the guards, despite the sergeant's now frantic gestures. But Juana's life was at stake – maybe Raul's as well, and the guards didn't look the type *anyone* could push. She turned, and marched back to the window. The duty officer stood and inclined his head for her to follow him to the far side of the room where he held a steel door open. *"Pase."* He waved her through. Another officer ushered her to a bare interrogation room. He indicated a chair. "Please sit. Somebody will be with you shortly." 'Shortly,' turned into a half-hour, then another one. Once, determined to leave, she tried the door. It was locked. A glass plate at one side of the room appeared to be the one-way window. Were they watching her? All she'd done was try to inform the duty officer that Marcos's sister was in danger, and maybe dead. Apparently, family was of little concern to Marcos Ortero.

Dina surveyed every corner of the room. There was little to see. No police bulletins or artwork decorated the bare walls. She pulled out her phone. Twice, her thumb hovered over Frederick's name on her speed dial list. Each time, she hesitated. Finally, she shoved it back in her purse. He'd already abandoned her when she needed him. Why would her current difficulties make any difference? She slumped into one of the hardback chairs. Whatever she had to do here, would have to be done on her own.

The door opened, and a tall, angular man in a regular police uniform strode into the room. His thinning, gray hair indicated middle age. The deep grooves on each side of his nose were matched in depth by worn spokes that flared away from the corners of his flinty, slate eyes. His assertive jawline hinted of Greek warriors, or more likely, Spanish Conquistadores. The lips were thin and hard with single quotation marks bracketing his too wide mouth. Dina knew immediately he was Juana's brother.

She stood as the man crossed the room. "You are Dina Rodríguez Roseman?" He offered his hand in the American fashion.

She nodded, and briefly touched his palm.

"It is a pleasure to meet you." The way he said it indicated the joy was about as welcome as a colonoscopy. "One of my men says you have news about my sister, Juana? This concerns me greatly. Please, sit." He contemptuously waved a hand at the chair from which Dina had risen.

For a moment their eyes sparred back and forth, searching for an opening, seeking whatever advantage there was to be had. Dina lost – but not badly. It was she who opened the conversation. "I guess you know who I am."

"I do. I've not had the pleasure of being personally acquainted with any of your family, but I can hardly be blamed for that. Historically, your family has been on a different side of the law."

Dina bit her bottom lip. She'd have liked nothing better than to shout out to this man the sacrifices her father had made to protect his country. But she couldn't. Long ago, CIA agents had instilled in her family the same secrecy her father had been subject to his whole life. For their own good, as well as ongoing operations along the border, Ricardo Rodríguez's true role could never be known. Still, it hurt to have this man think of her father as something less than a hero. Her face reddened, but she accepted the accusation in silence.

"Anyhow," Marcos continued, "we can discuss those details later if it becomes necessary."

Dina had no intention of listening to more innuendo, and she wondered why he was making such a big deal out of her father's activities. "Is that a threat?"

Marcos's lip curled. "That depends. However, I understand you came here to talk about Juana. Is my sister okay?"

"No, she is not okay. Juana was abducted last night, sometime before nine p.m. We think she may have been tortured before they even left the house with her."

Marcos's knuckles whitened as he gripped the edge of the table. "Who?"

"So far, nobody has claimed responsibility or left a ransom note."

Marcos's face darkened. He stood, then paced back and forth, his lips an even thinner slash. Suddenly, he placed his palms flat on the table and leaned over, his face close to hers.

"So, let me get this right, Señora Rodríguez Roseman. Your family is still involved in smuggling drugs and illegals across the U.S. border. You've now stepped on Amado Carrillo's toes, so he kidnaps Raul Altamirez's wife – who just happens to be my sister."

Dina shoved her chair out of the way and tried to back away from Marcos's anger as he punctuated each word with a stabbing index finger.

"I have gone to great expense and trouble to protect *my* wife and children from families like yours. As long as I have this job, they cannot ever come to Mexico, not even to visit."

Dina folded her arms, and shook her head. "We do not smuggle drugs or anything else, and besides – "

"Really?" Marcos chuckled derisively. You expect me to believe that? You and your criminal family expose my sister to your illegal activities, and now *she's* the one who suffers."

Dina turned and strode toward the door. Whatever she'd hoped to accomplish here lay in ruins. "Marcos, whether you realize it or not, we are on the same side, in every way. Juana is my friend, so either arrest me or let me out of here. My job is to find Juana – and Raul."

Marcos's eyes remained hooded and distant. His shoulders slumped, the anger drained from his face. "I wish I could help you with my sister." He stepped around the table, his jaw set, the muscles in his face twisting as if a seismic tumult were erupting inside his head. "Someday I will be so happy to walk away from this city. But until then, every decision I make is framed by how it will affect those officers who serve under me, never mind all the unfortunate people who live in this hellhole city." He glanced up at the one-way glass, as if he actually could see the officers watching and listening on the other side. "Until I have brought peace to this killing field, I can have no other goal. In the meantime, it seems my whole family continues to suffer. However, many in Mexico have had to bear the same cross in this war with the cartels." He turned and shuffled toward the door, his mammoth responsibility and defeat apparent in every bone of his body. When he reached it, he produced a key ring. "Come with me. And while we're at it, tell me more about your family." His voice hardened. "I will not attempt to disguise the low opinion I have of your late father – and my sister's husband. You're convinced I'm wrong, so if you care, you have five minutes to change my mind." He motioned Dina through the door, then closed it softly. Dina tried desperately to condense the lives of her family into that time frame. Five minutes was not enough. Five hours would have barely sufficed. They used the stairs. Dina spewed every good deed her family had ever done, but as they passed the second floor, she knew she'd failed. Marcos had lost none of his hostility.

Chapter 11
DINA

AT THE THIRD FLOOR landing, Marcos interrupted Dina's account of her family's history and fixed her with an icy glare. "You say Federal Police were there to investigate Juana's disappearance?"

Dina nodded.

"And they never notified me? Besides her criminal husband, not only am I next of kin, but I'm the police commander in charge of this district." His jaw clenched with renewed anger.

Dina brushed away his indignation. "First – Agua Prieta is out of this district, and secondly, they might not have known who to contact."

"No." Marcos waggled a finger in front of her face. "It may sound pompous, but that is no excuse. Every policeman along the border knows who I am." He grinned ruefully. "I may be hated, but I *am* well-known."

Dina shrugged. "What if they didn't want the family involved until they had some contact with whoever took her?"

Marcos grimaced. "That's valid. It is easier for police to deal with kidnappers without a weeping, emotional family.

If we rescue the victim, we're heroes. And, as so often happens, if the victim is dead, no officer has to go back and inform the family of our incompetence."

Dina eyed him suspiciously. "From all reports, you are quite content to not be bound by regulation, paperwork, or grieving families."

A muscle twitched on the right side of his jaw. "I make no apologies for the way I conduct police work. This city is a war zone, and let me tell you, *Señora*, if I do not treat it as such – I will lose. That won't happen. And, I have every intention of finding my sister. As for Raul, follow me."

Dina had no doubt Marcos would do whatever it took to clean up Juárez, the same as he'd done in Tijuana. If his police force beat up a few innocent bystanders in his search for information and ultimate justice, too bad for them.

Dina leaned against the stair railing on the third floor landing. "So you have Raul here?"

Marcos's eyes narrowed. "He's guilty of harboring a criminal – and we may charge him with being an accessory to murder. So, to answer your question – yes, I have Raul. And I'm not sure he should leave until we find Juana."

"That's ridiculous. Harboring a criminal? Accessory?" Dina's hands gripped the railing at her back. "What's this all about? Commander Ortero, you and the truth are not even on the same planet. Raul is one of the best horse trainers on the continent, and for your information, he isn't inclined toward murder. He can't even put a dog or horse down, never mind shoot somebody."

"That doesn't mean he didn't harbor the person who killed my police officers."

Dina's lips momentarily hardened. "If we did, it was

because we weren't aware that a man we hired had committed those crimes. You have my word; all of our employees, including Raul will cooperate in every way with an investigation." Her hands clenched inside the pockets of her vest. "I may not see everything that goes on at the ranch because I'm not always there. Besides, we have hired some new help lately. It's been ... well, let's just say a difficult time."

"I presume you speak of Rodrigo Carrillo?"

Dina's eyes riveted on Commander Ortero's face. "Perhaps. We have many employees."

Marcos studied her. When he spoke, his words were clipped, each one carefully measured. "I suspect my knowledge of Rodrigo Carrillo, *and* Raul is infinitely greater than yours."

"Please, do not use those names in the same sentence. They are two very different – "

"Are they?" Marcos was too professional to sneer, but his words dripped with barely veiled sarcasm. Rodrigo is Amado Carrillo's son. Amado and Raul Altamirez are first cousins. You are aware of that, are you not?"

Dina's face blanched. "No ... no, that's not true."

Marcos's eyes never left her face. He shook his head. "I am not mistaken. How is it that you don't know this?"

"Raul would have ... no, I do not believe you. Besides – "

"Besides what? His face hardened. "It doesn't matter? For the thirty years he's worked for you, he just forgot to disclose that little detail?" Marcos rose, and beckoned her to follow. "Come. You can ask him yourself."

"Why are you holding him?"

Marcos's lips flattened, anger written in every plane of his chiseled face. His curt reply was a four word condemnation. "For 'just in case.'"

"You have to release him. What you're doing is against the law."

A vague smile touched Marcos's thin lips. "A lecture on the law from *you*, Mrs. Rodríguez-Roseman, is more than I can endure. Rodrigo Carrillo has killed at least two of my policemen. Raul has harbored him, a fugitive, from justice. In fact, I could and may charge you with the same. Come with me." Abruptly, Marcos turned and walked down the hallway to a short flight of stairs. Dina followed, trying to swallow the rising sense of dread. What sort of trouble had Raul brought on them when he'd taken in Rodrigo?

Marcos led the way to a solid steel door. He unlocked it, knocked once, then entered. Dina followed. Raul sat at a small deal table, a cup of coffee between his hands. He smiled, and stood to meet her. She rushed over and hugged him.

"Dina, you were worried, and Juana will be as well. I am sorry. It was not possible to call."

Marcos's voice interrupted. "Good morning, Raul. You two may have as much time as you would like. Then, I want like to speak with both of you about Juana."

"Juana?" Raul's head swiveled back and forth between them. "Is something wrong?" Dina nodded, then told him of her disappearance, with as little of the bloody bedroom detail as possible. Marcos's face masked any emotion, his slate-gray eyes non-committal as she gave Raul the details of Juana's kidnapping. When Dina had finished, Marcos softly stepped through the door. Neither spoke until the sound of his footsteps had receded.

Raul slumped onto one of the wooden chairs at the small

table, his head in his hands. "This is my fault. Oh, my beautiful Juana. If Marcos hadn't held me here, this would not have happened."

"Raul, you can't say that. The men who took her are Marcos' enemies. If you had been there, they'd have killed you and then taken her anyway." She pulled a chair and sat across from him.

"I should have been there to protect her." He leaned back and stared at the ceiling, his big rope-scarred hands stuffed knuckle-deep into the pockets of his jeans. His voice was distant. "How did you find out I was here?"

Dina hesitated before answering. "I – I found Juana's cell phone and scrolled through the messages you'd sent. I didn't want to invade your privacy ... it just seemed the only way to discover where you might be. I'm sorry."

"No, don't be. I'm glad you found it. Do you have it with you?"

Dina nodded, dug in her purse and handed Juana's lavender phone to him before she burst out with the question.

"Raul, Marcos said you and Amado Carrillo were cousins, and that he's holding you because he thinks you are an accomplice to murder." She threw her purse on the table, then held her arms out and gestured with both hands. "Please, tell me what's going on? I know that's not true about you being a cousin to the Carrillo family, but why did you hire that scummy Rodrigo? Didn't you know he had a cocaine habit?"

Raul held Juana's cell phone in both hands, slowly caressing one side of it with his index finger as he stared at the floor.

"No Chiquita, when I agreed to hire Rodrigo, I didn't

know about the cocaine." He sighed. "But Marcos is right." His gentle brown eyes moved to her face. "We don't pick our families. I didn't ask for my mother to be the sister of Amado's father. Though Amado is my cousin, I've not spoken to him since we were teenagers. Our paths in life have been very different, and certainly if it had been up to me, they would have never again crossed."

"Why didn't you tell us?"

Raul shrugged. "Your father knew. After he died, I didn't think it necessary or wise to advertise my family connection to Amado."

Dina stared at her oldest friend. Were there other secrets that only her father had known? For a moment, fear gripped at her chest. But no! If she couldn't trust Raul, then there was nobody in the world she could trust. She stepped forward and hugged him. "You are right. That was something nobody needed to know, but the knowledge is a little frightening. I suppose it could be a danger to all of us, now that he has decided you are useful to his corrupt cause."

Raul patted her shoulder. "Yes, his evil has now engulfed our ranch, and family."

Dina ran her fingers through her hair. "So why did Amado call? I mean, after all these years with virtually no communication, he suddenly calls his long-lost cousin? He must have wanted something?"

"He did." Raul spread his hands, palms up. Amado wanted me to take Rodrigo as an apprentice. He claimed the boy had no interest in the family business, which of course is the drug trade, and that the boy had a desire to learn about the training of horses. It was all a lie. Rodrigo had committed some crimes in Juarez, and his father thought the ranch would be a good place for him to hide from the police." Raul shrugged. "Amado is a father. I'm sure he hoped it would be a chance for his son to get his life back together. It didn't work. Rodrigo *was* interested in the horses, and had some talent, but he was trouble. Within a day, I knew he had a cocaine habit. I should have sent him away then, but that could have created even more danger. Amado's anger would have come down on all of us. I have never been afraid for myself, but I am now very afraid for Juana and the rest of you."

Dina reached over and touched Raul's shoulder. "The Juárez police killed Rodrigo."

Raul sighed. "I'm not surprised, but it saddens me to hear it. Rodrigo didn't have to be a *Sicario*. He was the son of the boss. They have many others to do their killing. Even though I didn't get to know Rodrigo well, I think he was a psychopath, a born killer. Only God can change someone whose soul is that twisted, and Rodrigo was not interested in hearing anything about God and redemption. Maybe I should have tried harder to make him understand." Raul cleared his throat as he averted his eyes and stared at the far wall.

Dina understood. It was so like Raul. Rodrigo Carrillo, a sadistic killer deserved only death, but to Raul he was worth something – enough that he would never quit trying to help him reach for what was best in life. She squeezed Raul's shoulder, wishing she could take some of the hurt away.

"Raul, what about Oscar? Luis said he and Rodrigo spent a lot of time together."

Raul stood, and walked to the far end of the room. A

sink and small counter with a microwave made up the bulk of the kitchen. He filled a glass with water, then turned and leaned against the sink. In those few moments, he had seemingly consigned his nephew Rodrigo to God and eternity.

"Oscar bothers me. Somewhere in the past, I have seen that man, though I cannot remember where. But enough of those evil men." He slid the glass onto the counter, walked the few short steps to where Dina stood and placed his rough hands on her shoulders. "You are holding something back. Tell me about Juana. I will wait no longer." His voice carried an unusual sharpness. "I want to hear whatever you know."

Dina dropped her eyes. "I thought I told you everything."

Raul placed a finger under her chin and forced her to look into his gentle, sad eyes. "Little one, you cannot tell false stories to your old teacher. You are trying to protect me, and God knows I do not want to hear what these vile men did to my Juana, but I have to hear it." His voice hardened. "Now tell me – even the bad parts."

Tears she couldn't hold back streaked her face. She fell into his arms, and for a moment, she was the same little girl Raul had comforted after she'd fallen off her first pony. But this time it was Raul who hurt. She must stay strong for him. "I think they tortured Juana before they took her away, like they wanted some information she refused to give. Marcos thinks they are trying to get at him, so whatever they did to her was to send a message."

Raul groaned, the pain a searing, hot iron deep in his soul. "Not my Juana. Why, why? She has done nothing to deserve this."

Dina held his hands, trying to comfort him. "Frederick

doesn't think they killed her, so we have to hope this is only about money. We will do whatever we have to do – and Raul, no matter how much, if there's a ransom, we will pay."

Raul took a deep breath. "Thank you. I can only hope and pray that money is all they want."

"We will all be praying, old friend. Now, let's go talk to Marcos. I dislike the man, but as far as Juana is concerned, he's probably on our side."

Raul nodded. "True. From the time they were children, he and Juana never got along. But I believe he will do whatever he can to bring her back alive."

Dina walked to the door and pulled it open. A policeman beckoned them forward. "Follow me, please." He led them downstairs to a room, knocked, then held the door open for them to pass.

A large table with ornate wooden legs was the only furniture of value. Marcos sat on the far side, arms crossed. A heavy, attractive young woman sat next to him behind the desk. Marcos beckoned them toward the two chairs on the near side of the table. "Come in. This is Detective Teresa Valenzuela. Teresa is our in-house expert on cartel kidnappings, and I might add – especially when it involves women. Teresa, you've met Raul." Raul and Teresa nodded a stiff greeting. "And this is Dina Rodríguez Roseman, Raul's employer." Dina stepped forward and shook hands with the pretty young detective. Inwardly she grimaced. The woman appeared to barely be out of college – until one looked into her eyes. Those eyes belonged to a battle-weary veteran. Teresa Valenzuela might not be middle-aged, but she was no rookie.

"Dina," Teresa spoke warmly. "I have heard much of your

barrel racing, as I have of Raul's training. I love your horses. However, a detective grade pay scale does not lend itself to owning a Rodríguez horse." She laughed, a low, musical sound, and Dina warmed to her immediately.

"Please." Teresa indicated the chairs. "Have a seat." She focused on Dina. "Though Commander Ortero has given me an outline, I would like to hear your version of the kidnapping. No matter how unimportant they may seem, every detail is crucial."

Dina sat uncomfortably on the edge of the offered chair as she started to speak. "I saw Juana that evening. She had been in Agua Prieta to – "

Detective Valenzuela held up a hand. "Before we start; is it alright if I record this? It is only that if I miss something, I want to be able to go back and hear it again." The detective's brilliant smile disarmed any objection Dina might have had. She glanced sideways at Raul. His face betrayed nothing, though she thought he was probably as uncomfortable at being recorded as she was. This was Mexico – Napoleonic Code law. There was no such thing as innocent until proven guilty. It was up to you to prove your innocence. She well understood the way the system worked, especially in Marcos's hands. Both of them must be careful how they worded each statement, every answer.

With frequent interruptions, Dina reported everything to the woman detective that she'd told Marcos. The only new information she added was the disappearance of Oscar. From the first, his departure had seemed more connected to Rodrigo than Juana's kidnapping, but when she'd mentioned him, Teresa had shown a quickening interest. She wanted to know how long he'd been employed, what kind of work he did, and why they'd hired him.

Dina cautiously answered every question while she worried about the words she'd chosen.

Teresa noted every answer on the yellow scratch pad in front of her, then asked, "So your family knew this young man? Or did a friend or neighbor recommend him?"

"No, I think he just showed up in the yard, and my mother hired him." Dina shrugged. "My mother liked him, and he did his work well, often without being asked."

Teresa wrote some more. "Let's go back to the night after Raul and Juana's house burned. You saw a man standing close to what was left of the wall of the house, and yet you never went to investigate? Why?"

Dina squirmed. "I thought it was one of the ranch hands, or Luis checking to make sure the fire was no longer a danger to the other buildings."

"Luis? And he is …?"

"He is in charge when I am gone," Raul interrupted. "Luis has been with us since he was a boy."

Teresa stopped writing. Her eyes darted back and forth between them, her pen poised as the silence lengthened. All the laughter and false cheer had disappeared. When she spoke, there was no more nice-cop-I'm-your-friend routine. Each word was carefully weighed. "Mrs. Rodríguez-Roseman, is there anything else you can add that I should know?"

Dina stole a quick glance at Marcos. He'd not said a word through the whole interview, though his eyes had darted between her and Raul like a swooping chicken hawk intent on skewering a couple of foolish field mice. This wasn't going well. Teresa no longer called her by her first name, and after Raul's last interruption, she had ignored him. That seemed ominous. What had either of them said that had triggered this now hostile response?

Dina clutched at the vinyl chair arms to keep her hands from trembling. There wasn't anything else she could remember that would help in the investigation. Her last answer was abrupt, a natural response to the gathering animosity she felt toward the woman who sat across from her. "No, I have nothing more to tell you. That is all I can recall."

Teresa stared at Dina, then leaned back in her chair. "I have no more questions – for now. You both are free to go. That, however, may not last." She peered at Dina over her glasses. "Your story does not impress me. Something tells me there are some items you failed to mention."

Dina's face reddened. "What I told you is the truth – every word of it. My first priority was to find Raul, so we could work together to find Juana." She glared at Marcos, a building anger in her eyes.

"Obviously, your police force is better at bullying people than finding your sister, but whatever *you* think, we at the ranch love Juana and want her home safe." She strode to the door and jerked it open before she turned back to the chief of police and his female bulldog. "I guess I should thank you for at least not arresting me on some trumped up charge. Raul and I are going home."

Marcos drummed the tip of his pen on the table. His face showed no change in expression, nor did he try to stop them as Raul and Dina walked out the door.

Chapter 12
DINA

ON THE OUTSKIRTS of Juaréz, Dina nervously scanned the rearview mirror for the flashing lights of a police car, but the busy ribbon of pavement behind her was thankfully devoid of any of Marcos' troops. Later, she and Raul stopped at a roadside restaurant in Janos to eat, then drove on into the night. Just before midnight, she pulled through the ranch gates, with Raul's headlights close behind. The trip had produced no nasty surprises from Marcos, for which she was thankful.

After they'd parked in the expansive driveway, Dina walked with Raul to the burned-out hulk of his house. She stood beside him as he surveyed the ruins of what had been his life with Juana. She sensed his grief, and that he needed to be alone. Quietly, she slipped away and strolled through the corrals. Sometime later, she watched as Raul turned away from what had been his home. He found her waiting, and she laid a gentle hand on his shoulder.

"Do you want to move into a guest bedroom in the house?"

"No, the bunkhouse was my home for many years. I'm

more comfortable there, so I'll just return to my old hangout. It's not like there aren't any spare beds, with Rodrigo and Oscar gone." He gazed toward the stark walls where he and Juana Ortero Altamirez had found happiness together. Charred timbers, and blackened adobe were all that remained. Eventually, Raul stood, and without saying a word trudged toward the big multi-room bunkhouse that sat kitty-corner to the barn.

Dina called after him. "We need to make a plan. Come up to the house in the morning for coffee, and bring Luis – if you want."

Raul answered out of the darkness. "Yes. That will be necessary. I will be there at seven."

"Eight will be just fine. I'm exhausted."

Raul didn't answer.

Immediately she regretted her selfishness. Juana might be going through unimaginable horrors, and she wanted to *sleep*? Dina ran to catch up to Raul and placed a hand on his arm. "I'm sorry. I wasn't thinking. Let's get an early start. It would be unwise to waste even a minute."

For a moment Raul's weary eyes softened. "Seven it will be." He gently squeezed her shoulder, then disappeared into the dark bunkhouse. She walked the few steps to the house as the familiar night sounds pulsed around her. In the nearest pasture, a mare squealed her displeasure at an intruder in her chosen space. A nighthawk swooped low, its thrumming beat a signature sound that tomorrow would be a new day with fresh challenges, and trouble. This day was over. She'd done what she could do.

Quietly Dina slipped inside, and trudged up the stairs. Weariness sucked the last of her strength. She turned on the bedside lamp, slumped onto the edge of the bed and tugged at her boots. After sponging her face and brushing her teeth she leaned over to remove the throw pillows and of course Paulina's signature rolled-up towel, which she'd expertly shaped like a swan. It canted at a crazy angle in the middle of the bedspread, as if someone had jostled it, then tried to straighten the mess they'd made.

Dina stepped back and eyed the towel. It had been knocked over, come unwrapped, and then somebody had tried to put it all back together – unsuccessfully. Lupita? Hardly. She'd easily be able to right the damage. One of the workmen doing maintenance chores? It couldn't be. They had no reason to be in her room. Anything that needed fixing in the house would be Oscar's job, and he was gone. Besides, why would a workman disturb anything on her bed? Her eyes darted nervously toward every corner of the room.

Maybe Oscar had come back with a perfect explanation, and she'd be ashamed that she'd not trusted him. Perhaps he'd only gone to Agua Prieta and got too drunk to find his way home. It wouldn't be the first time one of the men had done that. Sometimes, even the steady hands thought they needed to blow off some steam, something she'd long ago decided not to judge. They were who they were. Her job was to stand by and support them. Let Almighty God be their Judge. Besides, a knocked over towel swan was nothing to worry about. Tomorrow ... well, tomorrow had enough grief of its own. She stumbled to the closet, found her nightgown, and within minutes was dead to the world.

Sometime before dawn, Dina's eyes opened. She lay still, unmoving and afraid. Some noise had caused her to be instantly awake. Her eyes ricocheted to every corner where a person could blend into the shadows. The minutes passed, each one like an hour. Cancerous fear held her immobile. What sound had awakened her? A momentary surge of exultation sluiced away the fear. Frederick had returned. But she knew he hadn't. Whatever had cut through her sleep hadn't been her husband, but though she stayed awake for most of an hour, there was no strange movement or sound. Eventually, she summoned the courage to turn the light on. Hardly daring to breathe, she tiptoed to the walk-in closet and stared at the door. Could somebody be behind it? Despite the throat-tightening fear, she pushed it back and turned on the closet light. There was no one there, and her breath escaped in a torrent of relief. It had only been a dream. Disgusted with her overwrought imagination, she crawled back into bed and drifted off to sleep.

The sun had barely crawled over the eastern horizon when Dina's alarm clock burped out its rude summons. She dragged her legs from under the covers and put her feet on the floor. Weariness tugged at her resolve. Surely Raul would understand if she slept an extra hour, but she knew he wouldn't, not with Juana in danger. Wearily, she pulled on a housecoat, before her tired body could betray her. Raul depended on her. She needed to be downstairs and waiting at the agreed upon time.

In the bathroom, Dina pressed a warm washcloth to her face. Though she sponged as much of the sleep out of her eyes as possible, they were still red-rimmed and puffy. After brushing her hair she pulled on a clean pair of jeans, then reached into the closet for a top. Her hands hovered over several. She chose an everyday pale yellow blouse and pulled it off the hanger, but it caught, slipped through her fingers, and landed on the floor. Exasperated at her clumsiness, she reached for the blouse, grabbed it – and snagged a fingernail. She stared at the broken nail, then shrugged. They were all too long anyhow.

None of her bureau drawers produced fingernail clippers. She turned to the purse she'd hung in the closet the night before. Two others dangled from brass hooks beside it. Several more sat on the overhead shelf. Not that she used them all. Though she hadn't decided what to do with them, two of them were too good to throw out. The other three just hadn't made it home to Albuquerque. Her hand rested on the shoulder bag she'd taken on the trip to Juárez, then froze. The main compartment zipper was open. She never left zippers open. Her eyes darted to the others. Each purse had been tampered with. Her mind returned to the dark hours of the night. Somebody *had* been in her room. Was it the same person she'd seen outside Raul's house? If so, what were they looking for – which brought up another question. Maybe Raul's house hadn't been torched to destroy evidence. Had the fire instead been a diversion, so the arsonist could search the main house undisturbed? Had he not found what he was looking for, then come back to try again? Fear sluiced through her veins. What was this all about? Was this connected to Juana, and if so, why? Did Juana's past have some sinister tie to Raul's arrest, and Marcos's war against the cartels? She tried to remember the few times Juana had mentioned anything about her life before coming to the ranch. There wasn't much, and she realized she knew few details about Raul's wife.

Dina's hands trembled as she dug into the purse to find the clippers. Carefully, she trimmed the broken nail, then filed the edges toward somewhat of an oval. Whoever had been in her room must have been there when she'd come in last night, possibly the same person who had inadvertently knocked over the towel swan on her bed. Both Lupita and Paulina would have been in the house, and Mama was always in her room, occasionally toddling downstairs when she felt well enough. Surely nobody could just waltz into the house without being noticed. But last night, somebody had been in her bedroom and rifled through her purses. Everything pointed to the fact that the person had still been here when she'd walked through the door last night. She'd interrupted them, and they'd hidden in her closet until she'd fallen asleep.

Dina checked her watch. In fifteen minutes, she needed to meet Raul. She fought the weariness that weighed on her like a lead blanket as she slipped on a pair of leather sandals and clumped down to the kitchen. By the time she got there, the malaise no longer dogged her steps. Adrenalin and a growing fear left of what was ahead left little room for despair or inaction. She greeted Lupita, and poured a glass of orange juice.

"Lupita, were you here all day yesterday?"

"No, yesterday was Thursday.

"Of course, shopping day. What time did you get home?"

"The usual, late afternoon. Do you want some breakfast?"

"Just a piece of toast. Raul will be here in a few minutes." Dina glanced at the coffee pot to make sure there was enough. "Was Paulina here all day?"

"As far as I know."

"And there would have been nobody else in the house?"

Out of the corner of her eye she observed Lupita's suspicious glance. Her answer was calculated and questioning. "Nobody except your mother. Is something wrong?"

Dina buttered the toast. "Maybe ... I'm not sure." There was no sense alarming anyone – at least not yet. Lupita's curious eyes felt like knives probing into her back, but she had no intention of offering any information, mostly because she had none.

Dina's mother padded into the kitchen, still in her housecoat. She slipped onto the stool at the small table built into the kitchen wall. Dina poured a cup of coffee, and patted her mother on the shoulder as she set it in front of her.

"Good morning, Mama. How are you feeling?"

"I'm fine, sweetheart. It just takes me a little longer to get started in the morning. I will get dressed after my coffee."

Dina gently rubbed her mother's shoulders while she swallowed the tears she could not allow to fall. Mama's health had deteriorated rapidly in the last two months. The cancer was back, and though she put up a brave front, her strength was failing, one more reason to spend as much time as possible here. She wished her husband could understand, but that concept seemed beyond him. Her hands clenched, the newly trimmed fingernails biting into her palms. No, she wouldn't think about Frederick and their marriage problems, at least not this morning.

A double knock on the side door announced Raul's arrival. Dina poured him coffee and nodded her head toward the study. She didn't want either her mother or Lupita to hear any of the details of their discussion. Mama was aware that Raul and Juana's house had burned, but Dina hadn't told her that Juana had been kidnapped, and it could stay that way. Mama had enough troubles without having to worry about the worst ranch tragedy they'd ever faced.

Dina mumbled an excuse about forage problems in the old Quintaro pasture, then quietly slipped out of the kitchen. Mama seemed engaged enough in a conversation with Lupita about Father Ignacio's recent sermon on the doctrine of God's grace that she hardly noticed Dina's retreat.

Dina poured her own cup of coffee, then slipped into the office and closed the door. Raul had taken his usual seat on the left side of her father's desk.

"Why didn't Luis come?"

Raul shrugged. "He said he had to go to the east range to check on the grass. He thinks we should move more yearlings up there."

That seemed a lame excuse. Paco or Sandy could have easily handled that chore. Luis had almost always been included in ranch management meetings, but this time, maybe it was better that he had stayed away. This morning might be better spent listening to her oldest friend's broken heart. All those other ranch problems could wait.

Raul removed his straw hat, his fingers idly plucking at the brim while his eyes roved around the familiar room.

Dina set her coffee on the desk, then slipped into her father's chair. "We need to figure out who has Juana, but first I want to tell you what happened last night."

Raul reached for his cup of coffee. His eyes narrowed as they searched her face.

"Somebody was in my room when I went up to bed."

Raul's hand paused, the cup halfway to his mouth. He set it back on the desk. "You woke up, and this person was in your room?"

"Yes. Probably he was there when I went to bed, though I'm not sure of that. All I know is that when he left, he made enough noise to wake me."

"Why do you think he was in your room when you went to bed?"

"When I walked into the room, Paulina's towel swan was out of place. She is such a perfectionist, and would never leave it that way. Then I discovered that someone had gone through all my purses, including the one I'd taken on the trip to Juárez."

The weathered grooves around Raul's mouth turned flat and hard as Dina talked. He laid a hand on her arm. "Whatever is going on may be very dangerous. I think you should go back to Albuquerque until this is over."

Dina's jaw dropped, and her face flushed. She pushed her chair back. "That's the best you can come up with – that I should cut and run; let you face this alone? Thanks a lot for your vote of – "

A slow smile spread over Raul's craggy face. "Whoa ... stop right there. You know what I'm saying. I don't want you hurt. Whoever was in your room is looking for something, and they think you have it. Removing you would – "

"But they've already searched my room. They've figured out I don't have whatever it is they're looking for." Dina paced to the far end of the room, her arms crossed. "I wish we knew what these people are after. They burned your house, then they break into mine and search my bedroom? What do they want that is so valuable – or incriminating?"

For a long time, Raul's fingers traced the outline of his hat brim. "Perhaps it is necessary to find who has taken Juana before we can figure out what they want." He rubbed the edge of the desk with his big, rope-scarred thumb. "Possibly it is my long-lost cousin Amado and the Juárez cartel. But he has no reason to kidnap Juana. I have given him everything he wanted. I took Rodrigo in, which nearly got me an aiding-and-abetting charge from Marcos. I have cooperated with his evil in too many ways." Raul ran his gnarled hand through his streaked black hair. "Agh ... I knew better."

Dina returned to her father's worn chair. "How about Chapo Guzman's Sinaloa cartel?"

Raul's jaw muscle twitched as he stared at some point on the opposite wall. "Possibly, but why? Give me a motive."

"Maybe they found out you're Amado's cousin, and they want to put the squeeze on him, or take revenge for a killing, or ... I don't know. You're well-known, and not exactly poor either. It could be simply for money?"

"How I wish that were so, but if it's a kidnapping for money, we would have already heard from them. I would gladly pay." Raul leaned forward, his fists clenched. "And then I would make them wish they'd never been born."

Dina reached over the desk and patted Raul's hand. "No, don't go there. This isn't the time to talk about it, but you must forgive. It was God himself who said, 'Vengeance is mine.'"

"*Dios mio, Chiquita.* Leaving that to the Almighty is beyond my ability."

Dina sighed, leaned back in the chair and stuffed her hands into her jeans as she stared at the ceiling. "And mine as well, though I know it does no good to drown ourselves in a thirst for vengeance. We must try to be calm, to think like they do, or we'll never get Juana back."

Raul's face momentarily crumpled with numbing grief and frustration. He walked to the wide window that looked out to the arena and barns and stood with shoulders hunched, thumbs tucked deep into the pockets of his jeans. "You are right, but under the circumstances, I find it difficult to dispassionately assess the disappearance of my dear wife."

Dina dabbed at her eyes as she swallowed unbidden tears for Raul's hurt. He and Juana had somehow preserved that passionate first love. She compared it with her own, and tonight – she knew Raul and Juana's had been infinitely better. Was there any chance of restoring what she and Frederick had squandered?

Raul's voice jarred her back to the present. "It may not be the Juarez or Sinaloa Cartels. It could be one of the offshoot gangs of 'wannabes'. They are hoodlums, and will do anything to get attention. Kidnapping is their bread and butter. Historically, they've targeted American tourists, but I suppose we look rich to them, and they may have decided we were an easy target. Now, any Mexican who has been fortunate enough to accumulate something beyond their daily bread is vulnerable." Raul threw his hands in the air in frustration. "I have no idea who Juana's kidnapper could be. All I know is that she's been gone since Wednesday evening, and we have no ransom demand. That says to me ..." Raul's voice broke, and he slipped back into the chair, his big, calloused hands wiping at the tears.

Dina gave him time to regain his composure. Her mind raced, searching for a way forward.

"Raul, let me talk to Frederick. With all his contacts in law enforcement on both sides of the border, he may have a better way to approach this."

"If you think that may be of value, I have no objection. Call him."

Dina pulled out her cell phone, her lips pressed together in an arrow straight line as she stabbed at the numbers. She tried not to think of the last chapter in their current arguments. Juana's situation was critical, much more important than whatever marriage problems she had with Frederick. Dina waited for the same old voicemail message, but Frederick picked it up after the first ring. "Hi. Can I call you back in five?"

"I suppose. Don't forget."

"I won't *forget*." His voice was testy.

Four minutes later, Dina's cell chimed. She glanced at the call display to make sure it was Frederick, then picked up the phone. No terms of endearment passed between them. Nor did she give any acknowledgement of their current rocky relationship.

"Hi. I'm sitting here in the office with Raul. There has been no word or communication about Juana. We're searching for answers. Who do *you* think would have grabbed her? What should we do? She's been gone since Wednesday night, which means she's been missing for nearly four days. We should have received a ransom demand or something, shouldn't we?"

"Whoa, slow down. Let me think a bit between questions."

"Okay, but before you answer, I'm going to put you on speaker phone. I want Raul to hear what you're saying."

Dina punched the appropriate button. "Okay, go ahead."

"Hi, Raul. I'm sorry to hear this. I will certainly try to help in any way I can."

Dina glared at the phone. Yeah, sure you will, she thought. As long as it doesn't take you away from your precious agents. She forced her attention back to what her husband was saying.

"You won't necessarily hear from the kidnappers right away. It's very common, especially if they're professionals, to hold the victim for days, maybe weeks before there's any communication. By this time, the family is desperate. When they receive a phone call from the kidnappers, their relief is hard to imagine. Any acknowledgment that their loved one is still alive is something they'd hardly dared hope for. Invariably, the police have advised them not to pay, but now they're desperate enough to do whatever the kidnappers demand. The police try to talk them into a coordinated plan so they can be at the money drop to nab the kidnappers. Meanwhile, the kidnapper is telling them if there is any police involvement, the victim will die. During this tug-of-war on their emotions, the family psychologically moves closer to the kidnapper. He's the one telling them they will see their loved one again – if they pay the required sum. He is even willing to negotiate. And what are the police telling them? Not to give in, or – to endanger the life of their loved one by letting the authorities handle the money drop. Often, because the family is so thrilled that the hostage is alive, they immediately peel off the demanded sum.

Raul scooted his chair closer to Dina's cell before he spoke. "So if these are professionals, what are the odds of Juana coming out of this alive?"

Frederick's answer carried the weight of a man who had dealt with a hundred tense standoffs. "If they're professionals, the percentages are in the fifty to sixty range. Kidnappers often slow negotiations to have time to identify any law enforcement on their trail. But if they're amateurs trying to make a quick buck, and they feel threatened, the percentage of a successful conclusion plummets. Another thing, and hopefully this is where we end up. When an exchange is made, it is always dangerous. The swap is usually made at night, in a place the kidnappers can easily monitor for police activity. The family is directed to leave the payment at the assigned venue. After the money is received, the victim is dropped at another location, usually within hours of the money drop."

"So if there is a ransom demand, why would we turn the money over without seeing Juana alive?" Dina asked.

"Because you don't have a choice. Unfortunately, trading cash for the victim at the same location happens more often on television than in real life. They're in control of the negotiations — not you."

Dina's face reddened at what sounded like a veiled insult to her intelligence.

"The kidnappers want to make sure of two important items before they turn their victim loose. One — the money is all there, and two — the bills are unmarked *and* untraceable. That takes time, and until they are sure, they don't deliver the goods. The upside is that once they have the money, the victim is only a liability. Their first choice then is to release the victim to get law enforcement off their trail." Frederick's sigh was audible over the phone. "I hope that helps, but I want you to understand the odds. At this stage, the chances of Juana's safe return are not good."

"And what if these are just small-time Barrio Azteca or Salvatrucha hoods?" Dina asked.

The momentary silence on the line was all the answer they needed.

"So what can we do? Is there any way you can find out who has her?" Dina asked.

"Possibly, but it would take time. Besides, my getting involved at this point would compromise – "

"Compromise what, Frederick?" Dina's voice dripped a potent mixture of anger and sarcasm. She was fed up with his offhand refusal to offer more than token assistance. This was the most traumatic event they had ever faced, and all he could do was run back to his office and wait for her to come cook his supper.

"What I meant was – "

"Never mind. You obviously have better things to do. We'll figure it out from here." Dina punched the 'end call' button and slammed her phone onto the desk.

Raul leaned back in his chair, a worried frown clouding his dark features. "Wow, you two really have some issues."

"Frederick and I have 'issues' because I care very much about you and Juana and as you heard – he doesn't."

"I'm not sure that *is* what I heard." His frown deepened.

"What do you mean? Didn't you hear what he said? 'No, it would compromise, blah, blah, blah.'"

"Ye-es. I think I tried to hear him. You never let him finish a sentence. Whatever other problems you have with your husband, he's a very intelligent man, and well-connected in the law enforcement community. He might have been able to help."

Dina stared at him, then dropped her face into her hands. "I'm sorry Raul. You're right. We're not getting along, but that should never hinder the search for Juana. Should I call him back?"

Raul wearily rubbed his eyes. "No. Let's wait and give him time to consider the alternatives."

"Meaning …"

Raul stood, and patted her shoulder before he walked to the door. "Perhaps Frederick can help, but in the meantime, I intend to search every hideout in all of Mexico."

"And then?"

"I will do what I must do." Raul stared at her, his craggy face hardened into a mask Dina had never seen before. Deep in her soul, she suddenly feared as much what his vengeance would do to him, as she did for Juana's life.

Chapter 13
FREDERICK

MONDAY MORNING, FREDERICK arrived at the office long before the sun tinged the eastern sky with any appreciable color. He flipped through the agent reports. Neither El Salvador nor Honduras had any pressing issues. The situation in Nicaragua was improving, but Venezuela continued to deteriorate, as expected. It was the Mexico agent, Pablo García who worried Frederick the most. Pablo had gained Amado Carrillo's trust way too soon – enough that the current most powerful drug lord in the western hemisphere trusted Pablo with his life. Amado was going under the knife. At forty-eight, the sands of time were running out, long life never being an option for a prince of the drug world, but Amado planned to extend it as much as possible. Plastic surgery would make him invisible enough he could start a new career somewhere else. And with most of a billion dollars stashed in safe-havens around the world, retirement would be a breeze.

Frederick swiveled far enough to the left he could look out over the industrial park. He laced his hands behind his neck as his mind deflected from the agent problems and back to what he'd thought about ever since his eyes had opened before dawn. How had last night's conversation with Dina gone so wrong? He cared deeply about Juana and Raul's agony, but even if it had been Dina who had been kidnapped, he couldn't leave – at least not now. All he could do was try to help, and last night's attempt had been disastrous. Dina failed to understand that some things were too dangerous for her to know, nor it seemed could she trust his judgment. She would always be headstrong, ready to jump in where no one else would or should tread … and he loved her for it. But sometimes –

The internal line buzzed beside him.

Carma, his personal secretary spoke in her usual efficient, clipped accent. "Bill Richardson is on line two. He said not to bother you if you're busy. He'll call back."

"No, put him through." Bill Richardson ran the Intelligence & Counter Surveillance program at a small junior college in the outback of Wyoming. All right – all of Wyoming was outback, but the school Bill Richardson represented was *really* out in the sticks. It didn't matter. Graduates from his program were fought over by every intelligence agency in the country. Frederick unashamedly bribed Bill with fishing and hunting trips to Montana and even to Canada to get first shot at their best. So – if it was Bill calling, everything else could wait.

They went through the usual niceties before engaging in a riveting discussion about a fishing trip for Steelhead on the Dean River up in British Columbia. Frederick had tantalized Bill before with that one. It would be the trip of a lifetime, on a world-class wilderness river.

The conversation eventually turned to the reason for

Bill's call.

"Listen, Frederick. I've got a decent graduating class this year. There are two – possibly three you'd be interested in. One is a young lady from Alabama, but she grew up in Iraq. She's fluent in Farsi, and has a good head on her shoulders. First-class, all the way."

"Sounds good. Get me an interview with her. We'll fly her out here if she'll come, and if she doesn't want to do that, I'll interview her on campus. I want a shot at her. What else do you have?"

A young fellow out of Vermont. Valedictorian type, top of the class, a hard worker. Also, he's cool, the type who will always come through in a tough situation. Several times I've thought he would do well with your organization."

"Let me have a look at him. Can you set up appointments for ... uh, let's see, today's the 12th – how about the 23rd or 24th?"

"Sure. I'll see what I can do. I'll get back to you by Friday with a definite."

"So who's the third one?" Frederick had enough years with Bill Richardson to know he always saved his ace for last.

"This one is a bit of a sleeper. He doesn't come to class all the time. His first semester he enrolled in education and business and nearly flunked out of both."

"Not interested. He doesn't sound like he has what it takes for us."

Bill's voice cut through Frederick's disapproving silence. "Let me finish. He has way above average intelligence. He has to, because he cuts classes, and still has a nearly perfect grade point average."

Frederick drummed his fingers on the desk in front of

him. If the guy didn't have the discipline to go to classes, it wasn't likely he'd make it with Stirling Associates. "So what's special about him?"

"Well, he's an Indian kid from somewhere up in Canada. Came down here on a scholarship, and yeah, it wasn't for academics."

"So what did he get a scholarship for, and don't tell me it was for being a minority or I'm going to cancel our fishing trip."

Bill chuckled. "Actually, it was a rodeo scholarship, which is neither here nor there, but the guy – "

"What's his name?"

Bill chuckled. "I thought you weren't interested."

"If this isn't your affirmative action project for the year, then tell me why you think he's so great."

"Frederick, this kid has a mental toughness that puts him in a class of his own. He's got savvy. I'm sorry; I don't know how else to explain him."

"Yeah, okay. Well put him on the list. I'd like to talk to him. You didn't tell me his name yet."

"Lonnie – Lonnie Bowers."

"Oka-ay. Plug me in for interviews with all three. And Bill?"

"Yeah?"

"Don't let that Indian kid get away."

That ended the conversation. Frederick checked the wall clock. He needed to get on with that business in Juárez, but after he'd hung up the phone, he sat quietly for a few minutes thinking about the young bronc rider he'd seen Saturday night. He understood exactly what Bill was talking about, and right there he made a decision. Sooner or later,

Lonnie Bowers was going to work for Stirling Associates.

The phone rang again, and he glanced at the number. An inside line. It was Ricky. Frederick immediately picked it up. "Yeah."

"Pablo just checked in. He says Amado plans to have the surgery done next week at the Jiménez Clinic in Juárez."

"Is that his best guess, or is he sure?"

"Still guessing, but he thinks the odds are high that it will be there. It's closer to the main hospital if something goes wrong, and to Amado, that's important. Apparently he's ready to turn operations over to his younger brother Vicente while he rides into the sunset."

"Okay, come to my office, and bring Carlos and Fernando with you." Frederick carefully replaced the receiver and leaned back in his chair. His index finger tapped a dissonant pattern on the edge of his desk. This had culminated too quickly. But ready or not, they had to react with whatever resources they had in place. Amado Carrillo was too big to lose, and once he had surgery, the odds of him disappearing forever were overwhelming.

One by one, the three men trooped in and sat on the far side of the conference table. Ricky had Pablo's file folder under one arm. The other two were empty-handed. Frederick was a stickler for security. Meeting notes were seldom allowed. When agent handlers walked out of the room, they were required to have every detail committed to memory; but then, only those who had that kind of mind were hired.

Frederick slipped into a chair across from his men. "Alright, we need to make some decisions. My first choice would be to have Amado Carrillo in our custody. So far, that hasn't worked. Second choice: make sure the man doesn't leave that operating table. Ricky, give us an update."

Frederick eyed the three grim faces across the table. Nobody spoke while Ricky opened the folder on his lap.

"Pablo says by tomorrow he will have the names of all three attending doctors. Pedro López Saucedo is Amado's personal physician. He will certainly be in the operating room, but I doubt we can sway him to do anything contradictory to Amado's well-being. Pablo will have the names of the anesthetist, and the surgeon who will do the actual operation by tomorrow night. Either may be an option."

Frederick leaned forward. "And if neither is willing to cooperate?"

"Ricky took a deep breath before he answered. "Then we'll have to find some other way."

What about post-operative care? Is there an option there?" Fernando asked.

"Pablo is convinced that after Amado leaves that operating room, we won't be able to touch him. They'll whisk him to some high-security hideout, with armed guards everywhere." He held up a hand. "Don't get me wrong. I'm all for exploring that option, but I have to agree with Pablo. Taking him out before or during the operation may be our only shot."

"And Amado's goons won't be in the operating room?" Up to now, Carlos had made no comment.

"Oh, they'll be on site. But because of contamination concerns they won't allow guards inside. Pablo's biggest concern is that they might change venues at the last moment. It's entirely possible that the Jiménez Clinic is only a smokescreen and the operation will be done elsewhere which means we need to plan for that."

Frederick's finger stopped drumming. "I don't think that's likely. They'll stay with a discrete private clinic where they can control security. Jiménez isn't perfect, but it fills in most of the security blanks. He'll not want to go through an operation like that only to wake up in handcuffs."

"Are there other facilities in or near Juárez that are possible sites?" Fernando asked.

Ricky pulled a sheet of paper from his folder and slid it over to Fernando. "There are only two we think they'll deem as professional enough to do the operation. The Jiménez and the Castañeda Surgical Clinic. Castañeda is on the outskirts of Juárez, a long way from any hospitals. That's a concern if there are operating complications. Besides, it would be more difficult to secure. Plenty go there for sagging jowls and belly tucks, so they must have a decent reputation, but Pablo doesn't think Amado will use it."

Ricky crossed his arms. "We have to go with Pablo's bet. The Jiménez clinic is a first-class facility. That's the location we should prepare for."

Carlos and Fernando both nodded.

"When will we have the final word?" Fernando asked.

Ricky shrugged and raised an eyebrow. "Probably the morning of the operation, when Amado checks in. Pablo's convinced there are no trust issues, but you never know. Amado didn't get to where he is by being stupid. Pablo wouldn't be the first agent he's had to ferret out."

Distant truck traffic on Valenzuela Boulevard rumbled through the silence in the room. Frederick eyed his men as he mulled through their reactions. "Okay, let's leave it there. Ricky, keep your finger on Pablo. If anything changes, let me know immediately.

"On another note, Fernando, we're pulling Hans out of Venezuela. I want you to drop that one and work with Ricky. Tomorrow morning, you need to go to Juárez. Find out everything you can about both clinics." Frederick motioned to Fernando's expanding waistline. Eat everything you can. You are a wealthy banker looking for ... what do they call it?"

Fernando scowled. "I think the word you're looking for is 'liposuction.' Have you ever heard of a more detestable word?"

"Yes, whatever. Anyhow, schedule an appointment, and of course if you're going to go under the knife for such a serious operation you must insist on a tour of the facility."

Fernando rubbed his ample stomach. His scowl turned into a groan. "Even the thought of it makes me suck in my belly."

Carlos and Ricky chuckled. Fernando's operational skills were second to none, but sucking in his substantial belly was like shrinking the pyramid of Giza.

"Anything else we need to discuss?" Frederick's eyes paused at each agent.

No one spoke.

"Alright, we'll meet late tomorrow afternoon." He turned to Fernando. "Unless for some reason you get held up in Juárez. Let me know if that happens. We don't have time to waste."

After the men filed out of the room, Frederick paced back and forth. Was Amado Carrillo responsible for Juana's kidnapping, because she was Marcos Ortero's sister. Or had it been the Sinaloa Cartel? This was their territory, and if Raul had refused to cooperate on a smuggling corridor through the ranch, they could have retaliated. One didn't say no to the cartels if you wanted to live a long and healthy life, but of course Raul would be well aware of that. He understood them, and knew their power.

Frederick slumped into the chair behind his desk. A familiar, foggy blanket of weariness crept into his brain, short-circuiting any further analytical thought. It was long past lunch time. He needed to go home – try to straighten things up, and at least get all the dirty dishes off the counter and into the dishwasher. He grabbed his jacket, flicked off the light switch, and listened for the familiar whir of the high-security locks as his office door clicked shut behind him.

When Frederick opened the door to their expansive adobe bungalow, a wall of silence hit him. He trudged into the kitchen to make a sandwich. Dishes still littered the counter. The beginning ulcer in his stomach started to burn. He wished Dina was here. She always organized things so well. Besides, it was lonely coming home when she was gone. He pulled a can of Coke Zero out of the fridge and carried it and the sandwich to the back deck. It looked out over the barn and three irrigated pastures that defined their small acreage. Often, he and Dina sat here enjoying the cool of a late evening, the distant sound of traffic masked by the cooing of the doves in the desert. Now, the pastures got only a cursory glance to make sure every horse was in its place.

This Juárez situation had way too many loose ends. Frederick reached for the antacid tablets he always carried, then remembered he'd run out and not bought any more. Dina usually made sure he had a good supply, but of course she wasn't here. His throat tightened like he was on the wrong side of a smoky fire in a drizzling October rain. He walked back into the kitchen and surveyed the pile of dishes. Should he deal with them now, or wait until later? Maybe he could get Nancy, their sometimes housekeeper, to come tomorrow. He'd call her tonight. He walked into the living room, kicked his shoes off and lay on the couch as he thumbed through his private emails. Nothing from Dina. Well, it wasn't as if he'd expected anything. His jaw clenched and worry like a cloud of crop-eating locusts settled on his shoulders. She wasn't happy, but when he thought about it – he wasn't either. How could she expect him to just drop everything here and stay at her family's ranch in Sonora? He couldn't do that. Not now. One little mistake and the Juárez situation would explode like a Roman candle, and an agent would be sucked into the relentless killing machine of the cartels.

Frederick threw his cell phone on the coffee table, then padded back to the kitchen. He tried to focus on the dirty dishes, but his mind marched two-hundred-and fifty miles south to the Mexican border where a few strands of rusty barbed-wire attempted to separate middle-class security, big-box stores, and high wages from Mexican poverty, tortilla and bean jobs, and the perpetual fear of the cartels. Frederick's jaw clenched with a sudden fear. What if he failed? Pablo had a wife and family. He had dreams. Who was he to order this man into the abyss where he might never return?

Chapter 14
RAUL

MY FATHER, GUILLERMO Raul Altamirez, was born on the wrong continent. He would have fit better with the Cossacks, or perhaps as ornery as he was, the Mongols. The man had infinite patience for horses, and there was little he didn't understand about them. He had none for children, and though we mostly ate on a regular basis, anything that resembled love was beyond his capacity.

My mother died when I was born, and that may be why my father turned against me. It seemed I got a beating every day of my childhood, whether I needed it or not. At fourteen, I had grown big enough to stand toe to toe with him and give back at least a portion of what he'd given me. That was the last of the beatings, but it also meant I had to make my way in the world. In the border country, there was little for work other than a few low-paid ranch positions. If one wanted more, you worked for the cartels. They promised big money, but the simple jobs they started you with soon turned to killing people that had done you no wrong. It wasn't in me to do that, so I put to use the only civilized skill I had. I'd watched my father, and observed the horses he worked –

enough that I learned early how they thought, and what made them react to humans. Because I wanted desperately to learn, every spare minute I had was spent with horses, and before I'd reached my twentieth birthday, the name of Raul Altamirez was known throughout northern Mexico. People brought their problem horses to me from all over Sonora, and even Chihuahua and Sinaloa. And though I was respected for my gentle ways, the same couldn't be said of my interactions with men. A smoldering anger burned inside me, and there were few who wanted any part of me in a bar brawl. I was strong, with big hands, hardened from work and the years of abuse from my father, and though I hated my old man, he'd made me tough, and taught me how to fight.

Despite those hard, early years, I've had a good life. Often, I thank God for the day I met Juana Ortero, though now I'm very afraid I will never see my sweetheart again. Amado's people took her, and there is no doubt in my mind they abused her. For that, I will not forgive them, nor will I go to the police. Too many are not trustworthy, and besides, their fear of the cartels is great. Vengeance will come by my own hand, and though Amado is a powerful man, there will be nowhere in our country for him to hide.

Late in the afternoon on the day after Dina and I returned from my incarceration in Juarez, I walked over to the sandy arena where we start the young horses. Luis had returned from the east pasture. He is a hard worker, and I knew at this hour of the day I would find him in the saddle. Often, to make it easier on the horses, we rode in the early morning or evening, especially in the heat of the summer. I sat in the shade of the loafing shed on the west side of the arena and watched him. Though he would never have the talent that Dina displayed, he was patient, and many times that is enough to make great strides with a horse. He loped the big, gangly roan colt we called Peyo in left-hand circles. With one glance, I could tell the horse's head was out of position. I half rose, intending to correct him, but instead I returned to my seat and stared toward the big coulee, determined to put my tongue on ice.

Most of the night, I'd thought about my future. I am so weary of this tortured land. If God gives me my Juana back, we will go to the United States, simply to be away from the corruption that threatens to ruin our country. I am tired of fighting the growing influence and barbarity of the cartels. Though blood runs deep in our culture, Amado and I have nothing in common. My family is Juana and those here at the Rodríguez Ranch, and I would do whatever it takes to stop the evil of my cousin's mafia from touching Dina or Mariela, but I can do nothing other than try to convince them to leave as well.

I watched Luis try to coax the colt into a flying lead change. Because the horse's head was out of position, he couldn't do it correctly, and again I wanted to walk out into the arena and tell him how to do it differently. Instead, I cupped my chin in my hands and clenched my fists. It would do no good for me to intervene. From now on, he would have to figure things out on his own. I would no longer be here to tell him how to set a horse's head or give the split-second cue a colt needed to do flying lead changes correctly, so he might as well start today.

After Luis had slowed the young gelding to a walk, I beckoned him over. He sat relaxed in the saddle and instantly cut off whatever I might have said. "You don't need to tell me. His head was a little high, and he still isn't as flexible as he should be in those small circles."

I nodded. "Yes, that is correct, but from now on *mi amigo*, I won't be looking over your shoulder."

Luis looked up from smoothing Peyo's mane. "You go to look for Juana?"

"Yes, and when I find her we will leave and not come back, possibly for a long time."

"Where will you go?"

"To Nevada or Montana. Many people there are aware of my work with horses, and there are several large ranches that have asked me to come and teach what I know."

Luis scowled, then stared off into the distance, avoiding my eyes. "I understand. But if all those who hate the cartels leave our country, there will only be evil left. What do we do then?"

I didn't answer. His words were my own, come back to taunt me. But whatever doubt I had was momentary. I only wanted Juana back. There wasn't enough fight left in me to stay and fight the corruption that had destroyed our country.

That night, long after all in the bunkhouse had gone to bed, I gathered what few belongings I had. There were few clothes or personal items. Those had burned in the fire. I threw my little bundle in the cab of my pickup with a few other odds and ends and loaded one of my horses in the three-horse slant. Quietly, I shut the door and stared up toward the main house. There was one last item to attend to, and not an easy one. I trudged up the path and knocked on the door as the many years the Rodríguez Ranch had been my home paraded through my mind.

Dina's brother, Alejandro, had never had an interest in horses or cattle. He'd followed his father's footsteps and now worked for the CIA in Washington. Dina, however, loved everything to do with the ranch, right from the time she was a little girl. Dina had always been special to me, partly because of her love of the horses, but more because of her spirit. She is a rare person in this world, though often I'd prayed to our Lord and Savior that she would learn humility and grace to overcome her sometimes headstrong, overconfident ways. How I wished her father Ricardo was here to shepherd her through more of life's trials.

When there was no response at the front door, I stepped to the side of the house to see if Dina's bedroom light was on. She was still awake, so I rapped at the side door.

Her feet instantly pattered down the stairs. I waited while she looked through the peephole, glad she was cautious. One had to be careful when opening to strangers. Some nights, it seemed like half of Central America was migrating north, right through the ranch. The bolt slid back and she swung the door wide. "Raul, what are you doing here at this hour? Is something wrong?"

I patted her back while I held her. "Chiquita, I am leaving for a while. I may be back in a few days. If I don't return by next weekend, then it means I probably won't be coming back."

"Raul, no." She stepped away and grabbed my arm. "I won't let you do this. You are upset and terribly worried about Juana, but it won't help if you get killed."

I patted her shoulder. "No, little one. I have no wish to die. Nevertheless, I think I know who has Juana, and where they have taken her."

Dina stared at me. "You discovered something on her cell phone, didn't you?"

I nodded, for I couldn't truthfully deny it.

Her shoulders slumped. "Tell me where you are going, so if there is trouble we at least have somewhere to look."

I hugged her because I loved her like the daughter I'd never had, and I had loved her father ... I suppose like that old story of Jonathan and David in the Bible.

"No. If I do not return, it means I have joined the thousands of others who have died at the hands of the cartels. To follow me would only add you to the list, and I could not bear that." Now I held her little brown face in my hands. I would always think of her face as exquisite and tiny, like a Chinese doll I'd once seen. "Sometimes you must let your Raul make decisions and trust they are good, even if you don't understand them."

I suppose she loved me as much as I loved her. We had worked together in the arena for many years, and certainly her passion for the horses was as much as my own. She nodded through the tears. "Then I will trust you, old friend, though I can hardly see how this is going to get Juana home. Go with all of my prayers to our great God."

"Thank you." I gathered her close, kissed the top of her head, and walked over to my rig. Once, I looked back. She still stood, hugging her yellow housecoat around her slight body to ward off the chilly night air of the Sonora desert. I waved, stepped into my pickup and drove east toward the little town of Janos. Amado had harmed the woman who had long ago taken my heart. Our common blood would not save him.

The three-quarter moon cast a soft light on the narrow ribbon of pavement in front of me. I pulled Juana's cell phone out of my jacket pocket and scrolled through the pictures, then thumbed the off button. I knew where to start my search. The possibility I might be wrong never entered my mind, and as I drove into the night, my thoughts were only of the woman I loved more than life. Then somewhere north of Janos, it was as if the pavement under my tires had suddenly turned to a muddy and impassable jungle trail, and my confidence melted like sun-rotted ice. What if I was wrong? Where else would I go to find her? I had no leads other than the pictures in my hand. I was one man alone against hundreds of evil men. What I'd do when I arrived at my destination was not at all clear, but my anger and grief were greater than any uncertainty and fear. Most times I believed there was a God who managed those kinds of decisions and had His hand on my affairs. Tonight, I didn't care. I wanted only to find Juana, and if they'd hurt her – vengeance.

Chapter 15
DINA

DINA HUGGED THE robe tighter around her shoulders to ward off the chill night air as Raul walked down the steps of the sprawling Rodríguez Ranch house. Would she ever see him again? Her whole world seemed to be falling apart, and now another of the people she cared for most was walking out of her life. Juana gone, and now what about Frederick? He had made it very plain they had differing priorities. Had it only been a week ago she'd won the barrel racing on her old horse Piñata at Ogallala, Nebraska? Everything had been normal, and life so good. She waved as Raul pulled out of the yard, wishing she could just roll back everything in life to what it had been. Now, with all the added stress and responsibilities of the ranch, it seemed she would never be able to return to the barrel racing she loved.

Much of the last year, Dina had shared the driving with Connie Mack. Last week, they'd done a wild run through five different states in three days. They'd both done well, and if they kept their present momentum, both would make it to the National Finals in December, Dina's first appearance and Connie's fifth. But now, it all seemed so ephemeral, as if the goal she'd dreamed about and worked for was not even worth pursuing. Though the cool night air raised goose bumps on her arms, she refused to go inside. She strolled across the veranda and perched on one of the rocker arms as she watched Raul's tail lights disappear over the north ridge. The night wrapped around her, familiar and warming. Crickets chirped in the grass while over in the west pasture a horse whinnied. At the bunk houses, a door slammed, and low laughter rippled across the yard.

Frederick had always supported her barrel racing. He loved rodeo, and he was proud of her ability – or at least he had been. Long before they'd met, his idea of a relaxing weekend was to drive five hundred miles to a rodeo and watch two or three performances before returning home, barely in time for work Monday morning. His secret passion had always been to be a saddle bronc rider, but he was physically not suited for it, and fortunately followed a path more in tune to his muscular frame and striking intellect. He was a genius at molding ordinary men and women into master agents, ready to meet every challenge in the intelligence field. She'd often heard from his agents that it had been Frederick's tireless efforts that had vaulted Stirling Associates to the top of their field.

From the day she and Frederick met, their relationship had been volcanic. With temperaments so different, their discussions were often heated. There were rough spots in their marriage, and probably there would be more, but he'd always made an effort to understand her needs – until now. How could he be so uncaring, and just walk away? In the intelligence business, her husband was the go-to guy. He dealt with drug cartel issues every day. Now, Juana had been tortured and kidnapped, yet he'd shrugged as if this wasn't his problem. Tears of anger and disappointment threatened to spill over, while somewhere down in the dry wash, a cow bawled at her calf, and a pair of coyotes sang their discordant song at the rising moon.

******

As she did every morning when she resided at the ranch, Dina had the barn feeding well-started before seven. Mid-morning, she walked back to the house to take care of some office work. After she'd checked to make sure Mama had eaten at least some breakfast, she settled into the office to check the bank accounts and sign paychecks. She'd hardly started before a vehicle pulled into the yard. She glanced out the office window, but whoever it was had already driven to the far side of the house, out of her sight line. Possibly somebody delivering bagged feed to the barn, she thought. Certainly they went through enough of that. It was their biggest expense. Or it might be a neighbor dropping in for a visit. Dina sighed. If that was it, she must be hospitable. Hopefully, they wouldn't stay long, or she would never get everything done.

As she walked through the *sala* to answer the front door, she caught a glimpse of the white pickup in the driveway. An ominous government seal sprawled across the door panel. An icy premonition of disaster rolled around in the pit of her stomach. No, that was foolish. Probably they were the water survey people from Agua Prieta. They'd been here before to dig holes along the old creek bed to do further studies on the underground aquifer.

Her heart sank as she watched two men step out of the pickup. It wasn't the water people. One sported a dark police uniform and a gun. Frantically, she wondered if she could reach Frederick. But what good would that do? He wouldn't help. Her fingers trembled as she punched in Luis's cell. He didn't answer. The men walked up onto the wide veranda and knocked. Dina opened the door but blocked the entrance. The one with the uniform sported a federal police insignia, the other a bureaucrat in a rumpled gray suit.

"You are Dina Rodríguez?" The gray suit seemed to be the spokesman.

"Yes." She opened the door a few inches wider and stood as tall as her five foot frame would allow.

"We would like to speak with you, and also Raul Altamirez. Is he here?"

"No, he isn't."

"When do you expect him back?"

Dina shuffled from one foot to the other. "I'm not sure. Raul took an extended leave of absence."

The two men exchanged glances, and Dina instantly realized she had said the wrong thing. Gray suit stepped forward, and thrust a sheaf of papers toward her. "Señora, this ranch and all assets are under seizure as proceeds of criminal activity. You are not under arrest at present, but under no circumstances is anything to leave this property – including you."

Dina gasped. "But ... but why? Who ordered this?"

"The orders come from the Office of the Attorney General for the United States of Mexico. Also, we will require your passport. Permission from the Attorney General's office will be necessary in order for you to leave the ranch. You will find any information you might need in the enclosed docket. Any questions can be directed to the underlined telephone number."

"What is the reason for all this?" Despite her resolve, her voice cracked with the fear that welled up inside her. She had little doubt these two were following the orders of Marcos Ortero. No one else had the political clout to obtain a court order of seizure. She tried desperately to mask the volcano of emotion that cascaded through every vein in her body as she turned and stumbled toward the office. Her Mexican passport lay on the desk. Would that satisfy them? She carried an American one as well, but if Marcos didn't know her father was a U.S. citizen who had worked for the CIA, then he probably had no idea she carried an American passport. It was worth a try.

She hurried back to the front hall. Both men had now crowded inside the house. She handed the pudgy one in the suit her Mexican passport. He shoved the document in a folder as his eyes flickered downward to her breasts. For a moment he leered, then nodded to his partner. "Thank you, Señora for your cooperation. *Buen día.*" His eyes scanned the room, greedily pausing over each piece of expensive furniture and original western art.

Dina's face flushed. She stepped forward until her face was inches away from the suit. Her eyes flashed with anger. "Yes, good day. Anytime you're ready to leave us to get on with our business will be just fine."

The gray suit puffed out his chest and scowled. He started to reply, then apparently thought better of it. Both turned and marched out to the pickup. Dina stared at the papers in her hand, but her eyes refused to focus beyond the Spanish "Whereas," at the beginning of the first sentence. Later on, there were two or three "wherefores." Those paragraphs were no more comprehensible than the first one. She stared at the words, wondering what horrors lay ahead and how to react. Quietly she closed the massive wooden door, leaned against it, then slid to the floor. Why was the ranch suddenly a target? But she knew why. To Marcos, her father was a smuggler. And his only sister had been gullible enough to marry Raul Altamirez, who happened to work here. Though Ricardo Rodríguez was dead, Marco would surmise that Raul had undoubtedly carried on with the drug-smuggling enterprise. And why wouldn't he? Raul was a cousin to Amado Carrillo. Amado's son Rodrigo had recently stayed on the ranch. Two of Marcos's policemen would never see their children grow up because of Rodrigo. That would be more than enough to indict Raul and the whole Rodríguez family. To top it all, Marcos's sister had now been kidnapped. He would strike back with every weapon he could command.

Dina grabbed the door handle, pushed to her feet, and walked outside. She sank into one of the porch rockers, her mind scrambling for a solution. It didn't matter that Marcos Ortero was wrong on every count. She'd sat in front of those steely eyes. He would stop at nothing if he thought it would help him clean up Juarez. If that meant putting pressure on the federal government to seize the Rodríguez Ranch, then so be it, even if it was two hundred miles away. To convince him he was wrong would be impossible.

Dina shivered. Surely, all it would take would be Frederick's word that Ricardo had been a CIA operative, that the ranch was a real operation, and they were not involved in any criminal activity. He would have the credibility in the law enforcement community to make them believe the truth, that Amado had asked Raul to teach his son how to train horses. Raul hadn't known that Rodrigo's arrival was only a ploy by his father to get him out of Juárez until things cooled down. How could Marcos hold Raul responsible for that?

Her mind made up, she walked into the house and picked up her cell where she'd left it on the kitchen counter. Idly, her fingers scrolled through the last text messages, all from rodeo friends. There was more in her hesitation to call Frederick than she wanted to admit. But now, no matter what their problems, it had become necessary. He could help end this nightmare. Swiftly she punched in the numbers – before she changed her mind.

She waited for the usual shuffle to voicemail, but on the third ring he answered.

"You need to get down here. Two federal police officers just left. They gave me an order of seizure for the ranch and took my Mexican passport. I don't know what to do – "

"Hang on just a minute."

She heard him giving rapid instructions as he moved the phone away from his mouth. He was in a meeting. Nobody in the world had more of those than Frederick. Minutes passed as she listened to the muted voices in the background. The occasional word filtered through, something about engine problems on a helicopter. Engine problems? How did that stack up with what was happening here? Obviously, her husband seemed to think it did. "Fred?"

"Yes, hold on. I'll only be a second."

"This is a scary situation. I need you."

Voices jammed the microphone of her husband's faraway cell phone. He obviously was too busy for her problems. She deliberately pressed the disconnect button. When her thumb touched the red icon, it was as traumatic as if she'd dialed the number of a divorce lawyer. As usual, Frederick would be no help now – or ever.

Chapter 16
FREDERICK

AT 7:28 P.M., Fernando handed his passport to the U.S. Customs officer on the Santa Fe Street Bridge. The woman scrutinized the photo, made him stand for a picture, then returned the document and waved him through. He walked north to the taxi stand, unaware that a man on the American side watched him as carefully as a mother sparrow watches over her young. Fernando wouldn't have been pleased to find the boss checking up on him.

Frederick sighed as he hiked back to where he'd parked his car. Long ago, it had become second nature to do an inordinate amount of both checking and babysitting for every agent. He desperately wanted every one of them to be as safe as their danger-filled occupation would allow, for each to come home to their families, though to make that happen, his own home life suffered. At least, that was Dina's perspective. He shrugged. Perhaps she was right, but what else could he do? His men depended on him to get them through, whatever the danger might be. Usually, he did.

Before Fernando even hit the taxi stand, Frederick was well on his way to headquarters. He had enough head-start that when Fernando arrived, the coffee pot was fresh with rich, black Columbian. The agent-handler had hardly poured a cup before Ricky and Carlos walked through the door of the Spartan conference room adjoining Frederick's office.

Any meeting involving agents was held in 'the room.' Minimal furniture and fixtures made it nearly impossible to bug. Even if that had been a possibility, the room was electronically swept on a daily basis.

When all had taken a chair, every eye turned to Fernando. He studiously ignored the others as he stirred sugar and two creamers into his coffee. The men waited while he licked the condiment off the plastic spoon, then savored the first taste of the hot liquid. Finally, he spoke.

"The Jiménez Clinic is by far the best. They have all the latest gizmos and gadgets, enough that they nearly convinced me to get on the operating table."

Straight-faced, Carlos said, "We could start an office fund and get you – "

It had been a long day. Fernando didn't even smile. "Up y'ers."

"What about Castañeda?" Ricky asked.

"Decent clinic. Amado would like that location better. Actually, it would be easier for him to secure, but they don't have the qualifications or the equipment. The knife-man at Jiménez is probably in his early fifties. He's done in the neighborhood of fifteen hundred operations. The guy isn't going to choke or screw things up if he encounters a problem. He's world-class, and the facility is as good as any we have up here. That will be more important than anything to Amado. He's going to want to wake up. Second, he'll want to be pretty sure whoever does the surgery can give him enough gain to be worth the risk. The guy at Jiménez can do that."

"And the surgeon at Castañeda can't?" Carlos asked.

Fernando shrugged. "He's probably fine, but not for what Amado wants. He figures on coming out of there with a completely different face." His eyes flickered around the room. "After visiting both clinics, I'm certain Amado will go with Jiménez. He'll compensate for whatever security concerns he might have ... which means on the thirteenth of August you can expect a small army around that clinic."

Frederick's body jacked forward in the chair. Fernando's exact date had surprised him. "What makes you think it's the thirteenth?"

The corner of Fernando's mouth tipped upward. "Yeah, we don't usually get that lucky." He heaved his considerable bulk out of the chair and over to the coffee pot. Everyone waited while he refilled his cup and stirred in more sugar and cream. "After each clinic gave me a tour, I, of course, booked an appointment. That required both secretaries to look at their appointment schedules, and I made sure I saw both screens. At the Jimenez clinic, next Friday was blocked out. Not half a day, or a few hours here or there. Eight in the morning, until eight that night. I don't think that's a coincidence."

"Makes sense to me." Frederick's index finger tapped a rapid staccato on the edge of the table.

Carlos scowled. "And what if they really do have surgeries booked all day? Based on an appointment book, you're saying they'll do Amado's face job at the Jimenez Clinic on the thirteenth?"

Fernando's face flushed with instant anger. "Yes, I am.

If you have a better theory, maybe you should have gone over there."

"Oh, settle down. That seems like pretty thin evidence, but I suppose we have to go with it." He glanced across the table at Frederick.

Frederick hesitated. Carlos had doubts, but so did they all. He had to back his agent. "I'm in, which means that by tomorrow morning, we need to develop a plan."

Up until now, Ricky had stayed out of the sword play between Fernando and Carlos. Now, he leaned forward in his chair. "We can't plan anything without Pablo's input. He's worked his way through the ranks and into that operating room because he has more medical experience than anybody else that's close to Amado, so we need to talk to him. Any decision has to hinge on his assessment."

Frederick suppressed a grin as he eyed the three agents. All were independent thinkers. Often, as on this issue, they clashed, but in the end, every one of them would put their life on the line for the other. Pablo's plan would have to be a fluid reaction to whatever opportunity presented itself, but they had to have some idea how to proceed.

"Alright, enough for now." Frederick stood. "You guys go home and think about this. Let's meet in the conference room at eight-thirty in the morning to finalize." Heads nodded, and Frederick dismissed them.

The three men filed out, glad the day was over. The door closed automatically, and the lock did its soft whir and click routine. Frederick stayed seated and watched as they left the room. Tomorrow, more decisions would have to be made, lives saved, and God forbid, some lost, but for tonight each one could go home and help tuck their kids in bed. They could eat a late supper, watch T.V., make love, and just live their normal lives.

Frederick mentally rehashed the meeting as he flicked through his appointment book. So much depended on the agent, Pablo. It was always that way. A very ordinary man was expected to do the extraordinary. And if he failed, too often it meant he or someone else would die. Frederick stared at the week's pages as the men's receding footsteps echoed on the tile flooring in the hallway. The pages in front of him had nothing recognizable written on them. In fact, the entries looked more like a junior art project. He scowled at the coded entry for tomorrow, then flipped to the back where he catalogued birthdays, anniversaries, and important moments in the lives of the men who worked for him. He kept that section as a reminder they needed time with their families and loved ones, and went to great lengths to make sure that happened on a regular basis.

Frederick watched the parking lot as his men walked to their vehicles. He so wanted to follow them. Tonight, that wasn't going to happen. Even if Dina didn't realize it, a long weekend in Agua Prieta had a cost. He reached for the first file on the back of the desk. If he didn't keep a handle on Venezuela ... well, it was just one more thing he needed to do. And then there was Ernesto in Colombia who had questions that needed immediate answers.

Just before midnight, Frederick switched off the lights, then wearily drove the few miles to the sprawling bungalow he and Dina called home. He wished he'd been able to leave earlier. Their parting bothered him, and not communicating would do little to clear up her resentment or dissolve his own frustration at her lack of understanding.

******

At six fifteen the next morning, Frederick flicked the same office light switch, and wondered why he'd even bothered to go home. Grudgingly, he mulled over Dina's frequent accusation. She was right. This office complex took up nearly every waking hour. He dumped coffee into a new filter. Was there any possibility of ever doing it differently? His jaw hardened. Agents didn't have regular work hours. That was the essence of what Dina was demanding. She expected him to be there when she was home, and yet if there was a rodeo halfway across the continent, she was gone in a flash. He was okay with that, and understood her passion to succeed. He just wished she would accept *his* need to excel. And there was a world of difference. If she failed to win, she didn't get a paycheck. If he failed to win, an agent lost his life.

Frederick spent most of the next hour on the secure interoffice phone talking to agent handlers, giving guidance, and making instant decisions, some of which affected people in the field a thousand miles away. By eight-fifteen, he was on top of all the current operational assignments. Only one was critical, but that might change before the end of the day. Sometime before noon, he would have to make a decision on the Venezuela agent. Evacuating him would mean sending a team of commandos into the dense jungle that lay between Venezuela and Columbia. That whole frontier was filled with government troops, bandits, and people fleeing for their lives. If caught, the commandos would have little immunity – and no help. Frederick sighed. That was nothing new. If the mission wasn't extremely dangerous and politically risky, Stirling wouldn't have the contract. It was why they existed.

Fernando and Carlos walked into the conference room

together. Ricky scurried through the door three minutes later.

"Sorry I'm late. There was a pile-up at the 15th Avenue exit and traffic on the loop is backed up for miles.

Frederick nodded. "Okay, let's get started."

Ricky finished filling his mug with coffee and slid into the chair at the far end of the conference table. Carlos sat on the side farthest from the door, Fernando across from him. Frederick took his usual seat at the head of the table.

"Alright. We've had time to consider the options. I don't think we should waste this opportunity, but I want to know what you guys think. As I see it, there are four issues. One – which clinic will they use? We think we have the answer to that. Two – what is Pablo going to need to get the job done? Three – what kind of security are we up against, and the last hurdle is the backup plan. What if Pablo can't get to Amado in the operating room? Can we expect a decent opportunity later?" Frederick's eyes flickered over each man. No one seemed inclined to volunteer to be first. He pointed at Ricky. "Last one here gets to start."

Ricky took one last slurp of coffee, then leaned forward. "This whole thing makes me queasy. We don't even know for sure where he's going for the operation. If Fernando has pegged it right, and they use the Jiménez Clinic, security will be a problem, which means they'll have a small army surrounding the facility. They will want to move him to a more secure location as quickly as possible after the operation. We don't have adequate time or information to plan a strike, and any immediate post-operative care they decide on won't be far from the city. That will be our best chance of success."

"So you don't think Pablo will be able to do anything in the operating room?" Frederick asked.

Ricky rasped the back of his hand over his two day stubble. "No. I don't. Amado's doctor will be extra vigilant, because if Amado doesn't come off that operating table alive, they're all dead men."

"Okay. You've made some good points." Frederick looked over at Carlos. "You're next."

Carlos chewed on his lip for a minute, while he tapped the table with his fingers. "Amado Carrillo is anything but predictable. He could surprise us and go to Castañeda, but we have to play the odds, and they're strongly in favor of the Jiménez Clinic. Either way, the key is Pablo. The question is whether he can be effective, and I certainly don't see how. Amado's team will vet every scalpel, each bottle of anesthetic. How Pablo will accomplish anything within that tight security is beyond me. However, he seems to think he can, and we have to respect that. I guess if he's unable to execute we have to try to use the post-op recovery location as a backup."

Nobody spoke, and Frederick's eyes circled the table. Briefly, he scrutinized each agonized face. These men were the best, every one a veteran of a hundred different operations. Finally, he turned to Fernando and nodded. "After sleeping on it, do you have any new concerns?"

Fernando heaved his bulky frame forward. He hunched over his laptop hooked to the massive computer screen on the west wall. Quickly he pulled up the Jiménez Clinic and surrounding residential areas. "I don't agree with Carlos. If we fail the first time, there will be no chance of a backup plan. They'll bury him so deep, nobody will find him. I think we're all in agreement. We want to go in and quietly do what we have to do, then get out." He circled three neighborhoods adjacent to the clinic. "The Jiménez Clinic is next to several densely populated residential areas, so any kind of shooting war leaves the possibility of unacceptable collateral damage. So if we can't get this murderer with our inside man – then I say we let him go. But we have to give Pablo the tools to succeed, and that means we have to doctor the anesthetic."

"With what?" Carlos asked. He probably hadn't meant to be as defensive as he sounded, but Fernando bristled.

"There are several options, any of which we can supply in lethal quantities. In an operative condition, either Dilaudid or Methadone will send Amado into the next life. He will never wake up."

"But that means Pablo has to find some way to add this stuff to the Propofol, or whatever else they use to knock him out," Ricky scoffed.

Fernando grimaced. "That's correct."

"That's crap. It won't work." Ricky waved his hand contemptuously. "They will already have a trusted supply on hand, and his doctor will guard it like his life depends on it – because it does. Pablo won't get near it."

This time, Fernando ignored Ricky's frustrated reply. "The only other way is to give him an overdose of the Propofol. That will kill him just as effectively. That is probably our best bet, though there's no guarantee Pablo will have an opportunity to do that either."

Frederick glanced at each of the men. Fernando's plan was meeting stiff opposition, for good reason. "Okay, Carlos and Ricky, you don't think slipping Amado an overdose is an option. With the information we have at present, I have to agree, but let's keep working on it. We all want to see this guy go down, but the same caveat applies. No matter what happens, if we don't have a solid plan to evacuate Pablo, then Amado walks. There's always another day."

The faint sound of traffic from Roy Avenue was the only noise, as every man in the room struggled with the logistics of the coming operation. Frederick restlessly tapped the table with his index finger.

"An overdose ain't going to happen," Ricky burst out. "They will have at least one operating room nurse and two doctors in the room. Amado's personal physician will monitor every procedure and drug. Bumping up anything to a lethal dosage will be impossible."

Frederick waited for one of the other men to speak, but no other strategies or input was forthcoming, which wasn't a good sign.

Fernando scratched at his armpit. "This whole discussion could be moot if we called Pablo in for a meeting."

"No." Frederick shook his head. "Too risky. If there's one moment of distrust, they will send him packing – or more likely kill him. As much as I'd like to give him more involvement in the planning process, we can't. Not at this late hour."

Ricky stood, then paced back and forth. "Frederick, we don't have a choice. We need to hear him. If it were my neck in the noose, I'd want to have a say. Pablo will want the same, even if there is a risk."

Like a woodpecker on steroids, Frederick's index finger tapped an increasingly faster beat. Everybody waited. The silence lengthened, and the discordant hum of the air conditioner now drowned out the distant traffic, competing in the silence with Frederick's tapping finger. He squared his jaw and scooted forward in his chair. "Ricky, you're right. I will go to Juárez. Meeting Pablo there is safer than discussing anything over the phone, or worse, making him cross the border. He is due to report in sometime today. Presuming that happens, I will arrange for a meeting tonight. Let's convene again tomorrow morning. Carlos, I want you to work with the IT guys and hack into the Jiménez computers. Do whatever you have to do to find out where they access their anesthetic. I will authorize it immediately."

Carlos's eyebrows rose, and for a moment, Frederick's drumming ceased. "I understand the difficulty. Twenty-four hours to access that is ridiculous, but see what you can do. Ricky, you and Fernando start working on a plan to get Pablo out of there immediately after the operation. The second they realize that Amado has passed to his well-deserved reward, they will round up everyone that was within a mile of that operating room. Pablo has to be out of their reach."

Frederick's face remained expressionless as the men filed out of the room. He was already planning tonight's meeting with Pablo. He knew he could have sent any of a dozen different men, but sometimes it was necessary to get a firsthand look. This was one of those times. He needed to assess the strength of Pablo's position in the cartel, his chances of success in neutralizing Amado Carrillo, and most of all, whether they could extract Pablo when it was over.

Frederick rolled back his chair, walked to the narrow privacy window and stared out at the parking lot. Amado held Juárez in the palm of his hand, and had for many years. How many agents did he have embedded at the border crossings? Would one of them recognize his face because of his connection to the Rodríguez Ranch? Or would they know of his role with Stirling Associates? All of which reminded him of Dina and all the problems that needed his attention at the ranch. He grimaced. If he disappeared tonight in Juárez, Dina would kill him.

Chapter 17
RAUL

A DOZEN MILES west of Janos, I hit the cruise control and fumbled Juana's cell phone out of the bottom of the leather saddle bags I tended to favor. They held the necessaries most men carry in a shaving kit, as well as other items I'd had need of through my years on the border. I brought up Juana's pictures, and choked up a bit as I scrolled through them. They were well-organized; the vacation in Disneyland with her sister and their kids, followed by a trip we'd done together into Colorado and Wyoming where I'd put on some training clinics. The last photos were taken when she'd gone to visit her aunt in the mountain town of Madera in the foothills of the Sierra Madre. The old lady was in her late eighties, and Juana had wanted to see her. A month ago, she'd driven up and spent the better part of a week, visiting and helping around the house. While there, she'd taken Aunty out for *comida* several times during the week. One afternoon, they had dined at a midtown restaurant, a quaint clapboard affair, not at all like our adobe and brick buildings in the desert. I had been there several times myself. The uniquely decorated restaurant was festooned with old tools and guns, memorabilia and photographs of politicians and plunderers, most of whom were long dead and gone. One could never mistake a photograph taken in that restaurant for any other place in Mexico. Juana must have stepped out of the booth, backed up a few paces and snapped the photo of her nearly toothless Aunty smiling over what appeared to be a delicious tamale. Nothing odd about that, except for the startled face of the man in the next booth. The look on his face indicated he'd not planned on posing for a photograph. He and Aunty appeared to be nearly sitting side by side. Though Juana and her brother Marcos were not on the best of terms, Juana had forwarded the pictures to him. She'd included a short text on Aunty's declining health, all while the old woman was finishing her tamale. Seconds after her police chief brother received Juana's text, he was on the phone. He wanted to know where she had taken that picture, and asked whether she had any idea who the man was behind Aunty. Of course Juana hadn't a clue until he informed her that it was Amado Carrillo, the biggest drug smuggler in Mexico, and that she should leave the restaurant as fast as she could get Aunty out the door.

Within twenty minutes, federal troops had surrounded the building, but the wily Amado was long gone. It may have taken a few days for Amado to discover who the woman was who had betrayed him, because it was nearly a week after Juana had returned home that she disappeared. Amado's gang were rabid killers. The only thing they knew was to hurt and destroy. They had probably discovered she was Marcos Ortero's sister, which made her an even bigger target, even without the photo. Even though Amado and I were related, his thirst for vengeance would have decreed that our house was burned to make sure Juana's cell phone camera was destroyed.

Dawn had painted the eastern sky with the first streaks of mauve and pink when I dropped off the high ridge and into Madera. I pulled my rig in beside a vacant lot not far from the plaza, unloaded my horse and watered him at a little nearby stream. After I'd filled a hay net and made him comfortable, I walked back to the cab and reached under the seat. I was not a violent man, nor was I one to lightly break the laws of the land, but these were difficult times in our country, and those who wished to protect their loved ones were wise to arm themselves.

My hand closed over the familiar grip of the short barreled .45. Juana would receive little help or justice from the authorities, and my cousin Amado Carrillo had become no better than a rabid coyote so I shoved the short barreled gun into my belt at the small of my back. I didn't want to kill anyone – even Amado, but whatever was required to rescue Juana, I would do.

I'd forgotten the exact location of the restaurant in Madero, other than it was in the old barrio Americano on the south side of town. I walked the streets until I found it. When I stepped inside and scanned the interior, only three other customers were being served. Some of the décor was new, though not much. Apparently, the *Federales* had fired enough rounds to impress the locals. Their efforts to capture Amado were still obvious, and probably added notoriety and paying customers to this back street restaurant's prestige.

I slid into a corner booth, my back to the wall. My position provided a good view of the wooden sidewalk that led to the door. I'd be able to see anyone who approached the restaurant, long before they entered. Those were precautions I'd learned long ago in those border years with Dina's father, before I became a trainer of horses.

A lady with streaky gray hair and a limp took my order for breakfast. She seemed to be the only one waiting tables so when she returned with my coffee, I didn't waste any time.

"Where did all the bullet holes come from?"

Her wary eyes had seen much of life, and she immediately sized me up as a stranger. "Federal police." With that short answer, she turned and stumped toward the kitchen.

I sipped my coffee until she returned with my eggs and chorizo. "What happened?"

Her expressive shrug needed no interpreter. "We do not talk to strangers. Those who are foolish enough to speak of the cartels or their activities end up dead." She left, her lips sealed.

I would get no information here. The whole time I ate, the waitress avoided my eyes, even when I would have only asked for more coffee. Eventually, she had to look at me, but only when I signaled for the bill. When she brought it, I started over.

"Señora, you misunderstood me. I was only asking because my wife's elderly aunt was here that day. I have come to make sure she has recovered. As you can imagine, that was a very traumatic experience for her."

The waitress peered at me less suspiciously. "And what is the name of this aunt?"

"Doña Luisa Ortero Portillo."

"Ah, yes. Doña Luisa used to come in often. She doesn't get around as well anymore. But yes, I remember the lady that was with her that day. That was your wife?"

"Yes, that would have been her." Right there, I decided to take another chance. "So you were working that day? You saw what happened?"

The waitress nodded, wariness and a hint of fear once more in her eyes.

"No." Quickly I held up my hand. "You do not have to speak of it. It's not your fault they took my wife. I will find – "

"They took your wife?" The woman backed away, and that was the last I saw of her. After five minutes, I left the money for my meal on the table and left. I'd have to find Doña Luisa's address some other way.

After walking through most of the town, and enduring a half-dozen shrugs at my questions regarding Doña Luisa, I found an old gentleman in a small plaza on the east side who pointed a gnarled finger toward a small pink adobe structure a half block away.

Doña Luisa's house was on a potholed side street that had never seen pavement. The ugliest hairless dog I'd ever seen lay in the middle of the dusty thoroughfare. His jowls slumped toward his narrow chest. He had a prominent backbone held up by a dozen razor ribs. A ropy tail seemed to barely suspend a pair of oversized testicles that drooped past his skinny hocks. He growled as I trudged toward him. It seemed wise to not antagonize any of God's creatures this devoid of attributes. I gave him a wide berth.

Juana's aunt definitely had the best cared-for address. Her small house was set back far enough from the street that only half the yard was filled with dust from passing cars. She had a sidewalk, and though it was a little tipsy, both walkway and yard were freshly swept. I knocked on the metal door. A barred window beside the door sported a pair of bedraggled, but clean chartreuse curtains. In this high mountain city, the winter cold forced most residents to install glass in their windows, an amenity we in the desert often did without. I knocked again, louder. This time, I could hear the tapping of a cane. The lock snicked open, and the old woman I'd seen on Juana's cell phone camera stood in front of me.

"Doña Luisa, I am Raul Altamirez, Juana's husband – "

"I know who you are. Juana showed me pictures of you." Her beady, old eyes surveyed me from head to toe. "You're not as handsome as she said. She must have Photoshopped your picture." Her voice was surprisingly robust for an eighty-eight-year-old woman.

I stuttered an apology. Photoshop? How would this old woman know anything about that?

Doña Luisa cackled, her black eyes sparkling with humor. *"Passè."* She swept her hand and me into the room. *"Sentarse."* She ushered me to a worn but neat sofa. "Juana is not with you. Why?"

"That is why I came to talk to you, Doña Luisa. Juana was kidnapped, I think by Amado Carrillo and the Juárez cartel. It may have had something to do with the afternoon you went to the Posada Rosario. Do you remember?"

"Of course I remember," she growled. "You make the mistake of most young people. You think my mind doesn't function any better than my old bones. Well, it works as well as it ever did, and don't forget it. When did this kidnapping take place?"

"Last Wednesday. Not long after she arrived home."

The old woman's sharp, ebony eyes flickered over my

face, possibly cementing her view that I was much less dashing than Juana had portrayed me. Or perhaps she was just trying to decide whether she would trust me.

"So you want to know what happened in the Posada Rosario?"

"Yes, that's where I need to start if I am to find Juana."

"And if you do find that scum Amado Carrillo, and he has her?"

I leaned farther forward on the couch, my voice soft in the silence. "I will do what is necessary."

Doña Luisa nodded. "Well spoken – and foolish. Though we have not met before, I think my sister's daughter chose badly. They will kill you." The old woman shrugged her bony shoulders. "I am not saying you shouldn't do what you need to do. You are obviously a strong man, as my husband was. And you will be stupid, because you are strong. It is not in you to be any other way." She sighed. "Like my Ruben, you will not return."

I didn't know how to respond to what she'd said. Possibly, there wasn't an answer. For a long time, Doña Luisa never spoke. Her eyes that had been so sharp, now stared vacantly out the window, focusing on scenes from the past, reliving a time and perhaps a horror of which I could never know. There seemed no sense in staying here longer. I stood to leave. "Thank you for talking to me. I will be going now – "

"Sit. You are going nowhere."

For the second time in scarcely more than ten minutes, this old woman had informed me who was running this show. Her plucky determination reminded me of Juana, and I understood why my wife was so fond of this old Aunty.

"I will help you all I can. They will kill you, but maybe Juana … ." Her voice trailed off. "The day we had *comida* at the Posada Rosario, Juana was scrolling through the messages on her phone while she waited for me to finish my meal. Some men came in and sat at the table behind us. I was facing away from the door, so I didn't see who it was until they sat. I would have known that evil man's face anywhere. We may have been at the table he wanted. I have no doubt they would have removed us, but possibly even Amado Carrillo has some reserve in manhandling an old lady, though I doubt it. While I finished eating, Juana stood and took a picture of me, then returned to her seat. After a few minutes, her phone rang. It was a very short conversation, and she put a hand on my arm, leaned across the table and whispered in my ear. "Aunty, we have to leave right now."

"I hadn't even finished, but I thought maybe … oh, you know, a woman problem, so I didn't argue, especially after she left two hundred pesos on the table. The bill could not have been more than a hundred and thirty, so I thought something had to be very wrong. Only a rich person would leave that much money – "

"So, then what happened?"

"We were hardly out of the restaurant when the shooting started. Juana nearly made me run. Can you imagine?" she said indignantly.

In other circumstances, Raul might have smiled at Auntie's pique, but between weariness and worry, his face muscles barely twitched. "I think Juana was very worried."

"Yes, I suppose she might have been, though she wouldn't tell me why we had to leave in such a hurry until we were here in my house with the door bolted. I suppose she did the right thing. The Posada was closed for a week while they repaired all the damage done by the *Federales*. For me, to have been killed wouldn't have mattered, and for Juana – it might have been better."

Raul's fists clenched, and his chest contracted with sudden panic. "Why do you say, 'It might have been better?'"

Tears softened the old woman's jet-black eyes. "Though I knew you would come, I've been so worried. Juana is very close to here."

Chapter 18
DINA

AS IF IN SLOW motion, Dina's eyes clumsily followed the lines of Spanish script. "The below described properties ... frozen ... forfeited to the state as proceeds of criminal activities ... all chattels ..." and on it went. Dina wasn't even sure she knew what chattels were, other than it probably meant the horses, cattle, and everything else on the property. How could they do that? She stared at the papers. They might as well have had Marcos Ortero scrawled all over them. He was the only one who had any reason to do this. Besides, no one else she knew had this kind of power at the federal level. Dina glanced at the stairs, then shoved the papers behind the sugar bowl. Mama had more than enough to worry about without the added stress of losing her home. She didn't need to see these.

Dina slipped out the side door next to the kitchen then trudged to the barn. She tiptoed inside, and leaned against the cool adobe wall, wishing Piñata was here. This would be a great morning to go for a long ride up the Big Coulee to clear her head and just think, but Piñata was enjoying a well-deserved rest at their small acreage in Albuquerque. That reminded her. She needed to call Norita to make sure everything was alright. Frederick was always too busy to do something as mundane as feeding horses. After the horses had missed several meals, Dina had hired a reliable neighbor to handle all the stall chores for the two barrel horses she kept at home. It was easier on their relationship just to have Norita take care of the horses. Besides, Norita, a single mother with two high-school-aged girls enjoyed doing it. Dina paid her well, and the extra income was probably more than welcome.

Dina strolled past the line of stalls. She stopped at the fourth one and stroked the gray filly's neck. She used to be able to recite the names and pedigrees of every horse in the barn. Now she could only recite a few. Benito now stood in the first stall. Farther up the alley, the big roan colt, Peyo, munched away at the oats in his feed trough. In the end stall, Pico, another one of Raul's charges, paced nervously back and forth in his stall. She walked back to his stall and scratched the tall, gangly colt at the base of his long, muscular neck. Luis had him going well, though it would be another year before he could start on the barrels.

What about Luis? If for some reason Raul never returned, should Luis be the new foreman? Dina leaned forward, elbows braced on her knees. Luis would be *so* hurt if she passed over him and brought in a stranger. But there was the *other* concern. She didn't want to even think about that, but it had to be considered. Luis had made it plain he still had feelings for her. If it had been anyone else, she'd have just let them go – no, she'd have fired them. But Luis? He'd been here since childhood. The ranch was his home as much as hers. On her worst day, she couldn't fire him. She shuddered. Maybe that was no longer a concern. If the government seized the ranch, a new foreman was the least of her worries.

Dina left Pico and walked down the alley to Benito's stall. Quietly she slipped a halter over his trim head and led him up to the tack room. After cross-tying him in the alley, she brushed his brilliant bay coat, then combed the black mane and tail until they shone. Would he be her next winner? Would he take his mother's place in America? Dina knew he was at least as fast as his mama, and the time was fast approaching when her old mare Piñata wouldn't be able to take the heavy travel schedule of a professional barrel racer. She stepped away from the colt and studied every line of his trim body. He certainly had the breeding. What she didn't know was whether he had the will to win. She turned to the tack room, threw the brush in the tray at the front, then slid a saddle off the rack. Benito's sire had the best blood lines in the business. His father was a son of the mighty Quick Charge. On his mother's side? Well, there were no bloodlines, at least none she was aware of. Piñata had come from the Miles City bucking horse sale. No papers – breeding unknown. It didn't matter. The mare could run with any horse in America. If they won just a few more times, she and Piñata would go to the biggest rodeo in the world, the National Finals in Las Vegas, Nevada.

She studied Benito's eyes and ears as she gently slid the saddle into place. His head never elevated so much as an inch. Good sign, she thought. Next, the snaffle bit bridle. No problems there. She led him outside, stepped into the stirrup, then picked his head up, one way and then the other. Benito did everything so right. There was no fear, no gaps in his training. She reached over to unlatch the gate at the end of the arena and rode outside, then let him break into a trot through the south pasture as they headed for the Big Coulee.

A mile later, the colt settled into a long-gaited, ambling walk. She urged him to pick up the pace, but his meandering stroll didn't seem to have a second gear. Oh well, if he could run, it didn't really matter if he didn't have a naturally fast walk. She sat back and let him mosey along. The pace fitted her mood. This wasn't a morning for training; it was a time to think and plan for the future. Fear again clutched at her chest. How would they fight this federal confiscation order? To lose the family ranch was unthinkable. Carefully she enumerated the charges, all listed on the second page. The first, of course, had been smuggling contraband. Could they make those stick? Sure, her father and Raul had helped a few of their countrymen on their way north, and had occasionally turned a blind eye to marijuana shipments through the ranch, but that had been part of her father's cover. He'd often been referred to in the underground community as '*El Rey.*' She never had figured out whether he had been called the king because of his smuggling activities or because he looked a bit like Elvis with his long flowing hair, and full-lipped, pouty mouth. He'd been the king alright. The king of disguises. Her father had spent a lifetime creating false impressions.

A deep sadness washed over Dina as Benito picked his way up the narrow trail. How she wished she'd have known the man behind the carefully cultivated façade; but long before she'd been born, Ricardo Rodríguez had in the service of his country been sworn to secrets which even his children could never know. His mandate from the CIA had been to unearth those along America's southern border who were a danger to the country. Dina swallowed the hurt and anger that sometimes still forced itself to the surface. Though she and her brother's relationship with their father had suffered, Ricardo's name would always be on the CIA wall of fame. He had accomplished what he'd been sent for, and done it superbly.

Dina shook her head. She could do nothing to fix the past. Those family events were history. She needed to deal with the present – the smuggling charges against the ranch. Why would a Mexican court even care about a few bales of marijuana that went into the States? And if it was Marcos Ortero who had drummed up this list of charges, what could he do to make them stick? Or was it something more? Had her father or Raul smuggled guns into Mexico? Dina scoffed, loud enough to startle Benito into jumping ahead on the trail. She tugged him back to his sedate pace. Neither of them would do that – or would they? Her father and Raul dealt with dangerous people, all armed with the best and latest weaponry. Though she'd never seen guns in the house, it didn't mean they weren't there. A Mexican court *might* find them guilty as charged.

Dina slumped in the saddle. A charge of gun smuggling would be all it would take for a federal court to seize the ranch. Then there were the other charges. Words like aiding-and-abetting, transport of dangerous and illegal substances; the list went on. Dina was all too aware of the differences between U.S. and Mexican law. It would not be difficult for a zealous prosecutor to make them look guilty. Unlike America, in Mexico you were guilty until proven innocent.

She and Raul would go to court with the onus on them to prove they had been falsely charged. How could they do that? In a tall, slate-gray building in Quantico, Virginia, their lips had long ago been sealed. Nothing, not even their deaths could change that. They could never divulge her father's role. But then – there was always Alejandro.

Chapter 19
FREDERICK

FREDERICK SPENT THE rest of the day on the phone with agent handlers, while he waited for that important call from Pablo. By four o'clock he was pacing the floor. Even though there were a hundred things that could keep an agent from calling at their regularly scheduled check in – and usually did, the antacid pills on his desk rapidly disappeared as he paced back and forth. Pablo was one of the best. He'd figure out a way to call. But while Frederick waited, his stomach burned with worry. He slumped into his chair, and popped the last two pills in the package while he filed the stack of papers on his desk.

At five o'clock, Frederick decided he'd waited long enough. He regretted his decision to be the one to go across and meet Pablo. He should have sent Carlos. He was Latino, and had less chance of standing out. He stuffed a few of the reports and papers in his briefcase, then grabbed his office emergency travel kit. That small carry-on suitcase had seen him through week-long stints in Los Angeles boardrooms, and the Guatemalan jungle. He slid it into the back seat of his Impala, then drove south toward El Paso. Three hours later, he reached the outskirts of the city, and stopped at a small cell phone store on Alameda Avenue. He paid cash for the cheapest pay-and-talk they had, then drove three blocks to a fast-food chain parking lot. He couldn't wait any longer for Pablo to call. He thumbed out the simple, and mostly foolproof text. It was not a message Pablo would want to explain to his wife, but over the years, Frederick had found it to be the safest one – for both parties. He grimaced as he stared at the screen. "Hey Luv, usual place and time tonight? XOX" As long as spouses cheated, that message would continue to work. If on the off chance the text message was suspect, they could scramble for a Plan B. That course of action, Pablo's wife wouldn't want to know about. It involved *real* escort services. In all the years Frederick had worked in intelligence, they'd only had to do that once. It had saved the agent's life. His marriage was eventually salvaged as well, though that took a little more time.

Frederick drove another three blocks before pulling to the side of the road. Pablo had answered. Quickly, he read through the text, then jerked the battery out and fired the phone into a dumpster. "Another thirty dollar text," he growled. The company did lots of those. Throwing cell phones away like confetti did nothing for the environment, but it kept agents alive.

This time of the day, traffic south from El Paso to Juárez was horrendous, but by seven o'clock he was within sight of Mexican customs at the Paso del Norte Bridge. He mulled over tonight's meeting with Pablo as he inched forward in the line of permitted Mexican workers and shoppers heading home. He checked his watch. It would take another hour just to get through Mexican Customs. He scowled at the inefficiency. His agents had frequently endured his soapbox rant on the deteriorating conditions and mindless security attempts that had overtaken U.S. Customs and Border Patrol. And if any agent was foolish enough to let him start on the farce that was Homeland Security ... Frederick gripped the wheel and inched ahead another two car lengths. He hit the radio button, hoping for a talk show in Spanish. He needed to practice more. Even after all his years on the border, he still had an atrocious accent. But there was nothing on the radio that piqued his interest. He pulled ahead another car length, growling over the stifling bureaucracy that hamstrung both countries. His jaw clenched. He was at it again. Enough!

Eventually, the line was conquered. Frederick handed a passport to the Mexican agent and waited for the cursory examination. He answered the few standard questions from the young officer, then was freed to make his way through the scarcely hidden multitude of guns, knives and death that defined the garbage-strewn alleys and tortured streets of Juárez. He hurriedly bypassed them all and hit the perimeter expressway toward the Juárez airport. Halfway there, the mostly manicured grounds of the Hotel Casa Grande appeared on the left. He exited, parked, and walked to the desk. The young woman checked him in efficiently and quickly. She glanced at the name on his credit card. "Nicholas Robertson." Her eyes stayed a moment too long. Had that name meant something to her? Was he guilty of the exact sin he'd often warned his agents against? He'd used that identity several times, but because he was seldom in the field, it should be safe enough. After this trip, he'd order a new set of documents.

As Frederick finished filling out the registration form, the first tingling dread built into a crescendo of warning. He peered over the top of his glasses at the young lady's face. She quickly dropped her eyes. Late twenties, with dark, round features, neither pretty nor plain. Jet-black hair with a streak of brown gathered into a bun at the back of her head. A black skirt topped by a sea-green blouse. She was clean and neat, a little overweight, but nothing that said drug cartel. Nevertheless, everything about her manner shouted danger.

Frederick finished checking in, decided against prying his valise from the bellboy's grasping fingers, and followed him to the elevator. On the third floor, the young man led him to room three-twenty-five, and unlocked the door. Frederick dropped thirty pesos in his palm. The boy's face lit up in a big grin, both of them aware that amount of money was a major overpayment for services rendered. The boy thanked him, and vowed to be instantly available if Frederick had need for any further services.

For the next twenty minutes, Frederick scoured every inch of the room. This was a hotel for business people. The chances of any bugs were close to one in a million. Nevertheless, what he did was a habit. Lives were lost through carelessness, a company principle he never let agents forget.

Eight o'clock rolled by, the time Pablo was supposed to show, then eight-thirty. Too early to panic, but definitely a question mark. He hated hotels and seldom used them for meetings, but it would never do for Pablo to be seen meeting with anyone, especially not a blond, and obvious foreigner. He stared at the pavement below. The usual assortment of vehicles nearly filled the parking lot, most in the front three rows. Frederick had backed the Impala into the back row which butted up to a vacant lot. He watched as a late model Ford pickup parked in a spot next to the Impala. A short, muscular man with long, curly black hair slid to the ground. A leather satchel swung from his shoulder. He sauntered toward the front of the Impala, his eyes roving over the New Mexico plates. Coincidence? Maybe, but Frederick had never been one to gamble on happenstance. He grabbed his valise, softly closed the door, and took the stairs to the lobby. As the man with the satchel spoke to the girl at the counter, he ducked into the adjacent restaurant. He distinctly heard the girl gave the man a room number. Every nerve in his body screamed danger as the satchel guy strode around the corner to the elevator. It was then that the girl looked up and saw him slip through the restaurant door. Her eyes widened, but at that moment the automatic doors opened for another customer. Pablo hurried up to the desk.

"Has Mr. Nicholas Robertson arrived?" Pablo used the name Frederick had given the girl when he'd checked in.

"Yes." Without a glance at the computer screen, the girl politely gave the correct room number, and added that Mr. Robertson was currently in the restaurant. Frederick froze. The girl remembered too much, spoke too fast while her eyes refused to meet Pablo's.

"Thank you." Pablo turned and walked briskly into the dining room. Frederick noted the consternation in his eyes. That was enough. He inclined his head as he led Pablo toward the table closest to the kitchen. Instead of taking a seat, he dived through the revolving kitchen doors. One of the cooks swore in Spanish and attempted to block his exit. Frederick never even slowed. The hand that held the valise made what seemed a lazy arc. The side of it connected just below the cook's left ear. He stumbled sideways, his knees buckling. Frederick paused, grabbed his collar, and lowered the man's head gently to the tiles. He then sprinted through the produce door and ran for the Impala, Pablo a step behind him. Neither spoke until they hit the perimeter expressway and sped south, away from the border and safety.

"They had a trace on you." Pablo's voice was quiet. Whatever fear he might have had was gone. He was again the cool, in-control professional.

"How do you know that?"

"Because I was sitting in Octavio Semilla's office when the call came in."

In spite of his long training, Frederick blanched. Not from fear, but from the realization that his mistake could have cost an agent's life. That possibility hit him with the punch of a thirty caliber bullet. "This is inexcusable ... but, how did they find out?"

Pablo's lips formed a hard line. "That passport you're using? You better chuck it."

Frederick stared at him. "I haven't used it for at least six months."

Pablo's eyebrows rose. "Maybe not, but the last word I heard when Octavio walked out of the room with the telephone was *'passeporte'*. I think you better get a passport with a different name, boss. They're onto that one."

Frederick wiped his damp face with a handkerchief. He was supposed to be the one who taught the professionals. He was the man who didn't make mistakes, the go-to-guy who agents in the field could trust with their lives. He'd failed. Now, an operation that could go a long ways toward changing the face of Mexico hung in the balance because he'd been too slipshod to switch identities.

"Pablo, I am so glad you were late. They already have an assassin upstairs in my room. Anyhow, you can't go back, not with what they now know."

"Boss, whoa – back up." Pablo turned in the seat and faced Frederick, who still drove south as fast as the Impala could navigate the multiple lanes of traffic. "We can't abandon the whole operation."

"And why not?"

"Because, this is our best chance to stop Amado Carrillo. If he leaves that clinic, he is a free man. Nobody can touch him. Sure there's DNA, but we'll never find him."

Frederick slowed and edged into the right-hand lane. "I don't want to quit either, but you've been compromised. There isn't time to embed another agent, so as far as I'm concerned, Amado walks." He shrugged. "Win some, lose some."

"No, listen to me. When I left Octavio's office, I had a tail. That's what took me so long. I had to lose him. So ... when I walked into that hotel lobby, I was clean. There was nobody watching me, which brings me to your end.

From the time you crossed the border, they were on to you. They knew you checked into that hotel. I'm sure the girl at the desk was told to call immediately if you tried to leave. Then I walked in and asked for you using the same name that is on the guilty passport. Ding-ding. She knows something is wrong here. But does she ever once look at me? No, because she's not a professional. In fact, she averts her eyes to avoid giving anything away. She's excited, already counting up the new clothes and cashola her Sicario boyfriend is going to spread her way after he kills you. Thirty seconds after I left the lobby, you can bet she got on the phone. The first thing boyfriend asks for is a description of me. She stutters, her confidence slipping, but tells him to wait a minute."

"Why's that?" Frederick asked, but he already knew the answer.

"She grabs a room-service bill or a piece of paper and rushes into the dining room to give it to a waiter — any excuse so she can get a look at my face. However, my face is no longer there. We're gone, and so are all her new clothes and presents."

"We don't pay you enough," Frederick growled.

Pablo snickered, and turned in the seat. "You can start rectifying that oversight tomorrow if you'd like. Listen, if I thought for even one minute I was wrong, I'd be outta here in a flash. But I'm not wrong."

Frederick grimaced. "You're betting your life on it?"

"I am. Someday, a bad guy might get me, but it won't be on this one. Drop me off at the corner of *Carrizal* and *Abrazo*. I'll make my way home from there."

"What about the operation?"

Pablo grinned. "It's a go, and I'm in." "That's what I was doing in Octavio's office. We were going over security. There will be me, Amado's doctor, and the plastic surgeon in that room."

"Not even an operating room nurse?"

"Oh yes, but only one, and of course the anesthesiologist as well. Because my training is in anesthesia, Amado wants me inside, even though I haven't had a lot of experience in operating room procedures. He knows if somebody has it in for him, the operating room is the obvious place. Very easy to have a 'whoops moment' with the anesthetic. He's adamant. He wants two people in there he can trust; his doctor and me."

"So, is there some way we can make sure Amado doesn't come out?"

"All I can do is continue to build a good cover story, and be ready when and if the opportunity presents itself."

"That's the best we've got?"

"Afraid so, but face it Frederick. This is the only opportunity we've ever had to take this guy out. We have to run with it."

Frederick scrubbed at his eyes with a thumb and forefinger. "I'm meeting with the team tomorrow morning. The first item on the agenda is to work up a method to extract you after it's over. As long as we can come up with a workable plan, it's a go. Otherwise …"

"… we ditch the whole thing." Pablo waved away Frederick's argument. "I appreciate your concern, because if we are able to take Amado out, I want out of there fast."

"What will happen in that room once they realize that Amado isn't going to wake up?" Frederick asked.

"It's going to be instant pandemonium. Everybody in that OR is going to know they're dead meat. They'll pull out all the stops to pump some air back into him." Pablo hunched forward, a pensive look on his face. "If anything happens, his doctor will insist they rush him to South Hospital. Everybody will know they can't get him there fast enough to do any good, but they're going to want to be seen as doing everything possible. Along with his doctor, I will demand his immediate evacuation as well. In fact, I've already insisted that we don't start the operation without an ambulance standing by. When everything blows up, they will stuff Amado in that ambulance and race for the hospital. That's where it all gets dicey, because I don't know where, or if I can give them the slip. I have to be ready to seize any chance. The same for your rescue team. They need to be ready to respond to whatever situation we will face. Any chance at escape will require split-second timing, and a bit of luck. After we load Amado in the ambulance to go to South Hospital, all their security personnel will be angry, scared, and suspicious of every person who was in that operating room."

Frederick took the exit to *Calle Carrizal*, pulled onto a side street and found a parking spot before he leaned toward Pablo. "That's too loosey-goosey for me. If we can't come up with an acceptable escape plan at tomorrow morning's meeting, then we're going to drop it, and you're heading for the border and safety. One thing I've learned in this business is that there's always another day. Don't forget that."

Pablo stuck out his hand. "Thanks, boss. I've always loved working with you. This one's going to fly. See you when it's over."

As their hands met, Frederick tried to feel the assurance in Pablo's voice, but the lead sinker in the pit of his stomach outweighed all the brash confidence in Pablo's grip.

Chapter 20
RAUL

LIKE TWO SMOLDERING shards of charcoal, the old woman's beady eyes held mine.

Juana here? Alive? I lunged forward and grabbed her hand. "Tell me where, Aunty, and how do you know this?"

A derisive scoff spewed from her toothless lips. "Amado has a hacienda here. It is in the mountains, not far from our town, but that miserable son of a female coyote must have people to wait on him, and of course he takes whatever woman he wants. The family of the young lady is usually well compensated for his lust. His dollars buy a certain amount of loyalty, but I think it is not the same as it used to be. Now there are too many who bear the scars of his evil." She picked up the knobby, dried ocotillo stick that lay across the coffee table, and pushed herself to her feet. I remembered that Juana had bought her a nicer, store-bought cane, but she'd refused to use it.

Doña Luisa pointed to a house on the other side of the street. "There." She pointed a gnarly appendage toward a magenta adobe house. "There is one who knows what happens in the mountains. Maria cooks for them. She is the one who told me about a woman they kidnapped. I am sure it is Juana."

"She saw her there?" My knees skidded on the tile floor as I knelt and clutched at Aunty's thin shoulders. "How would she know – ?"

"She told me three days ago they had a prisoner who looked like Juana. I thought Maria was making up stories, but then she said they had taken this woman because she is Marcos's sister, and that they'd tortured her." The old woman's eyes filled with tears. "Then I knew for sure."

I reeled to my feet and stared across the street at the house where this woman lived, and for a moment, an unreasonable hatred filled me for Juana's brother, Marcos. He had sent his wife and children out of the country so they would be safe, so now his enemies had taken Juana. He had put her at risk, and done nothing to insure her safety. He was the cause of this great tragedy. If he hadn't held me in Juárez, this might never have happened. For that, I could not find it in my heart to forgive. Nevertheless, today my anger would be directed at Amado. Marcos and I had our score to settle, and though he was stupidly blind to my *real* involvement along the border with Ricardo, I would address that another day. Now, nothing mattered more than Juana. I would find her, no matter the danger, and cousin Amado would have his day of reckoning. I would deal with Marcos later.

"Aunty, when does this Maria come home from Amado's mountain hideout?" I gently helped Juana's venerable relative back to a comfortable position on the couch, embarrassed that I'd lost the little composure I'd portrayed.

"Perhaps today she will come, but it might be tomorrow.

Her daughter lives here, and at least once a week she comes to town for the night, then returns to the mountains the following morning. I can watch and perhaps send you a message when she – "

"No, it is not in me to wait. I will find this mountain hacienda. Where is it located?"

The old woman pursed her toothless lips. "You go alone?"

"I have no time to wait for others, so yes, I will go alone."

"Ay, Juana is lucky to have married such a man."

"I think not. Nevertheless, I will find her."

"What will one man do against so many?" She spoke as if she'd forgotten I was there, her ancient eyes vacant, lost in a distant past of which I knew nothing.

I shrugged, for truly I had no answer to such an obvious question. Amado's hideouts would be guarded by many Sicarios.

Doña Luisa spoke again, her eyes rheumy, the words tumbling out in a rush of slurred syllables. "God and the Blessed Virgin, help this man to find his way. Show him the secret trail through the canyon and up to the mountains." She mumbled some other words, but I couldn't make them out. Then she lifted her chin and peered at me, once more sharp and focused. "Take the mountain trail to Casa Blanca. You will find what you search for on the west side of the Rio Yaqui."

It was foolish to think I could just ride in and take my Juana away, but the anger in my heart spoke louder than any caution. I patted Juana's old Aunty on the shoulder, thanked her, then trudged up the dusty street.

On my way back to my pickup and trailer, the few

people I met averted their eyes. One man even crossed to the other side of the street at my approach. I understood. Our country has succumbed to much evil, and people are close-mouthed. Amado's brutality had long ago silenced any who were foolish enough to give out the kind of information I needed. Few are inclined to talk to a stranger, and never about the cartels. To ask questions would be unwise. I would instantly be reported as one looking for trouble.

I loaded my horse, then drove north on the highway toward Casa Grande, looking for a secure place to park my truck and trailer where it might be reasonably safe. Halfway up a pine forested hill, a dirt road angled off toward the east. I eased onto it, searching for an appropriate place to park. The tire-rutted trail ended at a box canyon. Other than some corrals cobbled together with rusty barbed-wire and dried ocotillo sticks, a humble brick *casa* appeared to be the only building. A few cows and goats were shaded-up in the brush to the east of the house.

A wiry little guy in jeans and a blue and white checked shirt sauntered outside as I pulled into the yard. I wanted only to turn around and leave, but I could hardly do that when the owner had obviously come outside to discover my reason for being there.

The man leaned an elbow on the box rail of a decrepit Nissan pickup with a bent fender and three distinctly different paint jobs. He appeared trustworthy enough, so I stepped out and walked over to apologize for driving into his yard. His eyes roved over my late model Silverado and expensive slant-haul trailer. I cringed. By most standards, I was far from wealthy, but I'd look well-heeled to this young man.

I greeted him. "*Buenos tardes.*"

He politely returned my salutation, enough that I decided to pitch my mission to him.

"I want to ride in the mountains for a day or two. I am looking for a safe place to park my pickup and trailer. Would it be possible to leave it here in your care?"

The young man looked me over, which I considered a good sign. If his eyes had focused on the tires and wheels, I might have changed my mind. Finally, he nodded. "Perhaps?"

I dug in my pocket and came up with a five hundred peso note. This was no time to dicker or be cheap. He likely had a family to feed, and I needed a safe place to leave my rig. When I came out of those mountains, I might be coming in a hurry, desperately needing that pickup and trailer to be in one piece. I handed the five hundred peso note to him. "Will that be sufficient?"

He rubbed the bill between his thumb and forefinger for a moment, then nodded. "Your truck will be safe here."

"Thank you. I appreciate that very much." I turned my rig around so it was facing toward the road, and unloaded my horse.

The colt I'd brought with me was a well-muscled four-year-old. Though his dull sorrel coat and limited ability in the arena meant we'd never sell him for a premium dollar, he was big-hipped and strong. The more I rode him, the more I liked him. He had a calm, willing presence, and when I saddled him I was again glad I'd chosen him over any of those other hyped-up arena athletes.

While I saddled Sorrel Horse, the young man watched me, though he never once spoke. The tack door on the trailer was on the passenger side as they all are, so I picked up my saddlebags and took them around to the driver's side of the pickup. The young man didn't need to see what I had under the front seat. Illegal or not, that .45 was coming with me.

When I carefully placed my load behind the saddle, the young man cleared his throat and nodded at the saddlebags.

"You are a wise man. One always should have some protection against mountain lions."

My fingers stopped for a brief second. When I met the cool eyes across Sorrel Horse's rump, I understood I was putting nothing over on him.

"I do what I have to do. This is a time of trouble in our country. It seems only the strong survive. I plan to be one of those." I mounted, thinking I'd already said too much.

"If my rig is as I left it, there will be another five hundred for you when I return."

"That is not necessary. You have paid me well. No one will touch it."

"*Gracias, amigo.*" I reached over and shook his hand. "My name is Raul."

"And mine is Genaro. Go with God and all the angels. I think you will need them."

I nodded my thanks, turned Sorrel Horse around and broke him into a slow ground-eating trot to the west. We'd make time where we could. Later the trail would undoubtedly get steeper. I had no idea how far it would be, but I would find Juana, and neither Amado nor a hundred of his evil Sicarios were going to stand in my way.

By late afternoon, I'd found a well-traveled trail that led to the west. Whether it was the right one remained to be seen. This was unfamiliar country to me, but as long as it pointed toward the setting sun and the Rio Yaqui, I would follow it. Three hours later, the scuffed track in front of me still skirted the deep canyon I'd been in since I'd crossed to the west side of the trickling stream that watered Genaro's rancho. By now, I was certain this was the right trail. What would I find at the end of my search? For that, I had no answer.

It was nearly dark when the thumping drone of chopper blades sounded to the east. Was that Amado? Was that how he traveled from Juárez or Chihuahua to his mountain hideout? How could I expect to fight and win against this man who could buy helicopters and airplanes by the dozen? He had an army of men equipped with the latest and best assault rifles money could buy. I felt like a throwback to another time. I would go against them with nothing more than a good horse, and the ancient revolver in my saddlebag. That didn't make sense, but it wasn't in me to do anything else.

The trail ahead switch-backed upward through a narrow draw, and it was at the top where darkness forced me to stop and make a cold camp. I unsaddled Sorrel Horse and picketed him, then ate a cold tortilla and a piece of cheese. Sometime in the night, I reached over and opened the flap on the right saddle bag. There had been a period in my life when guns had been very much a part of me, but that era was long past. I was now more at home with horses, and the .45 felt strange in my hand. Nevertheless, as I rolled it back and forth in my palm, the old familiarity of the worn grip began to feel comfortable, like the old times when Ricardo was alive. I checked the loads and pointed the barrel out into the night. Never to my knowledge had I killed anyone, but tomorrow, if I had to fill a whole graveyard with men – I was ready.

Chapter 21
DINA

DINA URGED BENITO to pick up the pace as they headed back toward the barn. If only Frederick were here. He had contacts, would know where to look, who to call. But her husband obviously couldn't be bothered with her problems.

At the barn, Dina stepped off Benito, eased the bridle off and slipped on a halter. What about Alejandro? His job with the CIA gave him access to information she could never have. Maybe he could help? He might even be able to come home. There was only one way to find out. Tonight, she would call him.

Dina's older brother had followed their father's footsteps. He'd worked for the Central Intelligence Agency from the day he'd graduated from college. Six years older than Dina, Alejandro had been gone before she'd reached her teenage years. Those were turbulent times; years when she'd not understood her father's role on the border. Nor had she been able to fathom why her brother had all but abandoned their family because of his own perceptions of Ricardo Rodríguez's activities. It was only after their father's death that Dina had become reacquainted with the brother she'd adored. Not that she got to see much of him now. Alejandro officially worked in Washington D.C., but calling him usually meant you would be transferred to an official sounding voicemail message. Though Dina occasionally inquired as to what he did, he would either ignore the question or mutter some nonsense about being a paper-pusher in some hidden-away office at Quantico. She knew he was obscuring the truth, and his eyes said he was aware she knew. Both understood that was the way it had to be.

After Dina had unsaddled Benito, she brushed his sweat-soaked hide and led him into the barn. As she led him into a vacant stall, Luis appeared at the far end with another horse. He grinned at her as they met. "Been out for a ride?"

"Yes, I just needed to get out and clear my head. I followed the wash up the Big Coulee. The last flood did a lot of damage."

"Yes, it was the biggest we've seen in twenty years. The water undercut and brought down a lot of big boulders. Have you heard anything from Raul?"

"No, and I'm not sure I will – at least for a while. Will you add his horses to your string, or are you going to let one of the other trainers take them?"

"I'm going to take them."

"Okay, but I want you to put lots of time on Benito." She eyed the gelding's hip and back. "Do you think he has as much speed as his mother?"

Luis's eyes followed hers. "That horse has everything. He might even run faster than his mother, and he isn't as high-strung. He will be your next love."

Dina stared straight ahead, unwilling for Luis's smoky Latin eyes to lock with hers. He stepped forward to unlatch the door to Benito's stall. It put him physically close to her, and instantly, she was resentful of Frederick's absence. If he were here, Luis would not be a problem. She brushed by Luis as she led Benito into his stall. What should she do? Luis apparently hoped her husband had permanently disappeared, and that there was a chance for him. And what did she hope? If things were different, would she be interested in his probing advances? Her fingers trembled as she slipped the halter off Benito's head and scurried toward the barn door. "Gotta' go. We'll decide on the rest of the horses later." She gritted her teeth and refused to look back. Luis had hoped to ignite something from the past she did not want to happen. The best defense was to put as much distance between them as possible.

Dina's pace never slowed until she reached the back step at the house. Something had to change. If Raul didn't return, Luis would be the natural replacement as foreman, but then she'd have to interact with him even more. They would be thrown together, dependent on each other. Yet ... could she fire him? Had some moral depravity triggered his undying love? Was love like a kitchen faucet that could be turned cold, or regulated to run lukewarm? She kicked off her boots and padded into the kitchen. Maybe she wouldn't have to worry about all that. If they went through the horror of losing the ranch – then Luis was the least of her problems.

Lupita sat in the kitchen alcove reading a cookbook On her way by, Dina stopped and gave her a hug. "What smells so delicious?"

"Oaxacan rellenos with shrimp and green chilies. I made them yesterday, but the shrimp we get in Agua Prieta are never as good as fresh ones."

"Oh Lupita, they'll be fine. Where's Mama?"

Lupita pointed toward the living room. "In the *sala*,"

"Oh good. Is she feeling better today?"

"Yes, she's having a good day."

Dina opened the fridge, poured a glass of iced tea from the pitcher and walked into the spacious living room. Mariela was curled up in her favorite chair. The blinds were closed to keep the hot Sonora sun at bay.

"Mama, how are you doing?" Dina bent over and kissed her mother's forehead.

Her mother smiled. "I'm fine, just tired. I try to get up and get something done, but my energy fizzles about five minutes after I start."

"Mama, rest is the best thing for you. Both Doctor Larson in Tucson and Doctor Sanchez said you must not get overtired. We have to do what they say. We'll beat this, one day at a time."

Mariela reached over and took Dina's hand. "You're right, daughter. We will beat this, but you know something? If we don't, that's God's will too."

Dina shook her head. "Mama. Don't talk that way. I can't – "

"Sweetheart, you have to be strong. Probably, I'm going to die. I don't know when, but I have done all the studying I can stand, and the prognosis is not encouraging." She ruffled Dina's hair. "Even your old mother can surf the internet when it's necessary. The odds of beating ovarian cancer are not good."

"Mama, we can do this. We'll go back to Tucson. Dr. Larson said he could get you into the Mayo Clinic. I will make another appointment with him tomorrow."

Mariela patted Dina's arm, then pulled her closer. "No, tomorrow I want you to do something for me. We are not going to go to Tucson, not anymore. Tomorrow, I want you to call Alejandro. I want to see him before it's too late. I want to enjoy my last visit with my son."

"But Mama ..." She could only nod through the forming tears. "Yes, I will call him." Then, she hugged her mother as if she'd never let her go. Mariela fell asleep with her head on Dina's shoulder. She didn't see the tears that wouldn't stop, nor did she feel the heart-wrenching loneliness that swept over her daughter, a sorrow that would never go away.

Chapter 22
FREDERICK

MIDNIGHT, AND THE border crossing happened at the same time. Frederick had never been superstitious. He scoffed mightily at those who put any faith in astrology, the stars, or for that matter, luck of any kind. Though his astuteness and intellect was legendary in the intelligence world, he believed in a God who managed the affairs of men. Man could affect that management by his actions, but he could not change it. And so, when he made life and death decisions affecting an agent's well-being, Frederick prayed. Most of his colleagues scoffed at such a quaint approach. They thought it a waste of time – or worse. Nevertheless, Frederick believed in it – and did it regularly. And so he did tonight, because in spite of Pablo's confidence, he wasn't at all sure he'd made the right decision in leaving him to carry on with this dangerous assignment.

Tomorrow morning, several questionable phases in the operation had to be addressed. What they would never do was base the mission on some antediluvian hope that when Pablo appeared around some corner of that hospital building, an agent would be able to pick him up and escape. That would never work, not with dozens of Amado's security goons surrounding the building. They had to come up with a solid operational procedure. Frederick didn't know what that looked like, nor did he have a backup plan.

As always, Frederick was the first to the Stirling Associates building in the Alamitos Industrial Park, though Ricky was not far behind. As Frederick made coffee, he kept one eye on the parking lot. Fernando and Carlos pulled up in Fernando's Chevy. They lived in the same sector of the city, and often car-pooled. Every agent drove either a Ford Focus or a Chevy Cruz. The company had been known to daringly order cars beyond those models, but it was rare, so when Fernando pulled the Cruz into the lot, then parked in a row of five identical white Chevy cars, his wheels were indistinguishable from any of the others.

Carlos grimaced as he exited and walked past the rear bumper. Fernando hated noise, and he especially disliked the short horn honk that the car did when he pushed one of the buttons on the key tab. When he picked up a company car, he regularly spit on the bumper. The wet spot picked up enough road dust that he could immediately identify the correct vehicle without pushing the key locator. Carlos thought it was a gross way to find your car, but the two had worked together for nearly fifteen years with few disagreements or bad moments, so he put up with it. When they walked into the meeting room, both Ricky and Frederick were seated and waiting.

Frederick nodded at them "Morning gentlemen. Coffee's on. Grab one and let's get started."

Ricky rose and stood behind Carlos and Fernando to fill his cup. All sat and turned expectantly toward Frederick.

"Okay, first I'll fill you in on the details of my jaunt into Juárez last night." For the next twenty minutes, Frederick gave a recap of his meeting with Pablo. He purposely left out the part about the offending passport that had caused the panicked exit from the hotel. They would likely find out soon enough. He would be the butt of a dozen good-natured jokes. That was okay. They worked as a team, and laughed together at each other's mistakes – after they'd fixed them. Mistakes were costly. For that reason, this morning's planning session was deadly serious. Each detail would be committed to memory. There could be no errors.

Frederick's fingers nervously worked together in his lap as he scanned the three men's faces. Why was he so nervous? But from long experience, he knew. It was the possibility that he might fail the men in front of him, not to mention Pablo, whose life depended on their careful planning. He pushed that thought aside and tried to concentrate. "Fernando, our man didn't indicate anything different than what you reported. He says the operation is going to be at the Jiménez in spite of higher security risks. Amado figures if he puts enough guys on the street they can hold off anybody's army, long enough for him to get the operation and get out of there."

"What does he say about the operating room?" Carlos asked.

"He doesn't think there's any chance of being able to tamper with the anesthetic. That will be purchased by Amado's own doctor, and guarded like the crown jewels of Mexico. The best he can hope for is to be able to adjust the quantity administered during the operation; enough so that Amado Carrillo doesn't wake up in this world, which brings us to the next point. Fernando and Carlos, what did you find about the origin of the Propofol?"

Carlos ran his hands through his thinning hair, then opened the file folder which lay on the desk in front of him. "There are three different suppliers of Propofol in Mexico and a couple more in the U.S. It's a drug with a long expiration date, so Pablo is probably correct. They already have the supply they need. Nobody's going to be able to get near it, so if Pablo thinks there may be an opportunity to give him an overdose, that's great."

Frederick eyes locked on each of the intense faces around the table. He reached for an antacid pill before he spoke. "I'm not telling you guys anything you don't already know, but for too many years, Amado Carrillo Fuentes has killed with impunity. Neither we nor our Mexican counterparts have had any luck hauling him into a courtroom, and unless we can come up with a viable plan, it's never going to happen. Is there any way we can prevent him from leaving that operating table?"

Fernando, the eternal pessimist, scowled. "Even if we're successful, it won't change anything. The Juárez Cartel is no different than any of the others. Succession plans will already be in place, but by next week, there will be another crop of 'wannabes' vying for the crown, which means we'll have it to do this all over again." He ran his stubby fingers through his short hair. "Sometimes I get so tired of playing whack-a-mole with these guys."

Carlos's eyes moved from Fernando to Frederick. "And what about Pablo? How are we going to get him out?"

Frederick hunched forward over the table. "That's what stops me from moving forward. At our meeting last night,

I'd hoped we'd come up with something workable. We didn't. I think we should abandon it and evacuate Pablo. There's too much risk."

"What's Pablo's take?" Ricky asked.

"He wants to stay. Her thinks there may be an opportunity to increase the dosage – enough that Amado won't wake up. That's great. We're all for that, but we still have to get him out. He's sure there will be enough confusion after they discover Amado is dead that he will be able to slip out of the clinic and escape."

Ricky shook his head. "Not a chance." "Even if Pablo made it outside, the building will have been secured by Amado's people. He will never get through that wall of guns to where somebody can pick him up. That is not going to happen."

"Yeah, I agree with you, boss." Fernando nodded at Frederick. "I think we should call the whole thing off." He reached forward and with his index finger, tipped his binder closed.

"Hold it, guys." Ricky uncrossed his legs and leaned over the table. "There is going to be confusion, but not pandemonium, which is why I think Pablo trying to escape by going outside the building is a non-starter. A number of Amado's people have military training. They're capable and smart. The second they suspect something is wrong, they will turn that clinic into an impregnable fortress, at least to conventional weapons, and anyone coming out of the operating room will be suspect."

"So what do you propose?" Frederick asked.

Ricky pushed his chair back and stepped to the far wall. He pointed his pen at the men. "Pablo thinks he can slip a little extra anesthetic into Amado. As dangerous as that is, we don't have anything better. We *have* to go with whatever he tells us." Ricky flashed a picture onto the dry board, walked to the front and pointed to a building on the screen. "Here's the clinic. It's on the corner of Calle Vicente and Juan Carranza, with an entry on the Valenzuela street side. There's also another one back here in the alley. That is the door closest to the operating room, the one they'll use if they have to rush Amado to the waiting ambulance."

Ricky sauntered back to the table and took a sip of coffee. "If Pablo is able to use the extra anesthetic, and Amado actually quits breathing there's going to be big panic in the operating room. Their immediate response will be a bombshell of confusion, perplexity, and fear. They're the best doctors money can buy, but at this stage, they will have no idea why this is happening? So, they scramble to get Amado into an ambulance, and off to South Hospital where there are better resuscitation facilities and equipment. The two ambulance attendants will help to load Amado, but they will sit in the front. Amado's personal physician will have priority in the back, as well as the other doctor. Pablo is trusted. He'll definitely be there to assist. I considered the possibility that an armed guard could take the passenger seat, but I don't think that's reasonable. Nobody is going to want to jeopardize the boss's life. They're going to let the medical folks do their job – and hope they can pull off a miracle. There will be no room for security people on a short ride to the hospital, and truthfully, none of them will want to go. Even at this early stage, everybody involved is going to start backing away. They all know – if Amado dies, vengeance will be swift."

"What about the plastic surgeon?" Carlos asked.

"He may be in the ambulance, but I doubt it. Same for the anesthetist. At this point, they're extra baggage, and can do nothing to save Amado. Both will suspect that the cardiac event their patient has suffered is due to suspicious circumstances. The anesthetist will be the first to suspect Pablo. The man's a doctor – and a good one. He'll soon figure out that an overdose or some foreign substance in the anesthesia is responsible, but finger pointing to save himself will come later.

"So, good. I don't give a rip about either one of them. What about Pablo?" Fernando asked.

"Ricky held up a hand. "I know. Neither do I, but stay with me here. As the ambulance speeds toward the nearby hospital, there's a total of six inside, plus Amado. Two attendants in the front and four medical personnel in the back. Way overcrowded. The soldiers will all be in escort vehicles, with probably one in front of the ambulance, and two or more following."

Ricky directed their attention to the map. "Here's South Hospital, barely six blocks from the Jiménez Clinic. Amado's security team could have lined most of the route with soldiers if they'd had time, because there will probably be that many in the vicinity of the clinic."

Every eye was now riveted on Ricky.

"So, the ambulance will use the shortest route, which means they will exit here." Ricky placed an "x" on the alley where it intersected the street. "They are going to turn left onto Calle Vicente and almost immediately make a sharp right onto Guadalupe Street. Four blocks later they have to turn left on to Cuauhtémoc Avenue. One block later they arrive at the hospital emergency entrance."

Frederick eyed Ricky, wondering what he was going to propose. Nowhere on that whole route was there a reasonable escape for Pablo. If anyone got close to that ambulance, they would be shot to bloody ribbons. He watched Ricky's eyes flicker around the room, gauging each man's reaction.

Fernando leaned back in his chair and crossed one hairy arm over the other. "There's nothing on that route that gives us an opportunity. It's not possible to extricate Pablo. I still say we call it off."

Ricky nodded, but declined to offer any further response. He waited until each man had finished studying the route, then pulled up another picture. "Fernando, you're right. There is no way to get to Pablo at the Jiménez Clinic, or on the route to the hospital. So ... our only chance will be after they arrive at South Hospital. Remember, everybody's still in initial panic mode. People are looking for direction." He held up a hand. "Let me paint this for you. When that ambulance screams into the emergency bay at South Hospital, the attendants are going to bail out and wheel Amado inside as fast as they can. I'm thinking Pablo will be out front, opening doors, screaming for emergency room personnel, and yelling for everyone else to get out of the way. Soldiers and Sicarios are the only ones not in panic mode. They're doing what soldiers do best; securing the perimeter, clearing the decks. Nobody is going to risk getting in front of that gurney on its way to the operating room.

Ricky eyed each man before continuing. "Okay, once they get the gurney inside the emergency wing, there is a short hallway. The door to the stairwell is part way down on the other side. South Hospital is a four-story building with a helicopter landing pad on the roof. When he gets to the door that leads to the stairs, Pablo is going to duck into it, but two things have to happen for him to be successful. We have to presume he will have at least a five second head start before soldiers behind the gurney realize what is happening. It's imperative there be a lock on the door that leads to the stairs. When Pablo goes through, he jams that lock home and shoots up those stairs like he's never run before. He may have a small advantage. It's a hospital. Even these goons will hesitate before they start firing automatic rifles to blow the lock off. Not for long, mind you, but enough that Pablo should have a two-floor head start before they get into the stairwell. Also, the door that leads out onto the rooftop helicopter pad has to have a sturdy bar, something they can't blow off with an assault weapon. Pablo's going to need enough time to get to the chopper. Then, that pilot has to have fifteen to twenty seconds to get out of rifle range." Ricky's eye flickered around the room, pausing briefly at each man. "Everybody with me?"

All heads nodded.

Ricky turned to Frederick. "Boss, you see any holes?"

"Not as long as we can get somebody in to do the lock work on the bottom door today. The chopper commandos can carry the necessary tools and gear to install a bar across the top door. That shouldn't be difficult. Five or six lag bolts screwed into the door frames with a big cordless drill will do the job. It shouldn't take more than two to three minutes. They'll be finished and waiting before the commotion starts at the emergency entrance below."

"So you don't think when the chopper lands on their roof

pad, there's going to be trouble? That's hardly going to go unnoticed," Fernando pointed out.

"The pad is four floors up from administration," Ricky replied. "We're going to be okay. Even if somebody hears the chopper, they won't be concerned, because no emergency call has been logged. I doubt that will be an issue."

Frederick remained silent, studying Carlos and Fernando. "What do you guys think? Carlos?"

Carlos scrubbed at his unshaven face. "I don't like any escape plan that depends on a helicopter, but I don't have anything better. I'm in."

Fernando growled. "If the bad guys hit that bird with any ordnance bigger than a wad of bubblegum, it will go down like a plucked rooster. I don't know, maybe there isn't a better way ... I guess I'm okay with it."

Frederick stood. "Then it's a go. Make the necessary arrangements Ricky. I will get the information across the border to our agent, and may God help us all – especially Pablo."

Chapter 23
RAUL

MY CAMP LEFT much to be desired. No water trickled through the rocks to make morning coffee, not that it mattered. I had neither pot nor beans. I moved Sorrel Horse into the brush, then bedded down in a small side canyon, close enough I could still see the trail.

Sometime in the quiet before the first light of dawn, I awoke cold and stiff. My first thought was for my horse, which I suppose is typical of cowboys. Without a horse, I had no mobility. I'd picketed Sorrel Horse at the edge of some tall dry grass, and I could see in the predawn darkness that his head was up, nostrils distended like he was testing the air – or going to whinny.

Quietly, I rolled out of my thin blanket, stuck the .45 in my belt, and slipped over to stand beside him. My hand went to his nose. Until I knew what we faced, it might be best not to advertise our presence. Below us on the trail, five men marched west, all bent double with bundles of marijuana. Each wore the distinctive garb and footwear of the ancient Raramuri, the canyon people who were now the largest drug producers for the Juárez cartel. They'd not bother me, and

I had no quarrel with them, but I quickly saddled my horse because this was a gift from God. I wouldn't have to waste time searching for Amado's mountain lair. They'd take me right to it.

The packers were heavily loaded and staying far back from them was weary work. It was nearly noon before they climbed out of the canyon and made their way to the top of the rim. I watched from a distance as they split up, then just disappeared into the brush. A good part of my life had been spent tracking cattle, horses, and sometimes people, so I had a pretty good idea what they were about. I abandoned the faint scuff marks and made a big circle. A half mile farther, the tracks all came together again and followed what was now a distinct trail. I presumed it led toward the Rio Yaqui, the river that drains much of the Sierra Madre before it flows into the Sea of Cortez, south of Los Mochis.

Five or six miles farther, I broke out on the rim of a long canyon. There was no timber here, and little to break the skyline for many miles. Below me, the land fell away to a series of benches festooned with Mexican oak and the shrub they call Madroño. In the distance, the river wound its way to the sea. On the last bench, with the river far below, a forbidding concrete wall enclosed a large compound. For a long time, I stared at it. Was Juana there? If she was, how was I to rescue her? Even from this far away, I could see the place was capable of holding off an army, and I was alone, with nothing more than a .45 in my hand.

Nevertheless, I spurred Sorrel Horse over the edge. We skittered to the bottom on a big shale slide, his hooves scrambling for solid ground and not finding it. It was a wild ride, but we reached the bottom, Sorrel Horse trembling at the new experience, but hardly the worse for wear.

An hour later, I broke out of the timber on the flat above the river where Amado's opulent compound rested. It didn't look any easier up close than it had at a distance. The concrete wall topped with razor wire ran around three sides. From where I sat, it appeared the fourth side was protected by a hundred foot drop to the Rio Yaqui far below.

Though fear ate clear to my backbone, I rode up to the main gate and hollered for somebody to open it. I didn't get off my horse. Being mounted seemed a small measure of safety, though common sense told me that thought was laughable against modern weaponry.

A tough looking young man in a desert camo uniform sauntered out of a narrow man-gate. He carried an assault rifle. "Who are you, and what do you want?"

I stared at him, then spat at the ground. "I am Raul Altamirez, the cousin of Amado Carrillo. Open the gate, you cheeky peasant." That was going a little far. I didn't know whether he'd shoot me or not, and I wasn't sure whether I cared. He must have decided that if I was really a cousin to the great one, then he should have permission before he blew my brains all over the rough-tiled driveway. His rifle dropped slightly, and he touched a button inside the guardhouse. The wrought iron gate, topped with jagged spear points slid noiselessly back.

I didn't even look at him. "Where is Amado?" The gates behind me slid shut, as noiselessly as they had opened.

"He might be here and he might not. Get off that horse."

I hesitated.

"Now!"

He'd apparently decided he didn't like being called a peasant. Further insolence would only cause trouble, so I swung my leg over the cantle and stood beside Sorrel Horse while my eyes darted around the compound. Was I really within a few yards of Juana? Could she actually be here?

Two more goons appeared, both barely more than teenagers. I stared hard at them, my fists clenching beside me. Had either of these been at the ranch the night they hurt Juana and took her away?

The oldest one spoke. "Turn around, and walk straight ahead." One of them prodded me with the barrel of his AK-47. I glared at him, then slowly pushed the barrel away from my belly with the back of my hand. I am not especially brave, and I have tried to not do too many foolish things during my time on this earth. I enjoy life as much as the next man, but a cold anger had overtaken all reason. My lack of visible fear and the pronouncement that I was Amado's cousin had perhaps been enough. They exchanged nervous glances, and backed away.

One of them walked in front of me toward the buildings. The other waved his gun barrel for me to follow. We entered what I supposed was a house, though many a hotel I'd stayed at would have been smaller. After we'd walked through a spacious courtyard, the man in front of me opened one side of a double door. We entered what might have been a living room, though that didn't seem a grand enough name for a room as large as this. I barely glanced at it. All I wanted was to find Juana and leave.

The young hood waved me to a chair, but I declined and walked to the only window in the room. "Where is Amado?"

"Someone will be with you shortly. Please – " Again he

indicated that I should sit on Amado's expensive seat, but I stood with my back to the window. His face flushed with anger before he turned and both of them left. I was now alone with my hope and fear.

Within minutes, a silver-haired man quietly opened the door and walked into the room. He held out his hand. "Welcome to El Aguila, Señor Altamirez. I am Antonio Montiel. Please, sit." He said his name like I should recognize it, which I didn't, then indicated a couch that probably cost more than Aunty's whole house.

"You know why I am here. Where is my wife?"

"I – I, well I'm not the person to … ." The man's voice trailed into silence and his eyes slid away from mine. Whoever he was, he was used to being in charge. He'd perhaps not expected my direct question.

"How did you find this place?"

I saw no reason not to tell him. Maybe it would make this band of criminals less cocky, though I doubted that. "It wasn't difficult. I followed some of your drug mules delivering bags of marijuana."

He shrugged. "I just wondered. Your visit isn't entirely unexpected. May I order some coffee, or perhaps you would like something stronger?"

"Neither. Where is my wife?"

He ignored my question. "Amado himself would wish to have greeted you. However, that is not possible."

"I recently did him a favor, one I regret. I have no desire to see him."

Antonio's lips tightened. "Yes; so I understand. If you will sit, perhaps we can discuss the information you need."

I stared at Antonio's narrow, impassive face. A beginning

fear of what he might have to say started a ball of fear deep in my chest. I backed up three steps and sat on the edge of Amado's blood-tainted couch, my fingers intertwined in front of me.

Antonio sat on another piece of the fancy, brocade furniture, to my left, so I had to turn my head slightly to watch him, to hear the words that would change my life forever.

"Juana Ortero is dead."

I wanted to scream as I choked back the great sadness that washed over me like a massive wall of water, but I was left gasping, unable to speak. The blood left my face and drained right to my toes. Grief stabbed like a thousand knives, and though this man lied to me later, I knew now he had told me the truth.

"Why? Why did you do this?" The words cut through the painful constriction in my throat, one tortured syllable at a time.

"She was the sister of Marcos Ortero. He has caused much trouble for us. Nevertheless, whether you believe me or not, her death was not supposed to happen. It was a mistake. A young man overstepped his authority. Amado was not pleased."

"You killed the woman dearest to me, and Amado Carrillo was not pleased?" In two strides, I was in front of Antonio. My hands reached for his throat, the volcano of wrenching grief demanding a violent, passionate response. At the last second, I glanced up. Part of the opposite wall had soundlessly slid away to reveal a half-dozen men with assault rifles, all of them pointed at my chest. My heart was dead within me, and I cared little whether they fired. Nevertheless, my hands froze. I backed away, my fingers clenched, my chest heaving with anger and sadness. My life as I'd known it, would never be the same

Chapter 24
DINA

THOUGH DINA HAD never visited Alejandro's Georgetown apartment, she thought she knew how it would look. It would be a great brownstone building, with white shutters and a massive front entrance built from sculptured stone, or maybe even polished river rock. Two concrete lions would adorn the heavy railings that led from the street. At Christmas time, a giant wreath would encircle the polished bronze knocker. That was all a little much, and probably Alejandro didn't live in anything like that, but still, that's how she always imagined it.

She scowled. One had to envision something. The few times she'd tried to reach him had been frustrating. Whatever voice mail service he subscribed to required at least ten rings before the message kicked in. It had taken awhile to figure that out. Apparently, Alejandro only wanted to listen to messages from the most long-suffering of his friends and family.

Dina eyed the giant cuckoo clock high in the wall at the east end of the dining room. The last time she'd tried to reach Alejandro, the battery on her cell had nearly died before she finally gave up in disgust and left a curt message. In return, her brother had sent his usual five word text message. "I will call you later." He had not returned her call. It wasn't like they had a bad relationship. It was just distant – had been for years. Dina sighed. Maybe someday that would change.

Carefully, she punched in the only contact number he'd ever provided, and waited for the long series of rings. Instead, she was immediately transferred to his voice mail. Disgusted, she started to ask him to call when she heard him interrupt.

"Mama?"

"No, Alejandro, it's Dina."

"Oh, hi." He sounded disappointed. "Is everything alright?"

"Yes, and no. How am I so lucky to catch you at home?"

"I'm not. It's just the way the phone system works for us."

"Oh, so it patches through to your office?"

"Well – sort of."

She was used to Alejandro's clear as dishwater answers whenever she asked anything about his work or employer. "So, how are you, brother?"

"Good. Busy as usual, but yeah, things are good."

Dina shoved all the real issues and problems aside. For ten years, there had been few opportunities to connect. "Got a girlfriend yet?"

Alejandro laughed. "Wow, that's a loaded question, but no, I'm too busy for that. I do have a lady I hang out with a lot. Nothing serious. We're just friends."

"Well, that's no fun. You're almost thirty, and still no

wife to take care of you?"

He sighed. "Yes, you don't need to remind me. How are things at your house? How's Frederick?"

"Frederick's fine – I guess."

"You guess?" Alejandro chuckled. "Ooh ... and you're lecturing me on relationships?"

Tears touched her eyes. "Well, things have been better. I've been here at the ranch for the last week." A rush of sudden affection and need for this brother she hardly knew welled up from deep in her soul.

"What's happening there? Is Mama any better?"

"No." Dina bit her lower lip, determined not to cry. "She's – she asked me to call you. I was going to anyhow, but she wants to see you before the cancer gets worse."

"It's that bad? Mama's not overreacting?"

"No. I wish she was, but Alejandro, this doesn't look good. I think you should come as soon as you can."

"Okay, let me see how long it will take to shuffle my schedule here. Hang on a minute." Dina waited while her brother in his faraway brownstone apartment checked his schedule. She wondered; was that *really* where he lived, or was it one of those generic high-rises with floor upon floor of soulless flats peopled with humanoids, scurrying like ignominious ants to their places of labor.

Alejandro's voice jarred her into the present. "If I can catch a flight on Tuesday, I will be there either late afternoon or early evening."

"Do you want me to pick you up at the airport in Tucson?"

"No, I don't want you to go to any trouble. I'll just rent a car, but thanks anyhow, Sis."

"I would be glad to come up and get you. Anyhow, text me if you change your mind. Oh, you probably should be prepared; there are some problems with the ranch that we will need to discuss as well. It has to do with Papa."

"Papa?"

"Well, you know ... anyhow, we can't talk about it over the phone. I'll see you Tuesday evening."

"Okay. Give my love to Mama."

"For sure. Love you." Dina carefully replaced the receiver. Tuesday could not come soon enough. She was grateful that Alejandro had agreed to come so quickly. In the past, it had been months before he could apparently schedule time to be away from his work. This time, even a week's delay would be disastrous; for the ranch, and perhaps for Mama as well.

Dina tucked her feet under her in the leather-covered recliner and snatched her cell phone off the cherry-wood side table. A vase of flowers shared space with the desk phone she'd just used to call Alejandro. It was past time she and her husband talked, that is if he could spare a few moments of his precious time. She hit contacts and tapped Frederick's number. After the second ring, the call went to voicemail.

"Hello, I'm either in a meeting or on the phone. If you will leave your number ..."

Same old, same old ... couldn't he even pick up a call from his wife? What if it was an emergency? She'd have more success calling the dog catcher than him. A voice deep within her said that wasn't fair, that she was being petty and churlish, but she angrily pushed it away and left a message. "It's me – again. Call me." She slammed her phone back on the desk. This was just the last of a long string of snubs. Whatever was going on, she and her husband were rapidly moving toward different planets.

Dina padded to the side entry and jammed her feet into her boots. She should have waited until evening to call Frederick. Every time she dealt with him or his inane voicemail, it just made her angry, which was a bad way to start the day. As she made her way to the barn, she checked the two outdoor arenas. Luis was loping big figure eights on Peyo; his lean, chiseled features furrowed with concentration. He didn't notice her as she walked by, which was good. She had no desire to face him this morning.

As unobtrusively as she could manage, she walked through the barn, pausing to check each horse and stall to make sure they were up to the standard Raul always expected. If Raul had a long absence in mind, it wouldn't be any different under Luis. He would be the absolute best manager she could hope to find. But ... there was the other problem. What if she and Frederick – no, that could never happen. Whatever problems they were having could be solved. The weight of her failing marriage seemed like the final brick on an already unmanageable load. Why was Frederick so distant? Where was Raul – and what about Juana? Would Raul find her? How soon before Federal authorities seized the ranch? And now, worst of all, Mama was slipping away. Dina's shoulders slumped, and she fought back the tears that threatened to spill over. All those heart-rending questions, and she had no answers.

Chapter 25
FREDERICK

FREDERICK PUNCHED THE necessary numbers to reach Oso in Juárez. He smiled as he anticipated the response he'd get to this assignment. In Spanish, *El Oso* means "the bear." The name had been shortened to just Oso, which was the only name by which anyone in the agency knew the great lumbering giant. Of Peruvian descent, Oso had been a part of the agency long before Frederick had arrived, and when there was an assignment like this, the man proved his worth.

Oso Markani had been drafted as a center for the San Diego Chargers, but his sometimes uncontrollable temper had terminated his football career before the end of the first season. That had been a good thing for Stirling Associates. Oso would take any task, and was fanatically loyal to the company and his adopted country. He was too much of a loose cannon to handle long underground assignments, but for short jobs like this he was unbeatable. Frederick doodled on a scratch pad, the phone to his ear as his mind cataloged every phase of the coming operation.

"Yeah."

The deep growl startled Frederick from his reverie. "Oso

— Frederick here."

"I know."

Frederick didn't wait for pleasantries. Oso wasn't one for small talk. "I need you to do a job — different than usual. Can you put a deadbolt on a door?"

Oso's answer was immediate, and as usual, cocky. "You think I'm an idiot or what?"

Frederick let his surly response go by. "So you've done that before?"

"Well — not exactly."

"It's at South Hospital in Juárez — on the first-floor stairwell door. Are you sure you can do it?"

"I am supposed to do this in the daytime?"

"Yes." Frederick's stomach tightened. Maybe he should get someone else. But there was nobody. "You'll need to find out what the hospital maintenance people wear. Go in, get the deadbolt on and get out. There's a possibility that someone will notice and throw a fit, but any hospital bureaucracy will take at least a couple days to actually have someone take it off. By then, we'll have done what we need to do.

"How soon do you need it?"

"Tomorrow."

Frederick noted the quick intake of breath over the phone.

"I'll see what I can do."

"Call me when it's done — and thanks."

By eleven o'clock, Frederick's bottle of antacid pills was nearly empty. He screwed off the top, shook the last two out and called the appropriate players for a one p.m. meeting. None of the drawers in his desk yielded any more pills, which meant it would be a long afternoon. He walked down the hall toward flight operations. Pablo's rescue operation depended on too many people making the right moves at the right time. If events didn't unfold exactly right, disaster, like a hovering turkey vulture would pounce and eat them all. There was too much room for error, so to have any chance at success, it was imperative that there be no misunderstanding amongst those who would be on the front line. He rapped twice on Hugh Jorgenson's door, then entered.

"Hey Hugh, ..." He pulled out a chair in front of Hugh's desk. "How's it lining up?"

"Good." Hugh leaned back and crossed one leg over the other. "What I'm going to recommend is that we go in with a Bell 206. They're small and fast. We can get two or three gunners in along with the pilot and still have room for whoever we're evacuating." Hugh's dark eyebrows scrunched together. "You're sure there's just one man to evacuate?"

"I'm sure, and two commandos will be sufficient. If all goes according to plan, this should be a boring trip. The last thing those commandos will do before you skedaddle out of there is to bar the door to the hospital roof. They'll take the necessary materials in with them. That should let you get well away before any bad guys show up to make life miserable."

Hugh's eyes narrowed. "We need at least seventeen seconds to get out of range. I prefer twenty – if we can get it. After that, no assault rifle is going to reach us."

"You'll get it. Who's flying the mission?"

"Pete Derose. He's the best we've got."

"Okay, I'm still deciding who will be in the chopper with him."

Hugh scooted his chair up to the desk and scanned his

notes. "Just make sure they're good."

A long silence seemed to take all the oxygen out of the room. Hugh looked up into Frederick's cold blue eyes.

"We-Don't-Have-Any-Other-Kind." It was as if Frederick had accented each word with a finger in Hugh's chest. The result would have been the same.

Hugh held up a hand. "I know that. I didn't mean to—"

Frederick waved the apology away. After a tense moment, he stood. "We'll finalize the details at the one o'clock meeting. See you there." He left without a backward glance.

Precisely at one, Frederick walked into the conference room and faced the men who would be involved in the Pablo Martinez evacuation. Fernando and Carlos sat on the side of the table farthest from the door. Ricky lounged at the far end. Hugh and the pilot, Pete Derose, were tucked in at the right-hand corner farthest from Frederick's chair. On the nearside, two lean-faced young men sat silent and watchful. One was in his early thirties. The other was younger, in fact he looked hardly out of his teens except for the great flowing handlebar mustache that gave his face a rakish slant. For more than a few, it was that part of his features they'd focused on — before they'd died. Those who lived longer took in the quiet, watchful eyes. They weren't always cold. Sometimes, they were ice, and on rare occasions *a* sunny aqua. Frederick introduced the young man as Derek Parker, the newest recruit at Stirling Associates. "All of you know Bobby Knowlton. These are the two that will go in with the chopper. Pete's going to fly one of the Bell 206's, room for four guys, five at the most."

"Alright, listen up." Frederick beamed the first picture onto the screen, walked to the front, and for the next hour went through the precise, step-by-step plan to evacuate Pablo. As he talked, he searched for the strategic weak spot. At the clinic, Pablo would hopefully administer the anesthetic overdose. When they arrived at South Hospital with Amado he had to be ahead of the gurney like he was clearing the way, then have sufficient space to dart into the stairwell and slam the deadbolt before anyone could stop him. Those were the tough parts. After that it should be easy – shouldn't it? Pablo would scamper up the stairs and onto the roof. The two commandos would cover his escape. They'd bar the door, follow Pablo into the helicopter and skin for the border. Easy. Wasn't it? If the plan was as good as it looked on paper, why did his stomach feel like there were ball bearings rolling from one side to the other, all loaded with arsenic and approaching disaster? What if Pablo was caught administering the overdose? What if he wasn't allowed in the ambulance? At the hospital, everything could go wrong. He might never make it up those stairs alive.

After another hour of detailed questions, the meeting ended. Frederick and Hugh would meet Pete, Bobby, and Derek at the hangar tomorrow morning to answer final questions, or solve any last minute problems. He walked back to his office and checked the phone. Seventeen messages, none of them that couldn't wait for an answer. Dina had called twice. His stomach again knotted with fear. He reached for the familiar bottle of antacids in his jacket, his instant defense against the scalding in his stomach. They weren't there. He'd have to stop at Walgrens on the way home and put in a supply. What was happening at the ranch? Had Dina been able to unravel Juana's mysterious disappearance? He picked up the phone and tried to call her.

It immediately kicked over to voicemail, and he paced the floor. He should be at the ranch helping her. Possibly Ricky could have handled this? He tried to concentrate on tomorrow while he plunked a dollar and a half in quarters into the vending machine in the hallway. A roll of antacid pills plunked onto the tray. He tore off a couple while he attempted to dissect each phase of the mission, but Dina's voice kept getting in the way. She needed him, and once again, he'd let her down.

Chapter 26
RAUL

FOR A LONG MINUTE, my eyes flickered between the assault rifles and Antonio. He sat unmoving, his elbows resting on the arms of the chair, his hands folded under his chin. There was no malice in his gaze, and it came to me that I had no choice but to believe his explanation that Juana's death had been some horrible accident. But my heart hardened. Amado shouldn't have touched her in the first place. He could have found some other way to reach Marcos. A mistake? If it was, it was one that would cost him his life. These men who faced me were of no consequence. My quarrel was with my cousin, Amado Carrillo.

Slowly, I trudged to the door of the room. None of the rifles spoke, and Antonio did nothing to stop me. I walked outside to where I'd tied Sorrel Horse to an acacia tree. I talked softly to him while I tightened the cinch. I had no idea how to get where I was going, but I knew that before I was done, vengeance would be mine.

A low voice reached me from the wide veranda. "Would you like to see her?"

I dropped the latigo. Antonio stood at the top of the

steps, his hands stuffed into the pockets of his cotton britches. He probably had better clothes, but for whatever reason, he dressed like a common laborer. In a perverse way, it made me trust what he said.

"Where is she?"

"Follow me."

I nodded and fell into step beside him. For her to still be above ground in this scorching hot climate meant ... no, I didn't want to go there because it meant if I'd been here a day ago, she might have lived. If her brother Marcos hadn't kept me locked up in Juárez, I could have saved her.

We followed a trail that narrowed along the cliff edge, then dropped toward the river far below. Near the bottom, the track opened up into a small meadow. A tiny white church with a tall steeple looked out over the river. At the back of the building, a few weathered gravestones stood stark in the light of the rising moon.

Antonio opened the door, and pointed. I stumbled forward, the tears in my eyes blurring the rough cobblestone under my feet. At the front of the church, Juana lay in an open casket. She'd died no more than a few hours before I'd arrived, and again I vowed vengeance on Amado. I cursed her brother Marcos, and I blasphemed a God who would allow such injustice in the world as I knelt beside the wooden coffin where they'd laid her. I put my hand over hers and wept. Agony constricted my chest as I stared at the missing finger and the broken bones. She'd suffered terribly at the hands of these killers, and maybe couldn't have lived after that first night at the ranch.

Sometime later, Antonio cleared his throat behind me to announce his presence. "It may not mean anything right now, but the man who did this is dead. I made sure of that. We are not all depraved killers."

I stared with unseeing eyes at his face, then slipped the .45 out of my belt and aimed it between his eyes. Antonio never flinched, and I think if he had, he would have never left that little church alive, but in some perverse way, his lack of fear returned me to reason. I dropped the hammer and wearily tucked the gun back in my belt.

Antonio walked to the back of the church and slumped into a pew. "We will bury her tomorrow if you would like. It is a pretty spot here by the river."

"I don't want her buried with murderers," I grated.

"There are no cartel killers buried here. Only a few local village people from long ago."

I gazed one last time at the woman I'd loved more than any other on the face of the earth. My fingers rested on her face, but it was cold, and once more the tears ran down my face for what might have been, and for what now could never be. We would never have the children she'd so wanted, we'd never again laugh, play together, love each other. It was all gone.

After I'd composed myself, I walked to where Antonio sat. "I think Juana would like it if we buried her here by the river."

"I will see that it is done first thing in the morning."

"No, I would like to do that. If you can find me a shovel, I will dig Juana's grave tonight."

A few minutes later, Antonio returned with a serviceable spade. For hours, I hacked away at that rocky earth, and eventually there was a hole that was as tall as I am, and as long. There was nobody there in the moonlight but me, so

I manhandled Juana's box from the church to the bottom of the hole alone. When it was done, I crawled out, and stood over her grave. I'd wept enough that there were no more tears. It was over. I would weep no more, but as I stood there looking down at all that was left of Juana Ortero Altamirez, I wondered what to say. I looked to both sides, peering into the darkness, maybe hoping there was a priest or minister, but of course there wasn't. Other than two or three weddings, and about the same number of funerals, I'd never been a church-going man, though I hadn't anything against it. Once in a while, when I could get away from the ranch I'd take in a Lent or Easter Mass at our white church in Agua Prieta, but I'd gathered few words from the Book, so I just said what came to mind.

"God, you know I don't have the right words, but Lord, they come from my heart. First, I'm sorry for cursing you earlier tonight. I don't reckon it's your fault that men have rejected everything you ever stood for, so I shouldn't have blamed you. For that, and lots of other things, I'm sorry. God, please watch over Juana's soul, or whatever part you have of her, and I guess it's hard to say ... but thanks for the time we did have together." And then I started on the Lord's Prayer, because if you grow up saying it every morning before school, you don't forget it. It seemed appropriate, and I think God and Juana were both okay with it.

A streaky, cold dawn had broken over the eastern edge of the Sierra Madre when Sorrel Horse and I left Amado's luxurious hideout. I rode up the hill from where I'd buried my wife. There was a new man on guard, and though we never spoke, the gate slid silently back to let me ride silently through. Sorrel Horse and I picked our way around the shale slide, scrambled to the top of the ridge, then down the other side into the big canyon that I followed out of the mountains. Cold, foggy air seeped into my bones. I unrolled and shrugged into the thin denim jacket I'd carried behind my saddle. All the way down that long canyon trail, I thought about what Amado had allowed to happen to my sweet Juana. Did it matter if he hadn't actually ordered her abuse and torture? I thought not. He'd kidnapped Juana in order to get to Marcos Ortero, and by the time I rode into Genaro Chacon's yard where I'd left my rig, I'd weighed Amado on the scales of justice and found him more than guilty. That wasn't hard. My cousin was guilty of a thousand murders. He paid the right policemen, the right politicians to look the other way – and he continued to kill so he could smuggle his white death north to the American market. After today, he would do it no more.

I watered Sorrel Horse at the little stream that ran through Genaro's yard, then loaded him in the trailer. Genaro silently watched me, then managed to find a flake of hay for Sorrel Horse.

"Come. My wife has *comida* and I think it would be good if you ate."

I'd not touched any food since yesterday, but I wasn't hungry. The anger and sadness still ran too deep for me to feel such ordinary things as hunger, yet I knew it was necessary to eat if I was to accomplish what I needed to do.

Genaro ushered me inside his little *casa*. It was humble by any standard, but the *tortillas, beans*, *queso*, and *chorizo* his wife served, filled an empty spot in my belly. That other emptiness – food would never fill.

We'd finished eating before any words passed between

us.

"You found what you were searching for?" Genaro's question seemed more a way to make conversation than prying, and I considered how to answer.

"I did."

For fully five minutes, neither of us spoke. Genaro seemed a man of few words, and I've always respected that in a man. Finally, I rose from the table, thanked him and his wife for the meal and sauntered out to my pickup.

"And the mountain lions?"

"I survived." I stared at the low peaks in the distance. "It was my wife. They killed her."

"I am sorry. And now you seek vengeance?"

I nodded.

"Sometimes that is best left with God."

"And sometimes God uses the hand of man."

Genaro refused any more money for looking after my rig, but I'd managed to tuck another five hundred pesos under the salsa dish on his kitchen table. He'd been a friend when I needed one. I'd not ever forget that.

Chapter 27
DINA

DINA SADDLED BENITO and left the corrals at a high lope. Checking the yearlings in the east pasture was something she could have delegated to one of the hired men, but this morning she needed to ride. Staying active for at least part of the day gave her something to think about other than a future without the ranch, and even more tragic, without Mama.

Was Mama failing this quickly, or was she just having a bad week? Maybe tomorrow she would feel well enough they could take her back to Dr. Larson in Tucson. He would get them an appointment at one of the best cancer hospitals in America, perhaps even the Mayo Clinic. Yes, that was it. Mama would be fine. She was only seventy, still way too young to die.

For a couple miles, Dina let Benito jog-trot along the dirt trail. When he wanted to slow, she pushed him harder. She wanted to see whether he'd inherited the tenacity and toughness his mother had. What was his attitude when he was tired?

A mile before the east pasture, she broke Benito into a

slow lope. He was smooth, way easier to ride than his mother had been. For months, Piñata had been wild and crazy, her gait as unpredictable as her fear. Benito was solid, his eyes alert and willing. She smiled as they topped a slight rise, and came to the section of loosely fenced range they called the east pasture. She reached down and stroked the black mane in front of her saddle horn, pleased with the solid foundation Raul had given this valuable colt.

A mile farther, Dina stepped to the ground and tugged at one of the sagging wire gates. She scowled as she dragged it open, then led her horse through. Though the ranch used water and salt licks to control cattle much more effectively than actual barbed-wire barriers, it was time she sent someone out to do at least a minimum of repair on the fences. Two far-flung springs, and a well on the home section were the only sources of water on the ranch, so the number of cattle they could run was limited. It was why Dina's father had decided to allocate more of the ranch resources into running a high-quality horse facility rather than the traditional cattle operation. That, of course, came with a whole different set of problems. A multitude of government regulations made it difficult to ship horses back and forth across the border. However, south of the border, operating costs were less, and selling into the lucrative American market generally added substantially to the ranch's bottom line.

After Dina closed the gate, she rode southeast along a dry wash, constantly scanning the ground ahead for cattle sign. They used the east pasture for yearlings, calves they'd kept over from the previous year to be fattened. It was lower ground with some sub-irrigation, so the cattle didn't have to travel nearly as far to get full, not like the cows and calves that ran on the higher desert pastures. She didn't have to ride far before she started running into little groups of cattle. It was now the hottest part of the day, so most of them were shaded-up in the dense brush. She checked the mineral feeders. All were low. She'd have to send one of the men with more salt.

By early evening she was back at the barn, more impressed than ever with Piñata's offspring. The colt was keen and willing, and even toward the end of the afternoon when the sweat dripped off his bright bay coat, his eyes were alive and enthusiastic. He would be fun to train. But the big question would at least for a while remain unanswered. Had he inherited his mother's speed?

After brushing Benito down, Dina trudged slowly up the lane toward the house. Luis was nowhere to be seen, which suited her well. She had no desire to deal with unwanted, conflicting emotions. She wasn't sure it was the same with him. Were those old feelings just there, buried embers from the past, that given enough oxygen could burst into flame? She had no intention of supplying the oxygen. If Luis understood her marriage was solid, he should feel the same way. She stopped on the rock-strewn path and stared out toward the western sky. How unshakeable was her marriage? Today, it didn't feel that way. Frederick had always immediately returned her call if her number showed on his call display, and surely he'd seen it – or had he? What if something had happened to him? Had he been in a car accident, or worse? Enough of foolish pride. She'd try calling again. They needed to talk.

When Dina walked into the house, Mariela was in the kitchen making a cup of tea.

"Mama, let me get that for you. Where's Lupita? You could have had her do it."

Mariela raised an eyebrow. "It's Thursday. Lupita went to town."

"Oh, Mama, I'm so sorry. I should have stayed inside and looked after you. I forgot today was Lupita's day off. Here, let me do it."

"Oh, I can still make a cup of tea. Do you want one?"

"No, Mama. Frederick drinks the stuff by the gallon." She reached into the fridge and pulled out a can of Coke. "I drink it with him sometimes, but I've never learned to like it. Oh, that reminds me. Great news. Alejandro will be here Tuesday."

A warm smile lit Mariela's face. "I am so glad. I will look forward to that. Do you think Frederick will be able to come while he is here?"

"I don't know, Mama. I will ask him."

"Please do. If we could all be together, that would mean much to me."

Dina looked away, her jaw set. She tried to keep the anger out of her voice. "Then he will come." If this meant that much to Mama, her husband had better show up.

After her mother had gone upstairs, Dina fumbled in her jacket pocket for her cell phone. It wasn't there, nor was it on any of the counters. She must have left it in one of the saddlebags where she'd tucked it when she rode up to the pasture. Quickly, she slipped on an old pair of crocs and hurried to the barn. The night was clear, each star a brilliant pinpoint of light in a dark violet sky. She switched on a light, opened the tack room door and dug through the saddlebags. Of course, it was right where she'd left it. She was about to turn out the light and leave when Luis walked in leading a saddled horse.

"You're still riding?"

He nodded, and Dina noticed the weary lines around his eyes.

"Luis, you're riding too many horses. You're trying to ride your own, and now Raul's as well. Why don't you parcel some of them out to Sandy or Paco?"

"I'd love to, but I can't. All of Raul's horses are past their level of experience."

"Maybe they can't carry on with their training, but at least they can exercise them. That would be enough until you can get to them later in the summer. And Raul might be home soon."

"He might, but I suspect not." Luis met her eyes then looked away, the note of discontent unmistakable.

Dina studied his face. Luis and Raul were close, always had been. What had gone wrong? Was it simply that Luis was no longer content to orbit in a holding pattern, waiting for Raul to retire? What if Raul didn't come home? For a brief second, Dina observed the flaring ambition in Luis's eyes, and wondered. Was he really still in love with her, or was his attraction more that she would someday own the Rodríguez Ranch? She had no intention of finding out. Whether she was ready or not, the time had come for her to take the reins. Her next words to Luis were clipped and harsh. "Let Paco take Socks and give that fancy buckskin that Raul was riding to Sandy. I cannot afford for you to burn out." With that, she turned and left the barn. Those were the first orders she'd ever given Luis, or for that matter, anybody else. Those few words would change the dynamic between them, but now she knew she could handle the relationship between them, whether Raul returned or not.

She trudged toward the house. Halfway there, her phone did the little ring that indicated a caller, the least offensive of all the dopey options Movistar allowed. She dragged it out of her pocket, hoping – yes! He'd finally called.

"Hi. You finally returned my call."

"Yes." His voice sounded tired. "There's just a lot happening here, stuff I have to be personally involved in."

Frederick was his usual vague self, she thought. Stuff? What did that mean? His 'stuff' was obviously more important than any of her problems. However, she needed him. She drew a deep breath. Would he understand?

"Honey, there are some issues here at the ranch that aren't exactly small. When do you think you can get away for a few days? Mama is worse, and next week Alejandro will be here. And – we have some frightening problems with the government."

"Alejandro can deal with government stuff."

"I don't know – maybe. It's just that I would feel better if you did it."

Frederick's voice was clipped, impatience gnawing at the edge of each word. "He does little else to help out. I'm sure he can manage that."

Anger surged through every artery. The tips of her fingers turned white as she squeezed the phone. "Because of course you're too busy. Frederick. This isn't working. I'd get more of your time if I were one of your agents."

"That's not true. It's just that right now, we're busy with a – "

"You're always busy with a new operation. What about

me, Frederick? When will there be time for us, never mind anything I need, or that the ranch requires. You never have time for anything other than your work." She wasn't shouting, but her voice had certainly reached a new level of frustration. Quickly she scanned the yard to see if anyone was close enough to hear her angry outburst.

"Dina, let's not argue. I've had a long, stressful day, I'm tired and – "

"I'm tired too," Dina burst out. "And now Mama's dying, and I need help or at least a little support, and you're nowhere to be found. I refuse to go on like this."

A long silence followed Dina's eruption. Their disagreements over the amount of time Dina spent at the ranch had been increasingly rancorous, but neither had ever laid down ultimatums.

Frederick's voice was stiff, emotionless. "The phone probably isn't the best way to solve our problems. We need to talk about this."

"I couldn't agree more. Perhaps I could schedule an appointment." She squeezed the phone until she thought it would shatter in her hand. He's so good at this, she thought. He's a much better fighter than I am – because he really doesn't care.

"I'll be done with this early next week. Let's talk Sunday night."

"Fine ... talk to you then."

"Yes ... love you."

"Love you too." Dina grated out the words. She was too mad to mean them, but then ... his hadn't sounded that sincere either.

She jammed the cell phone in the pocket of her jeans and

stomped toward the house. One way or the other, she would win. Momma would beat the cancer, Juana and Raul would come home, she would save the ranch, and yes, most of all, her marriage would survive – though she didn't know how.

Chapter 28
FREDERICK

FREDERICK CAREFULLY SLID his cell into its holster, leaned back in his office chair, and scrubbed at his tired eyes. He should have waited and called Dina from home. Perhaps the tone would have been a little more relaxed, and things would have gone better between them. Why couldn't she understand? He did what he had to do. This was his work, and it was not part of his DNA to leave details to someone else. That's how agents were lost. He would not – could not – do that.

Their relationship had suffered in the past few months. A conversation was obviously long overdue, but for now, their personal issues would have to wait. He had to concentrate on every detail of the next 24 hours. He again reviewed every moment of the operation to extract Pablo. What if the chopper malfunctioned? That shouldn't happen, but they needed a realistic alternate plan. He reached across the desk, pulled the phone closer and dialed Hugh's office in El Paso. Hopefully, he was still in the building. If not, he'd have to try his cell, which meant Hugh would have to call back on a secure line before they could discuss anything.

"Hugh here."

Frederick breathed a sigh of relief. "Hi Hugh. Just checking last minute details. We do have a backup bird, don't we?"

"I don't think there's a need for one. The unit we're using only has a few hundred hours on it. There's no danger of it letting us down."

"I'm sure you're right. But you don't think we should have another unit and pilot on the tarmac, just in case something goes wrong? You know, a mechanical failure, somebody gets sick ... no never mind, I'm sure we're okay."

"We're fine," Hugh replied. "That emergency beeper your man carries? I know you've used them a number of times before, but they're new to me. We can count on it working?"

"All I can say is they're the highest quality available, so yes, I don't expect problems. The technology is similar to a medic alert, except they're about the size of a ladybug. We've used them before in situations where it's impossible for an agent to use a telephone, and they performed well. But like a helicopter, it's technology that can fail. We're going to back up every part of the operation that we can. I don't want our man to reach that rooftop landing pad and have nothing there to whisk him away."

"That won't happen. We'll be in the air as soon as we get the signal from him." Hugh nodded at the Lego-block sized transceiver on the corner of his desk. "At what point will he trigger the alert?"

"Just before they leave the Jiménez Clinic with the patient. We're figuring a total of sixteen minutes from the time the alarm is raised in that surgical room to the time they hit the hallway with Amado's body at South Hospital.

You have nine minutes of flight time, from warm-up to set-down, which should give Derek and Bobby seven minutes to secure the area and fasten the bar to the top door."

Hugh grimaced. "That's too tight."

"You can't go in earlier. It's too risky to sit up there. Even seven minutes is going to seem like an eternity."

Hugh's jaw muscles worked overtime. "Yeah, you're right. I'm just afraid if there's an unforeseen problem that takes a few extra minutes to solve, everything will get tense, and that's when people make mistakes."

"I totally agree," Frederick said. "There are way too many moving parts in this rescue. Trust me, if there was another way, I would be all for it. I'll talk to you on the tarmac in the morning." Frederick quietly disconnected.

Frederick's cell phone rang almost immediately. He glanced at the call display. A blocked number. He pressed the green telephone icon.

Oso's voice boomed the few miles from across the border. "It's done."

"Good. Any problems?"

"Nothing that's going to affect your operation. A floor supervisor didn't think what I was doing met hospital protocol. Ultimately, we agreed that the lock would be installed on the understanding that if my orders from the director of hospital operations were in error, then Monday morning I would come back and uninstall the lock. That seemed to satisfy him."

"Great. And *Oso*, as always, thanks for the great work."

"Send money."

Frederick chuckled. "Don't worry, I will. You cost a lot of dough."

"I can always not answer the phone."

"No, no, that's not an option. I'm just saying …"

Oso guffawed, and Frederick smiled. They were on the same page. *Oso* wasn't cheap; but his work for the company was often dangerous, and Frederick expected to pay him well. The banter was necessary, part of the survival process for men who toyed with death.

Afterward, Frederick pulled the spreadsheet up on his computer, and again went through every minute detail. The aerial part was critical, but just as important was Pablo's performance. What if he was caught turning up the anesthetic? One of the best in Mexico, and well-respected in the medical community, the surgeon was no dummy. The anesthetist was just as experienced. He tried not to think about what would happen to them after Amado died. But there was no way he could rescue the medical team as well as Pablo. Besides, both had agreed to do the operation, undoubtedly for an astronomical fee. If they were going to bank a swag full of dinero for rearranging drug lord's faces, they had to pay in the coin of the realm. If it all went wrong, they would pay the ultimate price. And Frederick had every intention of making sure Amado Carrillo's face job went very wrong.

Chapter 29
RAUL

I LEFT GENARO'S small rancho and drove north to Janos. Juana's killing had left me drained of any emotion other than my grief and anger. When I reached the crossroad where I could have turned left for home, it never occurred to me to do that. I made a right turn for Juárez, for it was in me to extract vengeance from those who had taken her from me. At times, I'd hear Genaro's voice. "Sometimes, vengeance is best left to God." Wise words for one so young, and yet I couldn't do it. Not this time.

Late that night, I pulled into Juárez and drove to the street and fortress that kept Marcos Ortero and his policemen safe from Amado Carrillo and the various other thugs that roamed the streets of that hellhole city. I shook my head. So many, like my Juana, had died needlessly. I parked the pickup and trailer in an alley and trudged into the police station. Anger trumped every other emotion as I elbowed my way to the front of the lineup. When I reached the desk, the sergeant stared back at me, the same one who had been on duty when Marcos had held me. Marcos was the one responsible. He'd held me on a laughable charge – long enough I couldn't go home to protect my wife and home from Amado Carrillo's murderers.

"Where is Marcos?"

He waved me away. "Take a seat and wait – "

I dived over the top of the glass, and before that cocky desk jockey could squeak, I had him against the wall with one of my hands on his pudgy throat. "I asked you a question, and I expect an answer – now." My hands are hard from many days handling ropes and horses, and when my calloused fingers squeezed, the man's eyes bulged. Suddenly his eyes flickered toward something behind me. We'd gathered trouble. I saw the baton just before it smashed into my skull. I ducked away, grabbed it and gave a quick twist, because I hadn't time for anything else. Then I cold-cocked the uniform behind the baton. His eyes crossed, and he slid to the floor. I whirled and looked for the desk sergeant, but he'd disappeared. Two more officers boiled out from the hallway at the back of the room. It was time to get serious, so I hit the one on my left with a right cross. He went down like he'd run into a freight train. The other one skidded to a stop, which just meant that my left hook didn't completely douse his lights. Nevertheless, he lay on the floor, groaning. He didn't appear capable of carrying out any arrest warrants. Directly in front of me, the sergeant tried to scramble under his desk, so I helped him with a foot to his ample rear. He somersaulted and took the furniture with him. I glanced around. The outer office had mysteriously cleared of petitioners. The people of Juárez, at least those who were still alive had long ago learned to find a hidey-hole at the first sign of trouble. I turned back to the hallway and faced the man I'd come to see. Marcos Ortero stood stock still as he surveyed the damage, the ever-present AR-15, held in his right hand like it was a pistol. It takes a man with a strong arm to do that, but at the moment I didn't much care how strong he was, or even whether he'd shoot.

I paced slowly toward him.

"What is going on here?" Each word he spoke, fired like a bullet, was shot through with anger and incredulity.

I kept walking.

"This was you?" Marcos inclined his head toward his groaning policemen, and the overturned desk.

I kept walking, my face grim and silent.

Marcos's arm relaxed, and he leaned the rifle against the wall behind him. "You're making a mistake, Raul."

"No, you made a mistake when you held me. They burned my house and killed my wife because you wouldn't believe me. You didn't care enough to find out the truth ... and now, and now she's gone!" The pain was so great, I nearly screamed the last words.

Maybe it was the fact that he'd laid that assault rifle down and walked toward me, or it may have been the horror in his face that stopped me, but I think it was Juana herself, because suddenly I heard her voice in my enraged brain, "Sweetheart, he's my brother. I love *him* too." I stopped, my face a foot from Marcos's and listened to Juana – and Marcos never suffered at my hands. His face crumpled, and in the distance I heard his tortured, mournful voice. "No, not Juana." And I knew it didn't matter that they weren't always on the best of terms. He *was* her brother – and he cared deeply that she was gone and that the life he'd chosen had made him part of the reason she had died.

Faces filled the room, and suddenly there were policemen

everywhere. They slammed me up against the wall and this time I knew better than to lash out, but Marcos spoke, and it was like that old Bible story when Jesus held out a hand and calmed the Sea of Galilee.

Every policeman in the room backed off and nearly stood at attention, and not for the first time did I marvel at the power this man had accumulated during the short time he'd been in Juárez. Marcos turned, picked up the AR-15 and motioned me to follow. We walked upstairs to his office. I sat heavily in one of the plastic chairs in front of his desk and massaged my rapidly swelling knuckles. Marcos sank into the one across from me and ran his hand through his thinning black hair. He appeared exhausted, momentarily drained of every emotion. It was an interlude where I glimpsed the soul of a man who had sacrificed much. Whatever I had against him now seemed unfair. Against gargantuan odds, Marcos had vastly reduced the terror and wanton slaughter that had taken Juárez to the brink of anarchy. Still, the cold anger in my heart wouldn't go away. Why had he held me? He had no evidence, and I'd been guilty of nothing but being married to his sister.

"What are you looking for, brother-in-law?" I asked contemptuously. "You arrested me and held me with no evidence, and now you have threatened Dina. Why? What have you got against us?"

Marcos looked at me like I had lost every bit of reason I'd ever possessed. "You think I can stand by and watch while you continue to work hand-in-glove with the Sinaloa Cartel. That causes enormous problems for me here in Juárez, because then there is a war between them and the Juárez Cartel for the most lucrative routes." He shook his finger in my face. "And who's adding fuel to the fire? You – you Raul, with your continued drug smuggling."

Stunned, I leaned forward in my chair. We studied each other like we were on different planets.

"And I suppose you are sure that when Ricardo was alive, that's what *he* did as well?"

The scorn in his laughter was layers thick. "And shouldn't I be?"

With a different man, I might have walked out, or at least tried to because there was no reason for further discussion. But Marcos was the closest connection I had to Juana. "We don't smuggle anything – at least not now. Nor do we have anything to do with the Sinaloa Cartel. When Ricardo was alive, we did small stuff; people, and a little marijuana."

"A little?" Marcos's dark eyebrows rose.

I crossed one leg over the other as I considered what to say. My involvement with Ricardo was not a subject I talked about – to anyone. This was different, so I did my best to explain. "Dina, nor anyone else in the Rodríguez family can divulge any of what happened when Ricardo was alive. Certain American agencies made sure of that. I am not under the same oath of secrecy. They forgot about me. Ricardo was the closest friend I will ever have in this life. I would never tell you anything that would hurt the operations he was involved in, and I suspect a number of them continue as we speak. But I think you now need to know. Ricardo worked for the CIA."

Marcos stared at me as if I'd just grown another nose. Nothing would have pleased me more than to rearrange his, but Juana's memory again saved him from a permanent disfigurement.

"You are telling me the truth?"

"I'm not in the habit of lying, to you, or anyone else."

"Then what I did ... the confiscation papers are all wrong?"

"What confiscation papers?"

Marcos stood, wiped at his face with a trembling hand, then paced back and forth across the small office. "I just can't see ... Raul, you swear by Juana's memory you're telling ... ." He held up a hand. I think you are telling the truth, but how could all that have happened without someone on our side knowing what was going on? All I ever saw was you and Ricardo making deals with El Chapo and the Sinaloa Cartel. Why? What were you really doing?"

Raul bit his lower lip. "Even today, I do not know everything, but even if I did, I could not answer, even to you. Whatever you heard was wrong. Trust me when I say that in a small way, what we did helped to make your job possible. You are winning here, but that would have been many times harder without Ricardo Rodríguez."

Marcos leaned against the far wall, his hands flexing as if he wanted to choke somebody, but I think it was himself because for once in his life he listened, and he wasn't a man who did that well. With a thumb and forefinger, he rubbed the bridge of his nose as if he had a splitting headache. "I have made many mistakes in my life, few that I will admit to in public, but this ... this one hurts. I was so sure."

"You were wrong."

Marcos's teeth clenched, and his jaw muscles worked back and forth.

There was little more to be said, but one thing still bothered me. "What are these confiscation papers?"

Marcos dug a handkerchief out of his pocket and noisily blew his nose. "Don't worry. Now they are nothing. I can, and will make them go away."

When I'd walked into Marcos's police station, I'd not been sure where this would end. My anger and grief were still too much to bear, but Juana's brother would not suffer harm at my hand. There was little sense in staying longer, so I walked out of the room, pushed through the outside doors and into the crowded street. I would have to find a place to take my horse where he could get a drink and a bite or two of good feed, something not available in downtown Juárez.

An hour later, Sorrel Horse was properly taken care of, and I'd made a lumpy bed in the bottom of a dry wash. It wasn't comfortable, and though I had friends close by, they weren't the kind I could call on at midnight. As I'd done so many times before, my bedroll would be rolled out on the ground. And tomorrow? Would the dawn bring the vengeance I sought? Amado wasn't aware of it yet, but he and I were going to meet. For the hundreds who had died at his bloody hands, and especially for Juana, tomorrow would be his day of atonement.

Chapter 30
FREDERICK

FRIDAY MORNING, FREDERICK woke long before the sun shed any light on the controversial small rooster weathervane at the top of the barn. Dina had been determined they should have the real thing. After all, how were they to wake up in the morning in the proper mood without a rooster announcing the beginning of the day? They fought. That battle he won, though he had to pay to have an extra stall built in the barn, and yes, there was the little tack shed that was extra as well. In the end, refusing to have a real live rooster had been expensive – at least an extra eight grand. He chuckled as he let the shower sluice the sleep from his eyes.

It was the small things that drove him crazy. "Don't you think we should plant flowers here or, wouldn't that new leather couch we bought at Furniture Mart look great under the window?" Those questions were afternoon questions, items to think about when no agent was in trouble, or when he didn't have to balance a multi-million dollar budget. Flowers or furniture before he'd had a chance to grapple with company cliff-hanger issues had never worked for him.

It wasn't that he didn't appreciate Dina's attempts to

make their home attractive. He did, and loved her all the more for it. The dilemma was his, not hers. In the morning, he hit the floor running, his mind rapidly compartmentalizing problems and people. Not that he was a lot better in the afternoon, but he was working on that. He needed to find a way to switch instantaneously from work to home. Most days, he made a concerted effort to forget company problems when he closed his office door. Though he tried to leave all the agent calls at the office, it seldom worked. If an agent died or was compromised because he was dealing with where the dahlias or posies should go ... no, he couldn't even imagine the guilt and remorse. He turned off the water and grabbed a towel. When there were sensitive operations like this one, there was little time or energy to think or react as a husband. Maybe he never should have married? No, it was too late for that. He loved Dina more than ever, and he couldn't imagine life without her. Somehow, they'd have to figure it all out. But last night's phone call wasn't a good start.

Frederick walked into the kitchen of the single story rancher and poured hot water over a tea bag. He didn't drink coffee – hadn't for years. The tea habit had come from a stint he'd done for the British in Wales. When he'd come back to the States, the habit followed him. At the kitchen counter, he spent a few minutes scanning the news and markets. Another financial scandal in the White House. He really needed to call Dina. Hmm ... he scrolled through the list of news items. There appeared to be no end of illegal behavior with this administration. Iraq ... he glanced at the clock. Just a few more minutes and he'd call her. The escalating situation in the Middle East was undoubtedly creating employment for Stirling Associates, and every other intelligence agency. The problem was none of them had the right people. They needed operatives who were fluent enough in Arabic or Farsi to pass for natives. In the shifting tribal sands of the Middle East, recruiting agents with unquestionable loyalty and integrity was nearly impossible. Anyhow, those problems could wait. He had fifteen minutes before he had to leave for the office. He punched in number one on his quick dial. She answered on the first ring.

"Hi Frederick." Her voice sounded tired.

"How are you doing? I thought I should call – I mean after last night." The long pause told him this wasn't going to be a happy conversation. She was still angry.

"Well, thanks. I guess I failed to get the message across. I need you. We have problems I can't solve, and there's no one to help. Can you come tomorrow?"

"Dina, we have a huge operation going, the most important one since I've been at the agency. Today is going to be rough, but I promise you – Monday I'm all yours. I'll drive down Sunday night."

The audible sigh on the other end didn't need hearing aids, and Frederick winced. She didn't get it. She wasn't even trying to understand. She thought he could somehow just drop everything and rush back to the ranch at Agua Prieta.

His jaw set. "Listen Dina, I will come, just not today."

"Well, of course. I understand. Gotta go. I have things to do."

Frederick's face burned as the disconnection silence hummed in his ears. He should have just left it alone. They were no more on the same page than last night. He grabbed his car keys, switched off the house lights and left the house.

For a few seconds, he stood on the front step and scanned the yard. Everything appeared fine. He glanced at his watch, then hurried the few feet to his car. Out of long habit, he walked around the outside, then opened the hood to make sure nothing had been tampered with before he stuck the key in the ignition. As he turned west on to Ramirez Avenue, he forced himself to focus on the task ahead. Would this operation prove to be worthwhile? Would what they were doing even slow the flow of cocaine? He knew in the depths of his soul that it wouldn't, at least not for long. So was it worth risking Pablo's life or the lives of the two commandos and pilot who would have to extricate him? For that, Frederick had no answer. All he could hope was that the temporary supply disruption would save a few lives from the escalating horror that too often led to an early grave.

The night sky had turned to a burnt sienna when Frederick walked through the front doors of the administration building. He paced through the silent halls toward his office, anxious to review, give last minute instructions – and bite his fingernails. He checked for any messages. There was one from Hugh. "Will be on the tarmac by seven. Have bird problems."

Helicopter problems at this late hour? Impossible! Anyhow, that wasn't a big deal. The company had three Bell 206's, all of them ready to go at a moment's notice. So why was Hugh telling him this? He'd find out soon enough. The whole team should be on site before eight.

Pablo's best estimate had been that the earliest hour they would need to be ready to scramble would be between ten and ten-thirty. The surgeon would do Amado's face first before he started the skin grafts on his thumbs and fingers.

The operation wasn't scheduled to begin until eight, and the odds were good that Pablo would not be able to do anything until later in the procedure, possibly towards noon. By that time, everybody would be exhausted. Somebody would hopefully go for a potty break, or who knew what else. The onus then would be on Pablo. If he performed – great, but there was nothing Frederick or any of his team could do to help facilitate anything. As usual, the agent was the gigantic weak link, one they could not tinker with, or fix.

After dealing with two more remote operational problems, Frederick drove to the company airfield at their Intelligence and Commando Training Center. A helicopter waited for the short run to the El Paso base. When Frederick walked into the hangar, Hugh paced back and forth, eyeing the Bell helicopter. He scowled as Frederick approached.

"What's wrong?" Frederick asked.

"Apparently, there's a worn bearing in the tail rotor that the mechanics don't like. For whatever reason, it wasn't reported. Probably, they thought they'd have it fixed before anyone would need it."

"I thought this thing was nearly new?"

Hugh's eloquent shrug didn't require words.

"So use another bird. We have three of them."

"Uh ... one is in Guatemala, and the other one is grounded until it gets an annual inspection sticker."

Frederick leaned forward, his voice rising with each accusing word. "You're telling me we are going into the most sensitive operation we've done in years and we don't have a helicopter? We're not ready?"

Hugh shuffled backward, trying to put distance between him and his boss. "They can use one of the bigger choppers."

"No, they bloody well can't. They're too slow off the ground, and when they leave that rooftop, they need to get out of range quickly. I'm not going to jeopardize those boys because some aircraft mechanic is covering his butt. That helicopter right there is going in." Frederick stabbed a finger at the offending aircraft. Even the helicopter seemed to shrink in front of his explosive outburst.

"Okay, I get it." Hugh grinned weakly.

"Good." Frederick stepped around him and strode toward the rear of the blue and white Bell helicopter. He stared at the tail rotor, then gingerly reached up and tried to move one of the blades. It seemed solid, at least there was no noticeable bearing play. But did that mean anything? He was doing what nobody should do. Stirling hired the best people they could find. One of their expert mechanics had made a call. He was overriding him, maybe putting the crew's lives in danger. Was it worth the risk? He glared at the Bell 206, then walked to the back of the hangar where the larger twin engine Gemini hulked in the far corner. Could they try the operation with it? He shook his head. It was too noisy, and far too slow getting off the deck. On this mission, that could be fatal. He walked outside the hangar into the already stifling hot morning sun. There wasn't time to change anything, and he decided he didn't care whether the mechanic, the FAA, or anybody else showed up. They could fine him, or do whatever else they thought was appropriate, but nobody was going to mess with the plan. He crossed his arms and surveyed the burnt hills across the border. As much as he wanted to bull his way through, there was one man he had to consult.

Ten minutes later, Pete Derose walked into the hangar.

In his late thirties, Pete was a veteran army pilot of both Iraq and Afghanistan. Frederick had complete confidence that no matter what happened, Pete wouldn't panic and do something stupid. There was nobody better. Frederick shook his hand, walked back inside and inclined his head toward the Bell 206 Jet Ranger. "Hugh says the mechanic grounded her yesterday – tail rotor bearing issue. We don't have anything else suitable, so if we can't use it, then we have to cancel everything. I'm for taking a chance, but the final decision is yours."

Pete walked over and grabbed both blades of the tail rotor. Gently he moved them back and forth like it was an offending loose tooth. "I've logged over eight thousand hours in these birds. In Afghanistan, the blowing sand would eat the bearings out in a few hundred hours, and we seldom had the luxury of a field mechanic. I've had to fly them back to Kandahar or Kabul with the tail rotor squawking like a wounded goose. Let me tell you, it ain't fun. This one's nowhere near that bad." He turned and looked Frederick in the eye. "We have a job that requires less than thirty minutes of flying time. I say we're good to go."

Derek Parker and Bobby Wilsall arrived. Frederick signaled them to follow him to the ordnance depot. He unlocked the door with two separate keys. "Okay guys. You know the plan. Gather whatever you need."

Both men exchanged quick glances, then walked along the aisles of assorted weapons. Frederick almost grinned. One of the great perks of being a part of Stirling Associates was how they took care of their people. No agent went into danger without the very best intelligence, and no commando took on trouble without the most advanced ordnance in the world. Frederick watched the new man, Derek, nod with quiet approval at the vast assortment of options. Excellent. He seemed to be a keeper, and Frederick was glad the young man was impressed. It was important for him to understand that as much as the company could, they would take care of him.

With no hesitation, each man selected a variety of grenades. Bobby picked up one of the short Bullpup FN HAR carbines, and Derek instantly chose a Remington 870 model 12 gauge with a 20-inch barrel. Both holstered Sig Sauer .40 caliber pistols. Derek already carried a short-bladed belt knife. For a brief second, Frederick shuddered. Both were nearly as deadly without the assortment of weapons they carried to the door. To meet either of these two in a combat situation would be certain death.

After they'd finished, Frederick nodded, wrote in the weekend log the ordnance they'd chosen, and locked the door. Hopefully, they'd need none of it, but the little worms that slithered around at the bottom of his belly were rapidly growing into great big snakes. The chances of leaving that hospital rooftop without a pitched battle were nearly non-existent.

Chapter 31
DINA

DINA KICKED OFF her boots in the usual corner of the hallway and glanced at the clock. With Papa gone, and Mama sick, supper was not like it used to be. Often, she didn't leave the barn until dark, and then ate by herself. Usually, the evening meal consisted of whatever Lupita had left in the refrigerator.

Her family had always followed the Mexican tradition. *Comida*, the main meal of the day was enjoyed in the midafternoon. Afterward, especially in the heat of summer, a short siesta was observed. It was much easier on horses to catch a short rest in the heat of the day, then finish whatever training chore was at hand later in the evening. For anyone on the ranch to be idle before eight at night was a rare occurrence, so at that late hour, spartan meals were the accepted fare.

Dina stared at the kitchen counters. When Papa was still alive, Lupita would have set out all the tidbits they'd enjoyed as a light meal before bedtime. Perhaps *quesadillas*, rich with *queso ranchero* or *tostaditos* along with a juicy cantaloupe or mangos from the south. Now, there was nothing but an overripe pineapple. The refrigerator produced a little more. Lupita tried to set out an appetizing spread before she went home to her family. But after a few mornings of throwing out food, she refused to leave anything on the counter.

Dina dug through the refrigerator until she found a tortilla and a small dish of guacamole. That, with a few pieces of fruit, would be plenty. She wasn't hungry anyway. The conversation with Frederick had set a new low in their relationship. More and more they lived separate lives. Why had it turned out this way? She spread a thin layer of guacamole on the tortilla, then sprinkled grated cheese on it as she contemplated her deteriorating relationship with her husband. She'd been thrilled when the company had moved Frederick to Albuquerque. She was closer to her family, and after Mama had taken ill, it had allowed her to spend way more time at the ranch than when they lived in Miles City or Omaha.

Was the time she spent at the ranch what had divided her and Frederick? Should she have let Mama and Raul make all the decisions? But how could Mama have carried on alone after Papa died? Would Alejandro have become more involved if she had shown less interest in the ranch? No. That was wishful thinking – mostly on Mama's part. Alejandro disliked horses and cattle, or anything else remotely connected to ranching. He loved his job and had always been quite content that somebody else in the family would carry on with the tradition he so thoroughly abhorred. As a teenager, he'd had a banner made for his room. It read: My Place – Where Horses don't Kick – and Cows don't Crap!" To Dina's knowledge, his outlook hadn't changed.

After she'd eaten, Dina put the food away and wandered out to the east porch. Everybody who wasn't company used that entrance – except Mama. Before Papa died, she'd refused, disparaging it as a servants' entrance. Dina's face creased in a tired smile. Mama's real character had been as carefully crafted as Papa's. Her role as a shrill and overbearing debutante had been as much a part of her father's cover as his simpering and inept pretentiousness, a necessary façade to protect not only themselves from discovery, but also those they loved. Though now she understood the necessity of her father's work with the CIA, her smile settled into a grimace. She and Alejandro had suffered as a result.

Dina slipped into the ancient rocking chair that graced the far end of the porch. This truly was her favorite place, especially at night. As a little girl she'd curled up in this chair, certain she could survey the whole ranch. She smiled into the caressing warmth of the night. Maybe she couldn't see everything, but this cozy corner did give a great view of the barns and *cabinas* that served as homes for the hired men. Beyond the stone fence surrounding the yard, the smoke-blackened adobe walls of Raul's house stood stark against the night sky. Where were they? Surely Raul and Juana would return and everything would be as it was in the past, and they'd all live happily ever after. Wasn't that how all decent stories turned out? She stood and walked to the railing. Yes, of course they did. Raul and Juana would come home and build a new house. Then they would live there until a ripe old age. Many more good horses would come from the Rodríguez Ranch, and she and Frederick would ... would what? The voice in her mind slowed to a floundering crawl, like her thought processes had suddenly galloped into a huge mud bog. What could they do? Frederick had responsibilities he could not leave. He was the director of the most elite private intelligence firm in the country, maybe in the world. Did she expect him to walk away, to come and help run the Rodríguez Ranch? He could probably do it, he might even like being a rancher, but a great part of his talent would be wasted. Is that what she hoped would happen, just so they could be together? And what about her? It seemed like a great unseen force was backing her into a corner. Either she had to abandon the ranch and her family, or she had to give up on her marriage to Frederick. Was there no way to strike a balance so their lives could truly meld into one committed entity? And what about her barrel racing career? Where did that fit in? A lone tear slid down her face. Right now, it would be nice if a deep voice came out of heaven with specific instructions. But as the minutes slipped by, there was no voice, and no answer.

Dina gripped the arms of the chair. It was time to go up to bed. Whatever else happened, morning came early. Raul's house was a silent sentinel of black against the night sky. Seconds passed. She started to exert enough pressure to push herself off the chair. Suddenly, a figure appeared along the front of Raul's burnt house. Was it Oscar? Had he been the one who torched Raul's house? If so, why was he back? Without thinking, she bounded off the porch and ran toward the burnt walls. When she arrived, there was no movement or sound. Had she imagined it? No, she knew she hadn't. Someone had been here. But where had he gone? She surveyed the empty yard around Raul's house. There was no way he could have escaped without her seeing him. Suddenly, she wished she'd called for Luis or one of the men. That would have been more prudent. Too late now. She'd walk to the other side of the house and check the hedge of Joshua trees Raul had planted. That would be enough, and she would stay far enough away from them to run to safety if need be.

She sensed rather than saw the movement behind her, and though she tried to whirl away and run, it was too late. A strong arm slipped around her throat and jerked her body upward until her feet no longer touched the ground. She tried to scream, but the chokehold cut off her wind. Desperately, she struggled to kick free, but the man was too strong. A red film obscured her vision. Within seconds, the red turned to black. She shouldn't have come out here alone, and that was her last conscious thought before the darkness trumped all her plans for the future.

Chapter 32
RAUL

I ROLLED OUT of the thin blanket and pushed to my knees. Every bone in my body ached. I was too old to be sleeping on the cold ground, though I have to admit at least a portion of my misery came from the scrap in that police station. Sore or not, I needed to get started. I knocked my boots together and shook them out to make sure there weren't any resident spiders or snakes, then hobbled over to the side view mirror on the Silverado. The old man staring back at me looked terrible, and today of all days I needed to look respectable, like I actually belonged to the upper-crust drug-running part of the Carrillo clan.

I hadn't needed to sleep out on the ground. I could have rented a hotel room, but there hadn't been any suitable place for Sorrel Horse, so I'd elected to camp outside with him. I loaded my horse, then drove until I found a feed store where I bought a bale of hay. A small Pemex gas station washroom had a good enough mirror I was able to scrape off the two day growth of whiskers before I drove into the city. Several times I'd considered dropping Sorrel Horse and the trailer somewhere close. There didn't seem to be a safe place to do that, and though pulling that horse trailer into the tony, upscale subdivision where I was going would attract attention, I wasn't sure that mattered. There would be no disguising my identity. Besides, a touch of reality might be more convincing to those who surrounded Amado.

My anger and grief weighed heavy, and though I couldn't remember the last time I'd eaten, I cared little for food, and after today, I'd not likely have need of any. Amado Carrillo had killed Juana as he had hundreds of others. Today, the killing would stop. Justice would be served. Though he was a man with much money, and though he had protection in high places, this time he would not walk away from the evil he'd done. From that silent grave beside the Rio Yaqui, Juana's blood cried for vengeance. Those who were charged with providing justice and equality before the law would not do their job, had never done it with the cartels in my country, so justice and retribution would happen another way. I checked the loads in the .45, then tucked it into my belt. My denim jacket covered it well. If I was searched, they would find it quickly, but I figured on being convincing enough, that wouldn't happen. And if they did find it? I stared at my bare hands. The knuckles were scarred, the palms calloused and hard, and I knew they had enough skill in them to quickly do what was necessary.

Juárez is all about *maquiladoras*, those huge factories that facilitate the cross-border commerce between the United States of America and the United States of Mexico. Every day of the year, thousands of vehicles run between the two countries carrying people and duty-free materials and goods across the border. It's why every Mexican cartel covets the corridors where the *maquiladoras* have been established. But it was Amado who now held every crossing, and tunnel into the United States from the city of Juárez. His cocaine flowed nearly unrestricted into the lucrative American market until he was one of the richest men in the world. But rich men have families. They want chic stores where their wives can shop, good schools, and safe neighborhoods for their kids. They won't live in the hellholes created by their drugs, and they don't want their families near the extortion, kidnapping, and death that is a by-product of their criminal activities. Those 'safe' places are limited in Juárez. But there is one. The gated community of Loma Linda is located on the southwestern edge of the city. Many of the rich who have money and American status have fled north. Those who are left live in Loma Linda. It is one of the few protected places, a well-guarded community of wealthy survivors, which included Amado Carrillo and a select few of his upper-level lieutenants. The other residents minded not at all. It was Amado's presence and power that kept the community free from the degradation he'd helped to create.

I pulled up to the gate. The guard swaggered out of the kiosk and handed me a ledger to sign while he scrutinized my truck and horse trailer. The drop-down windows were open on the horse trailer. Sorrel Horse inspected the man like he might have a gallon of sweet feed. The guard walked back and petted him, then asked me which address I was visiting. Of course, I had no idea what house number or street I wanted, so I just told him the truth.

"I am Raul Carrillo Altamirez, the cousin of Amado Carrillo. I am going to visit him, though I do not have his exact address. Could you please tell me his house number and street?" I gambled they'd have a map and name chart of everyone who lived inside these gates. The guard eyed me warily, but he never hesitated. A cousin to Amado wasn't going to be turned away. He took the ledger, swaggered into his little kiosk and punched in a number on his phone. A superior must have given permission because he yelled out the correct house number, apparently on Calle García. As I pulled through the gates, I decided I owed Sorrel Horse for our ticket past the gate. Between him and the horse trailer, we looked pretty harmless.

Loma Linda would fit in the swank part of any city. Kids kicked a football in the street. Upscale minivans and Cadillac SUV's cluttered the driveways of sprawling ranch-style bungalows, every one of them a status symbol of the occupants. At the end of a cul-de-sac, I found the address the guard had given me, by far the largest of any of those oversized houses. I parked on the street, took a deep breath and walked up to a double front door that would have made our barn doors look like rabbit holes.

A fancy pull-chain doorbell announced my presence. Nothing happened, so I jerked on it again. A strapping young bodybuilder type opened the door and stared at me.

"May I help you?" His surly voice indicated the only aid he had in mind was throwing me off the property.

"Yes, I think you might." I gave him the biggest and warmest smile I could muster, which may not have been that impressive. "I am looking for my cousin, Amado." I tried to sound as if Amado and I called or texted each other at least once a day.

The jock glanced past me at the truck and trailer in the street. His expression cooled further, if that were possible. "He is not here."

"Ah Señor, I had hoped to catch him before he left for the day. We have much to discuss. Rodrigo's last days with us at the ranch – I think Amado would like to – " I tried to sound heartbroken at Rodrigo's sudden and well-deserved death, and turned away.

"Oh, you're *that* cousin." His lip curled as he stepped away from the door. "Your grief is touching. Even his father thought his passing might have been for the best."

I wasn't getting far. "Do you know when Amado might return?"

His eyes narrowed and he again glanced at my rig in the street. "No, I don't." He moved to shut the door. I let him get it most of the way closed, then rammed it back in his face. It was a move he'd not expected, and it bumped him hard enough on the chin to give me an advantage. I followed the door back and gave him a straight hard right to match the red mark the door had left on his jaw. It seemed a good point to aim for. His feet went out from under him, and the first thing that hit the hard tile floor was the back of his pointed head. He was in good shape, and undoubtedly tough. He came off that floor faster than he should have, but I was ready. He'd no more than got to his knees when I stuck that .45 under his chin and backed him against the wall. I wanted no more noise. At my age, one of his kind was enough to handle.

"Now, you can die right here, or you can give me what I need. You are speaking to a Carrillo, so show some respect if you want to live. Your job is already gone. I haven't decided yet whether to kill you, so let's start over. I came here to see my cousin Amado, and you refuse to tell me – "

He crabbed to his feet and plastered himself even flatter

against the wall. "My job requires that I be careful."

"I am the one Amado trusted with his son, so let us understand each other. Amado would not be pleased that you play foolish games."

For a long time he stared at me, I suppose wondering whether I would kill him. "This is a house that pays well, where silence and discretion are required at all times. But perhaps ... well, Amado will not be coming back here – ever."

"Ever?" I asked incredulously.

"He went for an operation this morning. Few know, but when he comes out of surgery, he will be a man with a different face."

"Where is this magical surgery going to happen?" I put more pressure on the barrel at his throat.

He went up on his tiptoes, then winced as the gun sight bit into his skin. His eyes crossed as they followed my trigger finger. "It will be done at the Jiménez Clinic right here in Juárez."

"When?"

"Today."

I stepped back, the gun barrel now in line with his belly button. "Well then, I shall pray that the will of *Dios* be accomplished – in all things," I added sarcastically. I didn't tell him what else I had in mind, but though I considered myself a believer in God, praying hadn't been the first response that came to mind. "Thank you, *Señor. Hasta luego.*"

Contemptuously, I turned to the door. Leaving Amado's pit bull alive was a calculated risk, but I figured he'd not want to advertise his loose tongue to anyone who mattered. If they were going to operate on Amado today, there was no time to lose. The man responsible for Juana's death would not come out of that clinic alive. For Amado Carrillo, judgment day had arrived.

Chapter 33
DINA

WHEN DINA AWOKE, panic squeezed the breath from her lungs. Her fingers clawed at the dirt. Inky blackness surrounded her as she tried to spit the sandy grit from between her teeth. She rolled over, and pushed shakily to her knees. Her throat burned, and she leaned over and retched, the nausea instant and intense. Despite the dizziness that threatened to overcome her, she forced herself to stand. Like the blackened gates of Hades, the charcoal-streaked walls of Raul's burned house loomed in front of her. She peered fearfully into the dark shadows, but whoever had choked her was no longer there. Painfully, she limped toward the house. Why had Oscar done this? She was sure it was him, but what was it he wanted? He'd searched Raul's house and then her bedroom. Whatever item he'd looked for must be small enough to be tucked in a purse, because he'd rifled through every handbag in her closet. And now he'd been poking through the ruins of the fire. Had he known she was watching? Could it be that he'd let her glimpse his fleeing form, hoping she would come to investigate? But why? Terror pushed her battered body into a shuffling trot. Tomorrow, maybe she would come back with one of the men and do a thorough search. Now, she only wanted to get to the house and feel safe.

When Dina closed the side door that led into the utility room, she locked it and stood for a moment with her back to it. She should call Luis. Her fingers trembled as she scrolled down to Luis's number. But no, she couldn't do that. The last thing she wanted was for her foreman to think she had to depend on him to protect her. Her relationship with Luis had turned an important corner. It would be going backward to call him to make sure her house was safe from boogie men.

Dina shuffled toward the kitchen. The only other person in the house was Mama – she hoped. If it really had been Oscar who had choked her, had he come to the house? Was he now hiding, waiting to find what he'd been searching for? Dina's eyes searched every corner and crevice. She would get to her father's office where the menacing pistol still lay in the bottom file drawer of his desk. Shortly after he'd died, she'd discovered it tucked between two folders. After gingerly pulling the gun from the worn leather holster, she'd held it at arm's length, determined to someday shoot it enough to become proficient. That had never happened. Her arms involuntarily clutched each other, and she shivered. Why hadn't she taken the time to practice? But really, what good would that do? Aiming at a target was very different than shooting a human. Could she ever do that? She hoped she'd never have to find out.

Dina's heart did a rapid staccato beat against her chest as she quietly tiptoed to the corner of the kitchen door. A chair creaked in the living room – or was it the office? She peered through the hinge-side crack of the door to see if someone was behind it. The kitchen appeared empty, at least as much of it as she could see. Softly, she stepped forward. The room was as she'd left it, the counters bare and clean except for the pineapple ripening by the toaster. The dish rag she'd used sagged listlessly over the middle partition of the sinks. The clock above the window sounded loud in the silence, each tick a harbinger of what her pounding heart told her to fear.

Dina clenched her fists. This was silly. Nevertheless, she was in charge, which meant she should take every precaution. There was no need to call Luis – but she needed to have Papa's gun. That's the only way she would feel safe. A small voice whispered it was foolish pride that kept her from calling for help. She ignored it. What would the men think? How would she and Mama keep help who were committed to running a first-rate ranching operation when she called for one of them to hold her hand every time there was a crisis? But this wasn't a typical situation. None of them would mind – would they?

Dina clenched her hands to keep them from shaking, and moved her right foot toward the office. The other foot had to follow, and that's how she made it through the kitchen and into the dining room. From there, it was an easy half-a-dozen steps to the office door. It was open. She could get the gun, and then everything would be fine. The screeching voice in her head shouted, "The office door is never open. Don't go in there." Her common sense said, "You probably left it open after you telephoned for that truckload of sweet feed."

Dina shook off the feeling of doom and walked into the

office.

She stared at the man who sat in her father's chair behind the desk. His voice was menacingly quiet. "Close the door." The pistol from the bottom drawer was steady in Oscar's hand.

Dina stared at the gun. Terror blasted a thousand volts to the tips of her fingers. Every muscle group in her body was instantly immobilized. The black hole in the end of her father's pistol would be her last earthly glimpse before eternity became reality.

Chapter 34
FREDERICK

FREDERICK PACED BACk and forth in front of the helicopter. A FedEx van pulled onto the tarmac. Frederick signed for the package. He knew the contents, but at this late hour the bearing for the tail rotor would be of no value. A mechanic rushed across the hangar towing a tray of tools behind him. Impatiently, he motioned the man to take his tools away.

"I can have this changed in three hours, maybe less." The mechanic's eyes pleaded for a chance.

"No. This bird goes with the feathers she has. Pray that she makes it." Frederick turned away. He didn't want the man's opinion, nor was he in the mood to argue. The mechanic turned and pulled his toolbox to the far side of the cavernous hangar.

Frederick's jaw clenched. Had he made the right decision? Should he have tried to replace the bearing that might fail? Or used the larger Gemini? No. Right or wrong, it was the only decision he could have made. When Pablo called ,they had to immediately be in the air. So, no matter what happened, the 206 was going to Juárez with a worn out, or at least less than perfect tail rotor shaft bearing. He glanced at his watch. Nearly nine o'clock. The buzzer on Hugh's vest could activate anytime. Then again, maybe nothing would happen. He'd harped beyond reason to Pablo that if the operating room didn't provide a great opportunity then they should let it pass. Not even a good opportunity. It had to be a great one. He wondered. Had Pablo understood that? Would he try to play the hero? Be the man of the hour? Frederick didn't think so. Pablo should be at least ten years and three kids beyond that, but you never knew. Agents were human. Sometimes, they made egocentric decisions.

Two minutes later, Frederick checked his watch again, while he eyed Hugh. Had Hugh missed Pablo's alarm, or worse, maybe the emergency buzzer hadn't worked. He walked across the tarmac to where Bobby and Derek were checking weapons, attaching grenade pouches, and adjusting their gear. Both had the still, expressionless faces common to men used to putting their lives on the line. To them, this was another operation, a chance to do what they did best. As dangerous as it was, these two loved their work. Frederick turned around and walked away before they saw the ghost of a grin on his face. He could probably cut their pay by ninety percent – and neither of them would quit.

Frederick wandered back to the helicopter and stared at the tail rotor assembly. He hoped and prayed that one more short flight wouldn't be critical. And if the worst happened? He'd known, been advised of a situation that compromised the safety of his men. A top-notch mechanic had been ready to change the offending bearing, and he'd not allowed him to do his job. Four men might die because of a decision he'd made. His shoulders slumped. Every corporation in the world had courses on leadership. But when it came to the tough calls, those courses were mostly worthless. How could anyone teach you how to weigh in the balance national security decisions that were potentially dangerous or deadly to the men involved? You hoped you were right because when you were, you looked like a hero – for whatever that was worth. And when you lost ... well, he wouldn't go there. Not today.

As if twenty thousand volts had zapped the tarmac, the jangling discordant baying of Hugh's emergency buzzer galvanized everyone in the hangar. Bobby and Derek bailed into the back seats in the chopper. Pete started the engine, and proceeded to do a quick run-up. In the seconds before they lifted off, Frederick opened the door and slid into the front right-hand seat. It was a last minute decision he couldn't explain, a decision against every company directive. But he couldn't help it. He wanted to experience first-hand what his men faced. There would never be a better opportunity.

Within seconds, the slicing blades were fighting for altitude as the nose tipped south toward Juárez. Frederick shaded his eyes and watched for the border. Suddenly, the fence lay below him, and they were into Mexican airspace. He peered through the Plexiglas, searching for the red cross that would mark the hospital landing pad. They would either rescue Pablo there – or die. Frederick leaned back in his seat. The men behind him were the best. If anyone could get Pablo out of Juárez, this was the team to do it. And if they didn't? Frederick refused to even think about the consequences of that.

Five minutes later, the three-story hospital building came into view. The familiar, faded red cross was easily visible, the symbol used by most hospitals in the western world.

Pete angled to the west of the few downtown office buildings, then lined up his approach to the landing pad.

Frederick glanced back at the two commandos in the rear. Neither showed any awareness of his scrutiny. Both were busily scanning the surrounding area. He pulled the Glock out of his shoulder holster and checked the loads. Not that he'd need them. Bobby and Derek would not need that kind of puny firepower. Still, it was a comfort to have it handy. He checked his watch. They'd been in Mexican airspace for four minutes. They would be on the roof in another three. By now, Pablo should be somewhere between the Jiménez Clinic and South Hospital. He stared through the Plexiglas, searching each building within a ten block radius of the hospital. Which was the Jiménez Clinic, and where was the ambulance that should now be screaming toward the hospital?

Below, a tan pickup pulling a white horse trailer sat in the parking lot of a small building six blocks north of the hospital. Frederick's eyes moved past that, still searching for the clinic and the first sign of that ambulance because until it made its wild dash toward the hospital, they had nothing. What if – what if Amado died and they didn't rush him to South Hospital? How would they rescue Pablo? Or what if they took Amado farther away? They might even have a plane ready and waiting to take him to Guadalajara, or Mexico City. Wave after wave of fear ate into Frederick's chest. Unconsciously, he reached for the antacids in his shirt pocket. If Pablo had been wrong ... a man had stepped out of the tan pickup, but it was too late to see more of what he was doing.

Derek and Bobby were out the door and on the roof

before the helicopter even settled. Bobby carried the long iron bar in both hands, his rifle slung over his shoulder. Derek packed a big yellow drill and the other L-shaped piece of steel. Bobby threw the door open and checked the stairwell. Derek slammed one of the lag bolts into the door jamb and drove it home. He did the same for two more while Bobby held the big flat bar steady. The whole procedure had taken forty-three seconds. The screech of the last bolt as it ate into the wood of the jamb was interrupted by the first wail of a siren to the north. Frederick froze. Was that the one they were looking for? Had Pablo pulled the trigger?

Derek flung the drill aside. He and Bobby unslung their guns, checked their grenade belts, then quietly slipped down the stairs to the second landing.

Chapter 35
RAUL

THE DENSE MORNING traffic slowed my progress, and I worried that I would arrive at the clinic too late. Now, the horse trailer only slowed my progress. After my frustration with the traffic around me reached the boiling stage, I tried to calm my anger. I might not make it before they whisked him away, but there would be no such thing as too late. It really didn't matter whether Amado Carrillo died today. He might postpone judgment, but it would come. Wherever he went in the world, I would find him.

By the time I found the Jiménez Clinic, it was after ten o'clock. I maneuvered to the far end of the small parking lot and made a circle so my rig was facing the street. It might be necessary to leave here quickly.

I stared at the red brick building in front of me. Black Cadillac SUV's and King Ranch Ford pickups littered the parking lot. Hard-eyed young men loitered at every entrance. How would I get inside? Without a doubt, I would be stopped and searched for a weapon. I walked toward the front door. Two men stood on either side of the entrance, one barking orders into a cell phone. I tensed for the coming confrontation, but before I'd even reached the sidewalk, both men sprinted toward the parking lot, ignoring me as if I was a potted palm tree. My right hand slid to the small of my back to touch the butt of the .45. What was going on? Maybe it didn't matter. The important part was that Amado would feel the bullets when they slammed into his body. He'd spent his entire life killing others. He had to have known that this day would come, that he would never live to bounce his grandchildren on his knee. Momentarily, I wondered whether his wealth had compensated for the early and violent death he would face. I set my jaw as I left those thoughts behind and reached for the brass pull handle on the door. Today, he would leave the world the same way he entered it – with nothing. I had no illusions. I would not leave here alive either, but that no longer mattered.

The front door had nearly closed behind me when I heard a big commotion in the hallway that must have led to the side entrance of the building. An engine roared. Men shouted. I stepped outside and ran to the end of the sidewalk in time to watch an ambulance sway out of the parking lot and onto the street. It recklessly plunged through the traffic on Valenzuela, then dived onto Calle Vicente. Brakes screeched as mostly courteous drivers attempted to give the ambulance room. I stared as a dozen armed men jostled through the door. They hustled two medical personnel in scrubs into the nearest SUV, then squealed out of the parking lot and across Valenzuela. Perplexed, I walked back into the building.

The waiting room contained the usual row of chairs. A solid looking coffee table with oversized square legs supported the same magazines all clinics subscribe to, most so boring no one but medical junkies would ever read them. At the end of the room, a walled-off space kept the receptionist separate from the unwashed, or perhaps in this case, the unface lifted. Nobody manned the desk, so I pulled the gun out of my waistband and cautiously followed the long hallway toward the east end of the building. The first two doors opened into consultation rooms, both silent as death. The third door on the left appeared to be a storeroom, a place to keep bedding and supplies. The one opposite yielded more concrete answers. It appeared to be a hastily abandoned operating room. I eased the revolving door inward. A middle-aged woman mopped at the floor, unaware of my presence.

"Where's Amado?"

The question startled her, and she stifled a scream. Her eyes nervously dropped to the gun in my hand. "I didn't see you come in. Who are you?"

I considered how to answer that question. "Why Señora, I'm just a loving relative."

"Well, he's not here." Suddenly her face dissolved into tears. "They took him to the hospital. He went into cardiac arrest on the operating table."

I was no expert in psychology, but I could have sworn her tears had nothing to do with Amado, and everything to do with fear. "You mean he's dead?"

"Señor, I do not know for sure. Maybe if he got there soon enough – "

"Where did they take him?"

South Hospital. It is close, so perhaps they might have arrived in time. If not, our lives are all in danger. Doctor Gonzalez did not want to – "

I didn't hear the rest of whatever she had to say, nor did

I much care. She was right. If anything happened to Amado, the life of the doctor and everybody in that whole clinic would be worthless.

******

Frederick paced back and forth at the top of the stairs, wishing mightily he could follow Bobby and Derek into the action zone. But that would only complicate things. What they were doing required precision teamwork. He could be more effective by ensuring no hostiles used the elevator. Even legitimate hospital personnel who now showed up at the rooftop helicopter pad would be detained. He scanned the floor indicator panel above the two elevator doors. Both units were moving. The one on his left stopped at the second floor. His thumb automatically found the safety on the side of the Glock. He flicked it forward and crouched with the barrel centered on the right-hand doors, then breathed a sigh of relief as the elevator stopped at the floor below him.

Frederick slipped over to the stairwell and peered below. The angle was perfect. He watched as both commandos checked their grenades and slipped further down the stairs. Derek had wanted to leave a Claymore at the top of the stairs with a motion sensitive detonator on their way out, but Frederick had vetoed it. There wouldn't be time to set it. Besides, if it was detonated, it would be too close to the helicopter pad.

The ambulance siren in the street shrieked progressively louder, then stopped. Seconds ticked away, the only sound now the whirring of the elevator as it returned to the first floor. Three floors below where Frederick stood, panicked voices faintly broke the silence. The sound of heavy footsteps delineated the rapid shuffle of feet on the tile below. This was it. Bobby swiveled, and glanced upward. Frederick gave him a thumbs-up. Now, loud voices. The rapid clack of running feet sent a quick rush of adrenalin to Frederick's fingertips. His right hand involuntarily tightened on the familiar checkered pistol grip. His thumb caressed the safety as his eyes flickered from Bobby, down to Derek, then back to the elevator door. He should have planned this better, maybe grabbed one of the M-16's from the armory. What if Derek or Bobby were shot? Frederick's eyes narrowed. He'd be little help with only a handgun. The muffled click of a rifle safety sounded loud in the silence. Frederick followed suit. What if one or both of them went down? Pablo would die, and it wasn't likely Pete would get the helicopter off in time, so he'd die as well. He could already picture the headlines, but whatever they were, it really didn't matter. He'd not be alive to see them.

Chapter 36
DINA

DINA FUMBLED FOR the doorknob at her back. Could she escape before Oscar pulled the trigger? Because he hadn't killed her at Raul's, didn't mean he wouldn't now. Nevertheless, her voice was as calm as she could make it. "What do you want?"

"Only what will soon be mine." He walked slowly around the desk, the barrel of her father's pistol steady in his hand. When he reached her, he inched the barrel forward until the gun sight bit into the side of her throat. The pressure pushed her face upward. "That may include you." Savagely, he ripped the gun sight across the bottom of her jaw. Blood spewed down the front of her shirt, and she tried to sidestep away. Like a striking snake, Oscar grabbed her throat, choking any sound she might have made. Fear sluiced through every nerve ending in her body. She now knew, leaving this room alive was not an option. Escape for Oscar meant she had to be dead.

Her voice quivered with fear. "Take what's in the safe. I'll open it."

Oscar snickered, and shoved her away. "Yes, we can start

with that. If you cooperate, I may reconsider killing you."

She nodded, though terror held her immovable. Somehow, she needed to step forward, to do what he was demanding. Though her shoulders remained rigid, inside she slumped. There was no way out of this. Nobody would hear her scream except perhaps Mama, and she didn't want that. Her eyes dropped to the invisible concrete pad, cleverly set into the floor. Much of what her family had accumulated was in that safe.

"I suppose that's why you came to work for us, so you could steal everything my father and mother worked so hard to build?"

"Spare me." The corner of Oscar's mouth turned up in a sardonic grin. "What they got was off the backs of others. Call tonight a tax, plus penalties of course, long owed to those whose labor your parent's exploited."

A sudden unexplained courage caused her to respond. "That's not true. You've been here long enough to see how hard we work. My family's money has been earned with callouses on our own hands." She edged sideways, trying to get away from the sweaty stench of his body. "Was it you who burned Raul's house?"

Oscar shrugged. "How else was I going to get into the house unseen, though it did me little good. I would have preferred to open your stash quietly, to relieve you of what you've stolen. However, you've been very careful. Even with my best efforts, I still don't have the correct combination to the safe, so you're going to open it for me."

"That's why you went through every purse and drawer in my room?"

Oscar grinned. "I try to be thorough."

Dina stared at the still unwavering barrel. She hoped Mama was already asleep. Luis, or any of the other hands would never come up to the house unless called for at this time of the night, so there was no chance of rescue. After she opened the safe, he would either put a bullet into her head or more likely kill her in a more silent way. She had little chance against his strength.

"I was quite sure you would keep a written record of the combination hidden in your room. Perhaps I was wrong, but – we've talked long enough. It doesn't matter now. Open it." He pointed at the safe.

A sudden burst of defiance, defined her reply. "And if I refuse?"

Dina saw the hand too late. His backhand blow cannoned her head off the vertical wood planks on the wall. Blood dripped from her broken nose. She sobbed with pain, and a growing panic. She didn't want to die. Not here. Not this way.

Oscar slowly lowered the barrel of the gun. His face took on a new coldness, his eyes still and hooded, like a prairie rattler. "I would rather not shoot you, so I will forgive your insolence – at least for the moment. I am not one of your sycophantic ranch hands. Your death will mean no more to me than swatting a fly in one of your extravagant domiciles. Amado Carrillo sent me here to look after Rodrigo – for several reasons. But after he was killed, I decided to turn this into … let's say, more of a paying proposition. This little windfall at our feet, and perhaps you, I don't intend to split. All of it goes to a good cause – me."

Dina stared at him. Would it matter if she refused to open the safe? He was going to kill her regardless, either now or later. But as she staggered to the middle of the room, a sudden picture of Juana's bloody bedroom flashed in front of her eyes. She stared at the numbers on the dial of the safe. It took every bit of courage she could muster, and even as she said it, she knew if the pain became too intense she would probably fail. It didn't matter. Her chin came up. She clenched her teeth, and to avoid his eyes she stared at the far wall. "I'm not opening the safe."

"As you wish." Oscar slipped behind her. His steps clicked out an ominous message of danger. He grabbed her hair, shoved her forward and snickered. "You will not die. No, let me rephrase that. You won't die immediately. After I'm done with you, your body will be so broken that you *will* expire, but it will take much longer to happen. A few days from now, your suffering will be almost over."

Dina bit her bottom lip until she tasted blood. This man was capable of everything he'd threatened. So should she open the safe? Did she have a choice?

Suddenly, Oscar's right arm curled around her throat. An involuntary scream rose in her throat, but he immediately cut off her wind. His left hand slipped under the arm that stopped her breathing, the knife he now held, a shiny harbinger of death. Dina could see the blade, glittering and deadly. He placed it against her throat, and the ancient prayer crept to her lips with new meaning. "Holy Mary, Mother of God, pray for us sinners, now and at the hour of our death." The familiar words were as comforting today as they had been when she was a little girl. Whatever happened, God was here. He was in control of her life, and if He wanted her to die, then die she must, to be instantly transformed into His kingdom.

Oscar laughed, a guttural braying, malevolent and evil. "We must start." He jerked her head back and slid the dull side of the blade against her throat. "One flick of my wrist. That's all it will take. You could be dead at the end of your next heartbeat. Are you ready?"

Her resolve melted like spring ice. If she died, would anyone take care of Mama? Maybe if she opened the safe, Oscar wouldn't kill her. At least there was a chance.

Oscar suddenly dropped his arm from her throat. She didn't see his other hand move until it was too late. His fist smashed into her cheek, and she crumpled. Her face skidded across the sharp edge of the dial on the safe. Instantly, she felt the blood gush down the side of her face.

"Be quick. I have no time to play your stupid games."

Dina had never actually examined the contents of the safe. Once, she'd opened it, but only to see if the combination actually worked. She'd never thought about what was inside. At times she'd wondered why Papa hadn't found a different way to store the hard-earned dollars he'd accumulated. At least twice, she'd spoken to her mother about moving the contents to a bank safety deposit box, but Mama was adamant. Banks weren't trustworthy. Whatever wealth she held was to remain in the office safe. Dina had finally given up trying to convince her differently.

As her shaky hand twirled the giant knob back and forth, Dina's heart sank. When she'd finished, the heavy door swung back in her hand. The result of a lifetime of prudent saving and shrewd investment lay in front of her.

Oscar pushed her aside. He'd come prepared, and he wasted no time in scooping the contents of the safe into a burlap bag. The many ounces of gold coins and precious gems were a heavy load. Dina's eyes flickered toward the door. Why hadn't she been more persuasive with her mother? Though Papa had not trusted any bank to properly store the gems and precious metals, anything would have been better than this.

Suddenly, Oscar froze. Dina glanced up. Luis blocked the door. His eyes flickered from Dina's bruised and bleeding face to the man on his knees in front of the open safe. Oscar stood, then staggered back against the wall with the heavy bag between his feet. Luis ignored him, his eyes now transfixed on Dina's face. A low growl rose in his throat. He strode forward, his hands flexing at his side. Dina watched the animal rage transform his face as he kicked a chair aside and strode toward Oscar. At the last second, Oscar fumbled the gun out of his belt. Luis launched through the air, his work-roughened hands grasping for Oscar's throat. In the small room, the shot was deafening. Luis crumpled. Oscar edged around Luis's still form, then turned and pointed the gun at Dina's head. "If you move, you will die." With that, he disappeared.

Dina slumped to the floor, then crawled over to Luis. Her rescuer, the man she'd known and played with as a child, was gone. Blood stained his black hair a curious brown. His features, despite the violence of his departure, were peaceful. He lay quietly on his stomach, as if he'd fallen asleep. For Luis, death was only a stepping stone to love – and a different life.

Chapter 37
RAUL

I'D LEFT THAT PARKING lot faster than I should have, and likely caused some upset for Sorrel Horse, which was hardly fair. It wasn't his fault the humans he'd been stuck with had issues to settle. When I got to the street, I made that engine hum while I kept an eye out for South Hospital.

Several blocks ahead, a white, three-story building with a big sign loomed to my left. I pulled into the parking lot, blocking about five other vehicles with that truck and trailer. Too bad. They'd just have to wait until the business I had to transact was finished. If I wasn't able to return, I hoped someone would take good care of Sorrel Horse.

On the east side of the building, I could see an ambulance was backed up under a big sign that indicated it was the emergency entrance. I bypassed the main doors where all the people hung out in front, and wound my way toward that ambulance. My hand brushed the small of my back as I checked to make sure the .45 was still there. Suddenly, at the emergency entrance in front of me, shots rang out, and I could have sworn one of them was a shotgun rather than a rifle. That was followed by several bursts of automatic gunfire. A couple of tough looking cartel types who I suppose had been left outside to secure the outer doors left their post and ran inside. I followed them right into the gunfire, because, at that point, I had nothing to lose. I only wanted to kill the man who had been responsible for Juana's death. If I died in the process ... I hesitated. I've tried to live by the Book, but there have been times in my life I've failed to live by my own standard, never mind God's. The growing volcano of anger in my chest, and my driving need for vengeance was at odds with everything I'd ever read in the Book. Now, I pushed that aside. I refused to leave vengeance to the Creator. I would kill Amado Carrillo.

******

Frederick

Suddenly, the door at the bottom of the stairs cannoned back against the wall. Pablo's panicked face appeared. Frederick's teeth clenched. Beside him, the elevator light indicated it was headed upward. Below him, Derek moved down a step and beckoned Pablo to hurry. Pablo slammed the door and rammed Oso's deadbolt home. Frederick tensed. It was too far. Pablo would never have enough time to scurry out of sight around the first landing before those behind him realized he was trying to escape.

The hastily installed deadbolt proved a waste of time. Pablo was barely at the first landing before a rapid-fire machine gun burst made a mockery of the deadbolt, and most of the door. The opening filled with faces and assault rifles. Derek grabbed Pablo and shoved him further up the stairs, then blasted away with the shotgun, one devastating round after another. From farther up, Bobby punched three 7.62 rounds into the crowd. One of Derek's shells must have been too far to the right, because it demolished the top hinge. The door did a slow bow before it settled at a crazy angle against the wall.

Pablo's pain-filled face appeared at the second landing. He limped up the last few stairs toward Frederick who pointed him at the chopper. Blood trickled down his leg, the scarlet smudges leaving a smeared trail on the tile as he hopped out of the stairwell and onto the helicopter pad.

The acrid stink of old cordite and new gunpowder sucked every breath of oxygen from the narrow confined space in the stairwell. Three times Frederick watched as a hand appeared around the corner of the bottom door opening to lob a grenade into the stairwell. Two of them bounced harmlessly against the stairs and clattered to the bottom. The third rolled back into the hallway before detonating. The cartel gunmen quickly realized the grenades were more a danger to them than Derek and Bobby, and they quit trying to throw them up the stairs. Twice, one of them was brave enough to stick an assault rifle into the stairwell and fire off a burst. A bullet clipped Bobby in the arm. He flinched and retreated as blood spattered the floor at his elbow.

Both Derek and Bobby moved upwards in a leapfrog pattern, each covering the other's retreat. At the top, they signaled to Frederick to run for the chopper. After one last burst to cover Bobby's advance through the door and onto the roof, Derek backed through, slammed the roof door shut and dropped the three inch iron bar into place. Pete was already hovering, the skids barely maintaining contact with the red cross underneath the chopper. Bobby scrambled in behind Frederick, and Derek dived in behind him as the helicopter lifted off. Both unleashed all the mayhem they had left at the door at the top of the stairs. Within seconds, Pete was off the deck, ducking and diving, using other buildings for cover while he angled for the border as fast as Bell technology would allow.

******

Raul

When I stepped through those glass hospital doors, it was as if I'd opened the gates of hell. One hallway ran straight ahead, the other angled to my right. It wasn't hard to figure out where the action was. Semi-automatic rifle fire, and the odd grenade explosion were deafening. Thirty feet down the hallway, a wooden door hung crazily on its hinges, peppered from top to bottom with what appeared to be buckshot and grenade fragments. Inside, a man lay at the bottom of the stairs, his blood seeping out into the hallway. I walked forward and glimpsed a second corpse on the first stair landing, a stream of crimson spidering to the bottom to mix with the pool already formed.

As I watched, a half dozen men with AK-47's leapfrogged over the bodies and disappeared up the stairs. Seconds later, I heard the sound of a helicopter taking off, followed by the sound of more rifle fire. Who the chopper carried, or whether the cartel *sicarios* had brought it down was none of my business. What did concern me was at the nursing station directly ahead where a few men huddled around a gurney. None of them seemed interested in the gunshots, or the bodies that littered the stairwell behind them. I pulled the .45 out of my belt and elbowed my way to the front. Those that were armed didn't seem to notice or care that a stranger with a gun in his hand was in their midst. A team of medicos were trying to pump life into the grotesque figure on the gurney. Though his face was horribly mutilated, it appeared to be Amado. I surveyed the various machines, and though I knew the names of none of them I reckoned the flat lines running across the screens were a good sign. A large piece of the anger drained from my heart. A bullet from my gun would not make Amado any more dead.

******

Frederick

Frederick glanced back at the passengers. Bobby and Derek stared out the windows, hands glued to their weapons. In the middle, Pablo slumped forward, his face pale and strained. He managed a wan smile at Frederick's concerned look.

"Thanks, guys." Pablo reached over and shook hands with both Bobby and Derek as the border slid under them.

Derek nodded at Pablo's heart-felt thanks, then knelt on the floor of the chopper and slit Pablo's pant leg up past the widening blood stains below his knee. Frederick turned to Pete. "Get an ambulance on the tarmac. It doesn't look life-threatening, but he needs some care."

Pete radioed ahead with the request. Minutes later, they settled in front of the El Paso hangar. Frederick knelt on the floor and talked quietly to Pablo. Bobby and Derek paced back and forth, waiting for the ambulance.

"Was it a success?"

Pablo nodded. "The guy's dead – but I didn't do it."

"What do you mean? Amado Carrillo is dead and you ... no never mind. We'll talk later. Get that leg taken care of." He squeezed Pablo's arm and stepped back to give the paramedics room to work.

The attendants brushed aside Pablo's feeble protest and

eased him onto a stretcher. Derek and Bobby started toward the hangar. Bobby held a handkerchief to his bleeding arm.

Frederick's stern voice stopped them. "Bobby, you're going nowhere. Get in that ambulance."

"Boss, it's only a scratch. It hardly broke the skin. There's no need – "

Frederick pointed at the ambulance. "Get in."

One of the attendants dutifully attempted to help Bobby into the back. He shot a withering glance at the man and crawled in beside Pablo.

Frederick turned to Derek. "I wish Bobby was here to accept the congratulations as well. I just wanted you to know it was a privilege for me to be with you. Thanks for a job well done." He turned away, knowing there would only be embarrassment and discomfort at the praise. "Okay," he said, his voice now devoid of any sympathy or praise. "Presuming Bobby can make it, we will debrief tomorrow morning at nine hundred hours. See you then."

Derek nodded, then silently turned and swaggered toward the hangar. A slow smile creased Frederick's face. It wasn't really a swagger. Neither of the two commandos could be accused of being boastful, or proud. They were just confident – and capable. He tried to think of a word for how they carried themselves. It seemed there wasn't any, at least none in English. He chuckled. On top of their confident tread, neither were much good at saluting. They'd long ago left that regimen. Today's accomplishment was the kind of free-wheeling action they thrived on. And as dangerous as it was, he doubted either had any intention of quitting – or saluting.

Chapter 38
RAUL

I SLIPPED THE .45 back into my belt. None of Amado's goons seemed to notice, or care. With their boss dead, security was no longer a priority. They were more interested in escaping. Nobody appeared willing to loiter long enough for the Federal Police or Marines to arrive. I watched as they hurriedly gathered their dead and left, the squeal of tires loud in the silence. Amado's mortal remains lay in the hallway where they'd abandoned him.

I stood over him, wanting to curse him, to put a bullet in his dead body. The flat green lines on the monitor spoke louder than my anger and grief. A bullet wouldn't have helped – me or him, so I took one last look at my dead cousin and turned away. He'd deserved to die for what he did to Juana and a thousand others, but in a small part of my soul, I was glad his death was not a blot on my conscience. I trudged outside to my pickup. To remain here longer would be foolish. When the police arrived, they would round up everybody in the vicinity for questioning. If they found I had a connection to Amado, I'd have to prove my innocence, which as recent experience had taught me, might never happen. Besides, this was Mexico. If they found my pistol, I'd never get out of prison.

My recent dealings with the law had made me wary of policemen. I drove out to the street, then up a back alley to get out of the area as fast as possible. When I reached the far side of town, I figured I was safe enough to pull over to the side of the road and make a phone call. Dina answered before the second ring.

"Hey Chiquita, how are things at home."

"We're coping, but Raul, where are you? Are you okay?"

"I'm okay. But ... I had to find Juana."

"Is she okay?"

"No, Juana is ...,"the words swelled from deep in my chest until they wouldn't come out. I took a long, painful breath. "She has gone to heaven." I'd buried Juana's body, and maybe saying those words had been a start towards what those psychologist folks call "closure." I don't know as there's any such thing. The agony never goes away, at least it hasn't for me.

When Dina again spoke, her voice was tight, and I knew she was trying not to cry. "Raul, I am so sorry. I was praying you would find her alive."

If we had been together, I would have held her and probably we would have both cried, but over the phone, it all seemed colder, more distant. Later, there would be more tears, but for now they'd all been shed, and I was able to keep my voice steady. "The man who killed my wife is dead, but that is not why I called. You have been served with expropriation papers for the ranch?"

"Yes, they delivered them on Monday. Not only for the ranch, but everything on it, and they took my Mexican passport."

"I have talked to Marcos. He says it was a mistake. All the charges will be dropped. We will have no more trouble with my brother-in-law."

"Really? That is great news. I'm so glad to hear Marcos is going to be able to get them to drop the charges, especially after Oscar – "

"Oscar? What happened with that worthless coyote?"

"Raul, he was the one who torched your house to create a diversion. He wanted to get inside my room to search for the combination to Papa's safe. He never found it, so he then returned. When I interrupted him – "

"Are you alright?"

Dina sighed. "No, to be truthful, I guess I'm not." Despite her determination, silent tears slid down her face.

"Raul, There is more bad news. Luis is dead. He tried to protect me, and Oscar killed him."

"Oh, Chiquita, I am so sorry. I will be there by morning."

"No, Raul, I don't want you to come home. Go and do what you need to do. We will have a memorial service for Luis after you return, but for now, you need to have time to grieve for Juana."

"Yes, but Luis was my friend. He looked to me as a father and mentor. I need to be there."

"Raul, there is nothing any of us can do. Luis is gone. I don't want you to take this wrong, but Luis and I have always had a special relationship. It's a hurt that I need to process in my own space and time. You deal with the loss of your wife. Any responsibilities here, either to us or the ranch, can wait. When you return, I will need your support more than ever. So there, I have bared my soul."

"That you have, but Chiquita, I knew that Luis always loved you. That is nothing to be ashamed of. You have always been honest, and true to your vows. I would have expected nothing less from you – or Luis. I have known few men as well as Luis, so when I tell you he would never have done anything to cause you unhappiness, believe me, it is the truth. Luis might have flirted, but he loved you too much to have ever gone beyond that."

"I don't understand. What are you saying?"

"He cared more about your happiness than his gratification, and that's a rare commodity in our world."

For a long time Dina was unable to get any words past the hard lump in her throat. Luis's devotion had at times been uncomfortable, outside anything she'd ever thought of as acceptable, and yet she didn't doubt what Raul was saying. Luis had always loved her, and she had loved Frederick. For Luis, she had been the unwitting bearer of frustration and sadness. Tearful words burst past the lump of sadness. "But Raul, how could I have done it any diff – "

"No, don't get me wrong, Dina. The fault is not yours. I just want you to understand. Luis loved you for all the right reasons. He was a good man."

"I didn't always understand that. I do now, and I will never forget him."

"That goes for both of us. From the time he was a boy, he has always had a special place in my heart. I need to go, but how is everything else at the ranch?"

"Everything is fine, now that we know we're not going to lose it all. We will have a grand fiesta to celebrate the saving of our home."

"Chiquita, I don't think I am in the mood for a fiesta."

"Oh Raul, of course not. That will all happen whenever you decide to come home."

"That is good. I am sad about Juana, and need time to grieve, but I am as happy about the ranch as you are. It will always be my home, but for now, I am going to go on an extended holiday to Montana. When I return, perhaps we can have that fiesta."

"When will you be back?"

"Before the snow covers the ground in the north. I well remember when you and Frederick were there. Montana winters are too cold for me. I will see you in the autumn. *Hasta luego, Chiquita.*"

"*Vaya con Dios,* Raul."

I threw the phone on the dash and decided that what I'd told Dina was more than a good idea. Up until I'd talked to her, I'd not thought much beyond the needs of today. Montana had been a vague plan. Now, I was determined that plan would become reality. For a time, I needed to wipe the dust of Mexico from my feet, grieve for what might have been, and contemplate whatever future I would have without Juana. Though the ranch would always be my home, I needed to leave the violence and death that too often defines everyday life in my country. I pointed the hood of that pickup north, and drove toward the border and Montana.

Chapter 39
DINA

By late Monday morning, Dina would have sworn she'd been interrogated by every police agency Mexico had ever produced. All had been to the ranch, taken pictures, dusted for fingerprints, of which there were plenty, and generally did what police force detectives do anywhere else in the world. All denied any possibility that Oscar would be able to leave the country with what he'd stolen. She knew better – and so did they, but it didn't seem productive to argue the point.

Oscar didn't appear to have worried about leaving fingerprints, and honestly, Dina didn't understand why the police thought they were a big deal. Every person on the ranch could identify the man. Besides, they'd have to catch him to match any prints they'd lifted, and that wasn't likely. She spent a good part of the day attempting to grapple with a future where there now might be a ranch, but no money to run it. Tears welled in her eyes as she considered each employee who had spent their lives depending on her family. Where would they go? What would they do? Even if she sold part of the livestock, finances would be tight. And what if they had to sell part of the ranch to survive? New owners would refuse to support those on the ranch who were old, and could no longer work.

Dina sighed as she walked to the barn. How would she break the news to her mother who was fighting for her life, that she was now about to lose her home? That couldn't happen. She had to hold on, even if they had to sell some of the cattle. Could Frederick or maybe Alejandro help? It wasn't likely. After all, both were foreigners. Well, Alejandro wasn't, but he worked in Washington, and Frederick of course, *just wouldn't have time*. Nothing new there. A cascading wave of bitterness welled up in her chest as she thought of their last conversation. He'd promised to come last night, and of course that hadn't happened. She should have known better.

At the barn, Paco was saddling his first horse of the day, a big chestnut with a wide blaze in the middle of his face. The three-year-old had lots of color and class, however, that didn't make up for his attitude. The colt had bucked every day since Luis had started him.

"Good morning, Paco."

"*Buenos días.* Did you want to ride this one today?" Paco winked at her. Dina's eyes narrowed, until she realized he was only teasing.

"Uh ... no, I don't think I ever want to ride that hurricane. He's athletic though, isn't he?"

Paco flopped the saddle on the colt's back. "He is that, especially when he goes to bucking. I'm stiff and sore from his shenanigans."

"What's his problem? Is the saddle galling him? Are you sure he doesn't have an abscessed tooth, or pain in another part of his body that sets him off?"

Paco shrugged. "Honestly, I don't know."

"Raul says we never take into account how a horse feels. We just expect them to be the same every day of their lives. He says they have down days just like we do. Could he have a bad tooth, or is he sore enough from bucking that he just gets crankier?" She held up a hand. "I know, you've probably been through those and a dozen other options. But there has to be a reason. I'm just trying to understand why."

"Yeah, me too. And I appreciate what you're saying. But if he doesn't settle down, I'm going to turn him out for three months and see if that will fix whatever is wrong. Sometimes that works."

"Oh, for sure. If there's a physical ailment that is bothering him ..."

Her phone started its musical clamor. The call display said it was Frederick. Hmm. He wasn't usually available on a Monday morning – or any other for that matter. He must feel guilty for not showing up last night as he'd promised. "Be back in a while." She waved at Paco, then walked toward the privacy of the barn office. She certainly didn't need any of the crew close enough to hear her reenact the fight for the Alamo with her husband. When she'd scurried far enough away, she clenched her teeth and stabbed at the green answer icon.

"Hi, I thought you were going to call last night."

"Uh yeah. I'm sorry, but I didn't get in until late, and I didn't want to wake you up."

"It wouldn't have mattered. I was too upset over Juana to go to sleep anyhow."

"Oh no, you mean Juana – "

"The Juárez Cartel killed her. Raul found her at one of their mountain hideouts."

"I should have come. Maybe I couldn't have done anything, but – "

"But what, Frederick? I tried to tell you we needed you, but you wouldn't ... oh, never mind. It's too late now."

"Won't you *ever* understand? I can't just drop everything and walk away at a moment's notice."

Dina's voice was icy. "Oh, I understand exactly where I am on your list of priorities. You've made that abundantly clear."

"That's not fair, and you know it."

"It isn't? Last night I stayed up as long as I could. I needed you. You said you would call, but did you? Of course not. You were too busy. And it would have been nice if you'd been here Friday."

"Why, what happened?" His voice sounded weary.

"You remember Oscar?"

"The shifty-eyed guy who disappeared?"

"Yes. Unfortunately, he came back and stole everything in the office safe. He got it all. There's no money left."

"How did it happen? You and your mother were the only ones with the combination numbers."

"I walked into the office. He had a gun. I'll give you the details when you get here, but if you know any way to retrieve it all – "

"But you're alright?"

"I'm fine."

"I'll be there tonight. It will be late, so don't wait up. Just leave the side door open. I should be in by midnight."

"No, I'll wait up for you."

"Okay. I'll be there as quick as I can. We'll talk then."

A warm rush of security settled over her. Frederick would finally be here. He'd take care of her like he always had before. She hadn't had those warm feelings for a long time. They felt way better than the anger, though she still wanted to keep lashing out, to lay all the frustration and fear she'd suffered on him. Her body suddenly tensed. What had he just said? "We'll talk then?" Of course. He'd meant that this was *the* talk. Their sham of a marriage was over. She backed against the wall of the barn, the only support she would have. Her face flushed, and a lone tear of desperation overflowed and carried a miniscule portion of the anger and dread to the hoof-scoured floor. Dina's teeth clenched against the heartache to come. Now, she could never let him know how bad she hurt.

"Yeah, we need to spend more time together and really ..." His voice trailed away.

Dina knew what he'd meant to say. They needed to spend time together to jointly arrive at an amicable separation. It was *so* Frederick. Neither of them had ever admitted they had major marriage incompatibilities. She had little faith that an actual face-to-face meeting would solve their problems. But, she had to try. Her marriage meant too much to just abandon it. Once more she slumped against the wall. Mama was dying. All the money was gone which meant they'd lose the ranch. And the man who had promised to love her forever now belonged to an organization. He certainly didn't belong to her.

Chapter 40
FREDERICK

FREDERICK NODDED A greeting to the two Stirling commandos in the hallway before he slipped quietly into the darkened hospital room. Pablo's wife sat beside the bed. He steeled himself for whatever might come. They were the hardest to deal with – the wives and sweethearts of his agents. Most didn't understand why he sent their men into places in the world where they'd be shot and killed. To most, he was the quintessential bad guy. Maria, Pablo's wife, was no exception. He wished he'd have asked the men at the door whether anyone was in the room. He moved quietly toward the bed.

"Good morning, Pablo … Maria."

"Mornin' boss."

Pablo's cheery tone seemed a good start. Frederick watched Maria out of the corner of his eye. She nodded, and murmured a polite though reserved greeting.

"How are you feeling?" Frederick reached across the bed and shook Pablo's outstretched hand.

"I'm fine. Just a ricochet. The bullet lodged against the big artery that keeps your feet warm. I guess it took a little chunk out of it, so they had to mess around in there and straighten it out. I'll be okay. The Doc just wants that leg immobile for a day or so, which means I have to stay here at least until tomorrow."

"That's not what he said," Maria exploded. "He said you were to stay here until Monday."

"I know what he said, but they always exaggerate to cover their butts. I'll be fine. I just have to convince him to release me tomorrow. I'm not going to lay here any longer than that. There's no need for it."

Frederick winked at Maria and nodded toward the two commandos outside the door. "When I leave here, I'm giving Tommy and Rick explicit instructions that nobody is to leave this room until I give the word." He grinned at Pablo. "You will be lucky to get out Monday. We're going to make very sure you're well mended before you see any sunshine."

"Aw, that's not fair. You two ganged up on me. Maria, I'd do just fine on the couch at home, and the T.V there is at least twice the size of this Mickey Mouse excuse for entertainment." He jabbed at the pint-sized 16-inch Panasonic mounted on an arm over the bed.

Pablo's wife mussed his thick black hair. "You'll do fine on the couch at home when Dr. Patton says so, not before. Anyhow, I need to go to work. I will leave you two alone to rehash your crazy, dangerous schemes."

Frederick walked over to the window and gazed out at the early morning traffic while Pablo and his wife said their goodbyes. Then, he pulled a chair to the side of the bed. "Are you sure you're up to this? We can put it off if you want."

"No, I'm fine. There isn't even any pain, or at least not much." Pablo pushed the button to elevate the bed another few inches. "So yeah, let's get started."

"Alright, if you're sure."

Pablo nodded. "Go for it."

"First, give me a detailed rundown from the moment they wheeled Amado into the operating room."

Pablo cleared his throat. "Everything was normal, at least as much as it can be when you have men outside the door with automatic weapons who will shoot you if anything goes wrong. That factor adds considerable pressure to the operating room environment for a surgeon – for all the staff. We all chatted with Amado when he arrived. Like any other patient, there were a few minutes for him to talk with the Jiménez surgical team. Everybody was relaxed and professional. The nurse had gowned and prepped him, trying to make him as comfortable as any surgery patient can be. The anesthetist chatted with Amado while he inserted the intravenous needle. Then they wheeled him into the operating room. Despite what the Jiménez medical team might have thought about Amado's doctor and I being there to protect him, there was a professional acceptance and respect. We'd both been present for the pre-operative assessment. There was no indication of any problems. His history, blood pressure – everything was as perfect as one could expect. The anesthesiologist inserted the intravenous feed into the tube in Amado's right arm, and then we started the operation."

"What time was that?"

"The surgeon made his first incision at 9:15, give or take a few minutes. The Jiménez Clinic has the best and newest equipment money can buy. There was almost zero chance of a malfunction. I checked the drug. It was Propofol, all in unopened, new-condition bags."

"Okay." Frederick hunched forward. "Describe the drug in terms I can understand. How does it work?"

"Propofol is often marketed as Diprivan. There is no better general anesthetic available. It is safer for the patient, and the recovery time is less. Propofol is chemically described as diisopropylphenol – "

Frederick held up both hands. "Hold it. I don't care what chemicals are in the stuff. What I want to know is whether it was right or wrong?"

"Absolutely right. The surgeon started cutting on him. Amado's doctor stood at his shoulder and watched every move he made. It would have been impossible for him to have done anything to cause Amado's death. Same for the anesthesiologist. He refused to leave even for a minute. I watched everything he did. At no point could I have faulted his delivery of the anesthetic. But an hour into the operation, for no apparent reason Amado's vital signs slowed. Talk about panic. Both surgeons worked furiously over him, but it did no good. Exactly thirteen minutes later, Amado's heart flat-lined."

"Hold it. You're telling me you never did it? You never ..."

"That's what I'm saying."

"Then who killed him?"

"Frederick, I don't know if anybody killed him. If either the surgeon or the anesthetist slipped a drug ... no, they couldn't have."

"Was there a possibility that someone tampered with the Propofol?"

Pablo shrugged. "Anything's possible, but who could have had access to it, and what was their motive? Everybody in that room was well aware of the consequences if anything went wrong. I don't know who in that room was responsible for Amado's death, but something out of the ordinary happened on that operating table for which I have no answer."

For a long while, Frederick searched the agent's face. Was Pablo a part of the mystery? Was he telling the truth, or was he so afraid of the consequences that he would carry the secret of Amado's death to his grave. Frederick gave a measured nod, and stood. How Amado Carrillo had died might never be known. His future was more certain. God in his Heaven had long ago spoken the words: "Vengeance is mine. I will repay." Amado had the blood of a thousand victims on his hands. From lonely graves, they demanded retribution.

Chapter 41
DINA

DINA PACED BACK and forth through the living room while she held an ice-filled cloth to her face. The swelling around her nose and eyes had receded in the two days since Oscar's assault, but she still didn't look anywhere near normal. Seeing Mama the next morning was unavoidable. That hadn't gone well. In fact, Dina had fabricated a fanciful story about one of the new two-year-old colts that had bucked her off in the upper pasture. She felt bad about that. Lying was never right, but the story about her face skidding through the rocks and cactus would cause Mama to worry less than if she'd told her the truth about her confrontation with Oscar, and of course the loss of most of their savings.

Eventually, Dina gave up waiting for the sound of Frederick's car in the driveway, and returned to the office. She slumped into her father's chair as her eyes traveled between the still open safe and the spot on the floor where Luis had died. Frequently, she peered out the corner of the window to see if Frederick had crested the far-off hill. She crossed her arms, determined to be ready for whatever confrontation was to come.

Dina's thoughts ping-ponged between the two items she'd been mulling over since early afternoon. First, the robbery. Would the police ever find Oscar, and retrieve what her parents had worked so hard to accumulate? And what about the ranch confiscation papers that she'd tucked behind the canisters in the kitchen? Had Raul been right? Would the nightmare of losing their home now go away?

Frederick would know better than anyone whether the government could actually confiscate the ranch. And if it was to happen, he could find out how long before they had to leave. Her second, but more pressing worry was Mama. What could they do to beat the cancer? Perhaps when Alejandro came, he could convince her doctor to refer Mama to a top-notch clinic in the United States. But how would they pay for it? Any cancer treatment north of the border would cost thousands of dollars, money they no longer had.

"Dina?" Startled at the sound of her mother's unusually stern voice, she whirled. Mama stood in the office doorway with an envelope in her hand, a worried look on her thin face.

"Mama, what are you doing downstairs? I thought you'd gone to bed hours ago."

"I had, sweetheart, but I couldn't sleep. There was something I felt I needed to take care of in the office."

Dina rushed forward to embrace her mother. While she held her, she tried to block her mother's vision of the office, because the floor safe still stood as Oscar had left it.

Mama was no fool. She immediately noticed the open safe on the floor.

"So, what is this? We've been robbed?"

Dina's shoulders slumped in defeat. "Oh Mama, I was

hoping you wouldn't find out. You have enough to worry about."

Mariela took Dina's hand and led her into the office. She lowered herself heavily into her husband's big black office chair. "So, I think you need to tell me what really happened. I think your injuries had nothing to do with a horse, did they?"

Dina's shoulders slumped. "Mama, I just didn't want you to worry. I saw a man out by Raul's house and went to check. It was Oscar." Dina omitted any of the assault details. That would only worry Mama more. "When I finally made it back to the house, he was in the office with Papa's gun. He forced me to open the safe. There was nothing I could do."

Mariela grimaced. "Hmm, I made a mistake when I hired him, didn't I? Though he was a good worker, he is an evil man. It just goes to show, we're never too old to be duped, not that it matters now."

"What do you mean it doesn't *matter*? Except for our operating account at the bank, we are destitute. Everything you worked for was in there. Why did Papa leave all those valuable diamonds and – "

"Oh, Dina." Mariela's lined face broke into a tired smile. "On his worst days, your father was never that foolish."

"I don't understand. What are you talking about? Those gems ... that gold represented nearly everything – "

"Come with me." Mariela rose to her feet and held out her hand, a faint twinkle in her weary brown eyes.

Dina grasped her mother's hand and followed her to the backyard. For as long as she could remember, her mother had kept a flower garden there. It was the one Oscar had tended after the cancer had stopped Mariela from working outside. Several large rocks marked the boundaries, and near the middle, a huge boulder the size of a small car shaded the array of flowers Mama had lovingly planted around it.

Mariela led Dina over to the boulder and leaned her thin body against it. "Do you remember when your father had this big rock placed here?"

"No, I guess I don't. I just thought it was always here."

"When you were little, your father gave it to me as a present on our seventh anniversary."

Dina faced her mother and gasped. "Papa gave you a rock – for a present? On your anniversary?"

Mariela chuckled, the sound low and musical in her throat as her face mirrored the memory of that time in her life. "Yes, I wanted a big rock in my flower garden. Your father gave it to me because that huge, unmovable boulder was a symbol of our union; solidly anchored by our vows before an unchangeable God. No matter how bad things were, there was always the rock to remind us of our life-long commitment to each other."

"What a romantic, sweet thing for Papa to do." Dina swallowed the rising lump in her throat, once more faced with the stark evidence that she'd never known the man who was her real father. Her parents had made a vow to each other. Like the rock, their marriage had been solid, unmoved by time or circumstance, inviolable until death. A flush of humiliation rose from her neckline to her face at the thought of her wavering commitment to Frederick, and she was suddenly glad for the darkness.

"Let's go back to the house now, Mama. You shouldn't get overtired."

"No, not yet. There is another thing I need to tell you." Mariela held up the envelope in her hand. "I came down to put a note in the safe. God knows I should have taken care of that issue long before now. It was foolish not to have done it, especially after your father passed away, but I guess it worked out for the best. Now, I realize it should have gone into a safety deposit box, or some other place where it was protected from the Oscars of this world."

Dina took her mother's arm, and attempted to start for the house. Her mother resisted. "No, daughter. There may not be another opportunity to tell you this, and what I have to say is important for both you and Alejandro. Now, I think I won't leave that note, but you need to hear what I have written. It's true that this rock represents your father's and my commitment to each other. But ... he also thought it was an excellent place to store whatever material wealth God saw fit to bestow on us." Dina's mother leaned heavily on her daughter's arm. "There was little of value in that safe."

"Dina stared perplexed at her mother. "I don't understand what you're saying. Are you trying to tell me – ?"

"Yes." Mariela turned and pointed to the freshly spaded garden soil around the rock. "There is a large metal box underneath all that stone. Your father was a perceptive and careful man, and these are perilous times. There are many in our country who would take from those who have worked and saved." Your father decided this was a much more secure place than a safe in the house, or for that matter – banks.

"So what Oscar took was not the – "

"No, what he stole were mostly baubles and fakes. Little in that safe had any significant monetary value."

Dina sighed. "And so the note in the safe was to tell

Alejandro and I that you and Papa's real bank was under this rock?"

Mariela smiled. "Yes, all in code of course, in case … well, we don't know if the chemotherapy will work, do we?"

For a long time, Dina clung to her mother as she blinked back tears. "Mama, thank you so much. Thanks for you and Papa being such a shining example to me of what a marriage should be."

Mariela nodded. "It wasn't always easy. Your father's calling in life made for a difficult marriage, as you so well remember. And now, I think it's time we both went up to bed."

"No, I won't go, at least not yet. Frederick's coming tonight, and there are a couple items we really need to discuss." Dina scrubbed at her tired eyes with the back of her hand. "And Mama, thanks for everything. You and Papa will always be an inspiration to me."

After Dina had helped her mother up the stairs and to her bedroom, she returned to the living room and sunk into the coffee-colored cushions on the couch. Again she thought about what her mother had said about the rock. What did it take to create the solid base of unquestionable loyalty and devotion that had made her parent's marriage a sacred pact for life? She stared at the far wall. What had gone wrong between her and Frederick. Had their respective careers become more important than their commitment to each other? Was there any way to start over, or did they even want to?

Dina never saw the lights come over the hill. Nor did she notice the reflection on the picture over the fireplace. She only awoke when Frederick leaned down and kissed her forehead.

Instantly, she pulled him into the chair beside her. "I'm so glad you're here. How was the drive? You must have left right after work?"

"Yes, I drove straight through. How are you, my little sweet one?"

"Fine, if I forget about Oscar's attempt to rob us, and that he killed Luis."

Frederick pulled her close, the way he always did when she came home with a problem too big to handle, be it horse or human. "Dina, I should have been here. I am *so* sorry." He pushed away, stood, and paced around the room, his fists clenched at his sides. "I can tell myself it wasn't possible to be here, that it was the biggest cartel takedown in the last ten years, but believe me, that means nothing compared to you."

"If you come back here and kiss me, you're forgiven." She held out her hand as a slow fire ignited deep in her soul, one that hadn't been there for a long time. Her face flushed with pleasure. This man was a keeper, but then – she'd always known that.

Relief melted the worried lines of exhaustion on Frederick's face. He studied her oval face and dark brown eyes. "You're serious?"

"Only if you hurry."

In three paces, Frederick reached the couch. He pulled her close, then kissed her while his fingers ran through her hair. "Dina, I love you. I always will, and I will do whatever I have to do to make sure this never happens again. I want you to know, I'm committed to you, to our marriage. Somehow, we will make this work – the ranch, my job, and your barrel racing career. Perhaps it's time for me to walk away from Stirling and move into another field?"

Dina gently placed her finger on his lips. "No, my Rico. Nobody else could do what you do. You are the best. You have a special calling. Only God can give the kind of talent you have, and to be truly happy, you need to use it."

Frederick placed his lips gently on hers, then held her face in his hands as he gazed into her dark brown eyes. "Thank you. I can't say I have any answers in regard to our future, but above everything else, you are the first priority in my life."

Dina pulled his head down and pressed her lips to his. What she wanted was non-negotiable. She'd chosen this man to be her husband because she loved him. Now, more than any time in the past, she knew; nothing had changed.

Sometime later, they talked. Dina lay in Frederick's arms, content, determined that their relationship would move to a new level. "Rico, this has been a difficult time, and I've had moments where I've been tied up in my own wants and selfishness. I'm sorry."

"Why? It's me who needs forgiveness. I should have been here. You were forced to deal with all this wrenching loss on your own."

"That is true. I did need you, but for whatever reason, God had you busy elsewhere, and I couldn't accept that. I've been resentful and angry. Probably there was nothing different you could have done – except called more."

Frederick's finger traced a line through her hair. "You are so awesome, and yes, I could have called more. That will not happen again."

"So," Dina poked a gentle finger into his ribs. "Which drug cartel chief did you capture? I haven't turned the T.V.

on in days. This week we had enough problems of our own."

"Amado Carrillo. He died on the operating table during plastic surgery. We had an agent in the room. That's all I can say, other than it was very dangerous bringing the agent back across the border."

"So the agent killed Amado?"

Frederick gently touched her lips with the tip of his finger. "You know I can't tell you that – for your own good."

"Oh, I understand. Anyhow, if Amado is dead, your agent must have done it."

Frederick didn't answer, and she knew from experience, he never would. But there were a few answers she needed, answers that couldn't wait. "Rico, how are we going to manage?

Frederick pushed away, sat on the edge of the couch and faced her. "You tell me. This is the first time in months we've had a productive conversation about our two very separate lives."

"I know," Dina said quietly, "but I think it's time we put the knives away and recognized where we're at and how we are feeling?"

"What do you mean, *how we are feeling*? We're just flat not connecting because such a large part of our lives are lived in different circles."

Dina rubbed the fingers of her left hand against Frederick's knee. "Maybe we first need to decide whether we want to change things."

"What do you mean?" Frederick's voice was devoid of expression.

"Just what I said. Since you took over the Albuquerque agency, it has consumed every waking minute of your time.

I try to understand that. I'm just having trouble trying to prop up our marriage at a distance, manage the ranch and Mama's health, all while trying to keep my barrel racing career going. I feel like I'm a rubber doll tied between two opposing teams of wild horses."

Frederick's eyes dropped to the floor. "So what do you suggest we do?"

"Communication would be a start." Dina reached across and touched his wrist. "It's not just you. We both have cell phones that text, call, and email. I could use mine way more than I have. When things go wrong, I get angry and resentful, and – yeah, I guess I go into silent mode."

Frederick wrapped her small brown hand in his. "We both do. I get wrapped up in my work, and with the operation to take Amado down, my life has been beyond crazy." Frederick scrubbed at his eyes and shook his head. "And Dina, I don't agree. Our lives haven't taken different directions, but they have gotten more intense. We don't schedule enough time together. That's devastating to our marriage, and we need to figure out how to change that."

"I agree, Rico, and please understand. What you're doing is important to so many people, and I *do* support you – one hundred percent."

Frederick ran his hands through her thick black tresses. "Sweetheart, we're going to make it, and if I have to drive to the ranch every weekend to spend two precious days with you, I will do it. You are that important to me, and what you're doing here is part of who we are." He knelt in front of her and held her hands. "This is not going to be easy. You are going to want more of me than I can give, and probably I'm going to expect more than you are able to do. We'll make whatever sacrifices are necessary. I love you, and I'm willing to do whatever is necessary."

"Oh Rico, I love you too – and I always will. And thanks for taking the time to talk this through. I needed to know I have your support."

"You'll always have my support. I want to be a part of everything that is happening in your life, and I promise to be there for you – always." He nestled beside her and pulled her close, as outside, the soft coo of a white-winged dove broke the desert silence.

For a long time, Dina lay in Frederick's arms. When she finally spoke, her voice resonated with the heavy load of tragedy she'd faced alone. "Rico, you need to know. Mama is dying. It won't be long now. And … and … That was all she could say. The tears she'd bottled up inside for too many days burst like a tropical storm.

Frederick continued to stroke her hair. This was not the time to talk. Mere words could never take this hurt away. Sometime after the tears had stopped, he took her hand and led her upstairs. Sadness was replaced with passion, as it should be, Dina thought. Grief could not consume her every waking moment, or she would not survive. Mama would want laughter after the sadness; she would want her daughter to live and love, create new life, and hold every moment as if it were her last. And so she did.

THE END

Epilogue

|MARK FINEMAN | TIMES STAFF WRITER

MEXICO CITY – Federal prosecutors Saturday were investigating widespread reports that Amado Carrillo Fuentes, identified by U.S. and Mexican law enforcement agencies as Mexico's most powerful drug baron, has died. Amid wildly contradictory versions of Carrillo's reported death, a communiqué released by the Mexican attorney general's office said that forensic experts were trying "to gain access to the corpse." Members of Carrillo's family told local reporters in their home state of Sinaloa that they have identified his body.

|MARY BETH SHERIDAN | TIMES STAFF WRITER

MEXICO CITY – One of the doctors believed to have operated on top Mexican drug lord Amado Carrillo Fuentes just hours before his death has been found stuffed into a cement-filled barrel, authorities said Wednesday.

The remains of Jaime Godoy were discovered with two other bodies Monday inside oil drums along the Mexico City-Acapulco highway. In a sign of a mob hit, their fingernails had been yanked; their blindfolded bodies bore burn marks. Two were strangled and one shot.

The identification of Godoy's body late Wednesday solved one of the many mysteries surrounding the bizarre July 4 death of Mexico's No. 1 drug trafficker following plastic surgery.

The three doctors believed to have performed the botched operation had disappeared. News reports speculated that the other two tortured bodies might be Carrillo's medical team, but there was no confirmation.

******

This is a work of fiction, but in much of fiction there is truth. Some details may never be known about the death of drug lord, Amado Carrillo Fuentes. *"El Señor de Los Cielos* (the lord of the skies)" died during or immediately after a botched operation to change his facial features so he would escape recognition by American and Mexican lawmen.

Since Amado's death, little has changed in the drug world. Amado's Juárez Cartel, under the leadership of his brother Vicente, still maintains control over a significant portion of the U.S. drug trade. Despite herculean efforts, and millions of dollars spent, every year, upwards of $60 billion worth of drugs flood across the border from Mexico to feed the ravenous appetite of over 5 million American drug users.